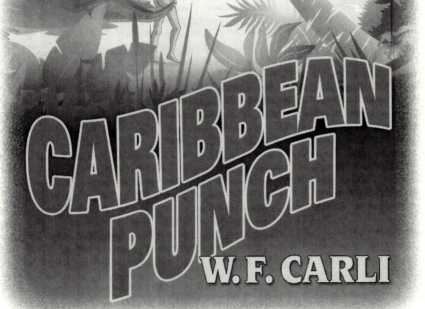

signed: W.F. Carli, St. Thomas 2015

This book is a work of fiction. Names, characters, places and incidents are products of the author's imagination or are used fictitiously. Any resemblance to actual events or locales or persons living or dead is entirely coincidental.

Published by Shooting Star Publishing
Friday Harbor, WA 98250
Copyright © 2011 by W. F. Carli

All rights reserved, including the right to reproduce this book or portions thereof in any form whatsoever.

ISBN: 978-0-9787311-2-0
Library of Congress Control Number: 2010913443

10 9 8 7 6 5 4 3 2 1

Cover design by A. Shull Designs, Friday Harbor, WA
Book design by www.FreelanceBookDesign.com

Printed in the U.S.A.

SHOOTING STAR PUBLISHING
Friday Harbor

*This book is dedicated to Maggie and the Big Chief.
Thank you for everything!*

Special thanks to

*Lee Gerard
Mike and Grace Aarhaus
C.M.C (you know who you are)
Alice Shull
Robert Warren
Shelia Deeth
Mad Jack BVI
Ariel Walden
Tony Fyrqvist*

Chapter 1

The ninety-eight foot motor-yacht Delta Rose lay at anchor a quarter of a mile from the island. Wisps of fog hugged the tree covered shoreline and small swells crashed against the rocks. Captain Burt Foster tried to peer through the gloom but the fog danced before him as if it had a mind of its own. The knot in Burt's stomach continued to grow, and his palms were now sweaty and he couldn't get that damn dream out of his head. Whenever he had that dream bad things always happened.

In the growing light of dawn the sleepy village of Washport Bay looked like many other little towns Delta Rose had visited this summer on her voyage to Alaska. But Washport Bay was different and Burt knew it. This little island with its small harbor was a port of entry for all vessels entering the United States and because his ship was returning from Canadian waters it was a mandatory stop. Soon Burt would have to bring Delta Rose alongside the Customs dock, tie up, and then submit himself to a bunch of government crap. Damn bullshit anyway, he thought.

It wasn't the paperwork that he disliked, or even the time wasted, it was the fact that he was going to have to put up with a bunch of heavily armed United States Customs officers as they crawled over his yacht and all he could do was try not to piss them off and stay out of their way.

Burt reached into his starched shirt pocket and pulled out a pack of cigarettes, flipping one from the open box to his lips as he continued trying to see Washport Bay. Here he was in one of the most beautiful places in the world, with air so fresh and clean he could taste it, and he was killing himself with another evil, stinking, cancer stick. Oh well, tough shit, he said out loud as if there was somebody standing next to him. He almost flipped the half smoked cigarette overboard but instead he smoked it down to the butt before he flung the stinking filter into the wind and out of sight. He hacked up a cough and spit it over the rail before he walked back inside, closing the door to the starboard deck bridge behind him. He grabbed a small handheld walkie-talkie off the chart table, dropped down into his helm seat and hit the transmit button.

"Sanders," he said, his voice harsh from the first smoke of the day.

"Yes Captain."

He could picture first-mate Chris Sanders somewhere near the galley making sure the cook was up and going about her morning ritual.

"Sanders, bring me a cup of coffee, would you?"

"Absolutely, Captain."

"What about our guests. Have any of them showed up?"

"Negative sir, I did hear some noise from the forward stateroom earlier this morning, but nobody has called for anything."

"Good."

"Coffee's on the way."

Captain Foster turned the radio off and set it back on the chart table in its holder.

The guests haven't stirred, well that was good, he thought, it's always a nuisance to have the guests milling around first thing in the morning.

"Coffee," Chris said as he put the steaming cup down next to the radio a minute later.

"Thanks."

"Think we'll have any problems with Customs?"

"Possibly, every port is different you know."

"Right, Captain," then Chris turned and disappeared down the steps that led from the pilothouse to the galley and dining area.

Chris's simple question was the same question that had been running through Burt's mind since he climbed out of bed this morning. Having a problem with Customs was not an option, not today, not with the guests that he had on board.

"No, not with these four," he muttered under his breath, his voice soft, sounding more like a prayer than anything else.

The three men and one beautiful young blonde airhead had arrived on a chartered sea plane at Saltor Bay, a small Indian coastal town in British Columbia five days ago with all the gear of big time salmon fishing enthusiasts. They lugged on board all sorts of bags and brand new stuff, looking like they were ready for a damn safari, Burt had thought when he first saw them. They paraded on board in their finest attire, but it was pretty easy to tell by the end of the first day that nobody was very interested in fishing. Mr. Joseph Flynn, who had chartered Desert Rose for the return trip from Alaska had only mentioned the day before that he was even expecting guests. That was strange in itself and it was even stranger when the guests finally arrived and Burt was personally introduced to only two of the group by name, Jake and Lefty, and each of them looked more like two hundred and fifty pound linebackers than fishing guides, and unless they were going to run into a grizzly bear up some river these two were definitely overkill.

The unnamed man, in his early thirties reminded Burt of a weasel from the moment he climbed on board, and he didn't like him one bit. He was constantly in motion, never sitting still, always moving, like some over amped coke head who just couldn't stop. In the last five days the weasel hadn't spent one hour salmon fishing. Burt wondered what the hell these four were doing on board, although he didn't have much doubt about what the blonde was up to, the way she hung on the weasel all day. The weasel guy was funny looking as well. His skinny frame was accentuated by his long nose and a crooked smile. He had jet black hair pulled back into a pony tail that just reached his shoulders and it looked greased down with motor oil. He had a gold front tooth and three small stones, probably fake diamonds in his right earlobe, but the thing that drove Burt crazy about the guy was the little strut he did as he walked around Delta Rose, like a peacock in heat which Burt doubted was possible, not with the blonde. No this group made absolutely no sense to him but that wouldn't matter much longer because once through Customs it was one long day to Seattle and by tomorrow Mr. Flynn and company would be long gone.

Burt stopped thinking about the weasel and his entourage and looked up at the digital readout of the twenty-four hour clock on his instrument panel, it was 07: 40. Well, he thought it's probably time to make sure everybody on board is awake.

He reached over and hit the glow plug for the Northern Lights generator pushing it in for fifteen seconds before he hit the start button. A small shudder ran through Delta Rose and he wondered if anybody else felt it. With a sense of apprehension that he tried to dismiss, he fired up both of the Detroit diesel engines. A deep rumble, like a growl from the belly of a beast reverberated through his ship. He glanced at another digital readout that showed engine functions, rpms, oil pressure steady, engine temperature cold but soon to be climbing. Satisfied he reached over and grabbed the radio.

"Chris, I want the anchor up in five minutes, have the fenders on starboard, and we'll need at least two mid-ship spring lines, plus bow and stern."

"Right, Captain."

One of the crew was soon at the windlass waiting for Chris's instructions to raise the anchor. Another crewperson was hanging large fenders over the starboard rail, as another was snaking out long two inch braided line for tying up at the dock. Captain Foster waited until the crewperson with the lines had them all cleated off and coiled on deck then gave the command to raise the anchor and prepare to dock.

Burt hated coming into marinas and having to tie up at a dock. It wasn't just the fact that maneuvering a boat as big as Delta Rose in tight spaces was difficult, which it was, but he just simply preferred to anchor out away from the crazies and craziness of shore-side life. He learned the hard way years ago that people who lived on land were too damn obnoxious for him. Yet this summer he had been forced for one reason or another to tie up at overpriced marinas more than he wished. In Juneau, Delta Rose had to spend a week at the dock waiting for clients, what a mad house that had been. The gawkers that came in droves to stare at his ship, the stupid questions they asked, the dirt bag hippies looking for crewing jobs, it was all enough to make him sick. Then there was security that was a nightmare, rotating the crew twenty-four–seven, always two on duty. Talk about some pissed off crew. No, he liked being at anchor, in his own private world, with no umbilical cord to the insanity of shore.

As soon as the anchor was secured he engaged the engines and watched the rpms jump up to 900. Slowly Desert Rose headed for the breakwater. He could see his crew was ready, everybody in position, the docking routine hopefully to be like clockwork, once again. Skillfully using both engines, plus bow and stern thrusters he soon had Delta Rose secured to the dock.

It was now eight-twenty. He reached over and grabbed the cell phone on the chart table and dialed Washport Bay Customs office.

"Good morning," he said, sounding more cheerful than he felt, "this is the captain of the ninety-eight foot Delta Rose. We have just tied up at your dock arriving from Canada and wish to clear customs."

He stood there hoping against hope that this was going to be painless. Maybe they would be to busy to come down and inspect his ship, maybe just ask for names and passport numbers, then give him a clearance number and off he would go, it had happened before. Somehow he doubted it today, but he could always hope.

"Yes," he said politely a minute later, "I understand, two officers will be arriving for inspection. Alright, I will have all the crew and guest's passports ready, anything else?"

"What?" he said surprised by their request, "you want all passengers and crew available, certainly passports should be sufficient."

The phone clicked dead without a reply and he knew this was not going to be easy. That bastard, he thought. How the hell was he going to tell Mr. Flynn and his guests that United States Custom agents may choose to interrogate them? It was very unusual for the crew and guests to be involved in a Customs inspection. Normally just glancing at their passports was more than sufficient. Burt shook his head in disgust as another small warning, something just beyond his ability to grasp went off in his mind, but he absentmindedly dismissed it once again.

He took a few deep breaths, straightened his tie and tried to brush any wrinkles from his shirt before he turned and walked down the stairs into the main salon.

"Good morning Captain," the cook said as he walked by her. He just smiled and kept going making his way forward to the main cabins. Taking another deep breath he knocked twice on Mr. Flynn's solid mahogany door.

"Mr. Flynn, sorry to bother you, sir, I need to talk to you," he said through the door.

A moment later the door opened and Mr. Flynn, dressed in a robe, looked at him with an expression that was impossible to discern.

"Sorry sir," Burt said, feeling stupid, "it's Customs. For some reason they are requesting all passengers be available to meet them if they choose. I wanted to notify you of this ahead of time."

"Is this normal?"

"No, sir, actually it isn't."

"I see, well . . . it seems we haven't much of a choice. I will let our guests know, keep me posted," then without another word Mr. Flynn closed the door.

Captain Foster felt like going back up to the pilothouse and having another smoke. Instead he made his way outside and walked down the boarding ramp onto the floating dock that his ship was securely tied to. He figured he might as well greet the damn Custom agents himself and escort them on board all official and proper like.

"Good morning, Captain," he heard someone say from above him. He glanced up, smiled half heartedly and nodded his head, but he couldn't see who had just spoken to him.

He turned his gaze down the long walkway that led away from the harbor and up to the small grey building that housed the Customs office. It was easy to see, the huge American flag hanging limp in the now breathless morning. He pulled out a smoke, lit it and sucked deep, bringing that foul concoction of evil into his lungs. By the time he was finished he could see two Customs officers dressed in blue uniforms making their way down the dock. With each step they took he felt a growing tension in his gut.

"Gentleman, welcome to the Delta Rose," he said a few minutes later as the two Customs officers stood before him.

"I'm agent Alonso, Timothy Alonso," the taller of the two said as he reached his hand out in a firm handshake.

"I am agent Robert Dexter," the second man said as he extended his hand.

"I am Captain Burt Foster," he replied before beckoning them on board by saying, "this way please. I have the passports in the pilothouse."

It never entered Burt's mind to ask for some form of picture identification.

The three walked up the boarding ramp in silence and continued in silence as they walked through the boat. That was strange Burt thought, most Custom agents in the past had always been full of questions, mostly friendly ones about the yacht, but not these two. The agents followed Burt up to the pilothouse then stood in the doorway a few feet apart as Burt walked to a small cabinet next to the chart table, knelt down and opened the door exposing a metal safe. He spun the dial back and forth with the experience of time and pulled the door open. He glanced back at the two agents as he stood holding all the passports of everybody on board.

"Here you are," he said handing ten passports to Agent Alonso.

"This is all on board?" he asked looking at Burt with a strange stare that didn't help the Captain feel at ease.

"That's all, five crew members, including myself, and five guests."

Agent Alonso quickly thumbed through the passports and selected Mr. Flynn and his guests then handed back the remaining crew passports.

"I will need to talk to them, should only take a few minutes," agent

Alonso said as he held the selected passports up for Burt to see.

"Aren't you interested in what we have to declare, you know . . . booze, smokes, wild women," Burt said trying to get these two to lighten up.

The agents looked at each other, laughed, but it wasn't humorous, "maybe, but now I want to see these people on the back deck," then Alonso followed by his sidekick turned and started down the stairs holding the passports.

Burt was speechless, but only for a moment, "why do you want to see them on the back deck? That's ridiculous."

Agent Alonso stopped, turned and looked up the pilothouse stairway at Burt, then gave him a stare that burned right through him, and in that moment Burt knew something was terribly wrong.

"Captain, don't ask me another question. I have my reasons, my orders, and I want them on the back deck with you, like right now!" then he turned and followed by Dexter, another asshole Burt was sure, they disappeared down the steps. The moment they were gone Burt rushed to his chart table, grabbed his cell phone and dialed the number for the Customs office in Washport Bay, hoping to file a complaint. It rang and rang before going to an answering machine.

"Shit," he said out loud.

He thought about calling his Customs agent buddy in Key West and running this crazy situation by him to see what he thought, but then hell, he'd feel like an idiot after this was all over.

"Okay asshole," he said loud enough that anyone listening downstairs could have heard him, "have it your way."

He walked down the stairs and once again had to knock on Mr. Flynn's mahogany door.

"Sorry sir," he said having a hard time hiding his anger when the door was opened, "but Customs requests that you and your guests meet them outside on the back deck."

Mr. Flynn looked at Burt with a stare that made him feel very small, like if he had any balls Flynn and his group would not be having to go through this run around. Burt almost told him to go to hell but he didn't.

"Sorry sir," he repeated before he turned and headed for the aft deck.

Agent Alonso and his shadow Dexter were standing near the stern rail inspecting the passports. Captain Foster walked over to them and stopped a few feet away. His anger was evident even before he said a word.

"I feel this is very uncalled for. Making my guests appear before you like this. What is this, a fucking inspection, some damn parade? You could have met them in my cabin or in the pilothouse but here . . . this is bullshit!"

Both agents looked at him but neither of them said a word. Alonso just kept flicking the top passport with his thumb, like a poker player holding his cards watching Burt without any emotion in his face. Burt felt like hitting him, but they both had guns so he kept his anger in check. Soon Mr. Flynn along with the weasel and his entourage appeared on the back deck and walked up to the custom agents and Burt.

"Agent Alonso and Agent Dexter," Alonso said reaching his right hand out to Mr. Flynn. Burt felt he was watching an actor.

"We are sorry to bother you but we have just a few quest . . ."he never finished his sentence. In that second a shot rang out from somewhere exploding the upper half of the weasel's head sending brains and bones flying, causing his already lifeless body to careen forward, slamming into the aft rail before flipping overboard and disappearing into the water. In horror Burt watched Alonso and Dexter reach for their side arms. Alonso aimed and fired, his first shot throwing Mr. Flynn backward, a look of complete shock on the poor man's face. Lefty and Jake both dove for cover, but Burt was frozen, his mind momentarily incapable of understanding. Dexter cut the fleeing Lefty down with two rapid shots sending the big man spinning before he fell gasping to the deck. Alonso fired the first shot into Jake smashing him into the hard steel of the deckhouse. Jake spun around, a pistol in his hand as another shot slammed into him causing the pistol to fall from his grip, as his knees slowly buckled and he slid down the wall and landed in a puddle of his own blood.

Burt finally moved as the blonde let out a scream and fainted. He turned, dove to his left, aiming for the protection of the hydraulic arm that raised and lowered the dinghy. He landed on his belly sliding painfully on the coarse deck before scrambling to his hands and knees desperately trying to gain the ten feet to safety. Suddenly a burning punch slammed into his back sending a spasm of pain that raced through his body as it knocked him flat. Knowing that every second could be his last he pulled himself to his knees then lunged forward rolling, trying to put any distance possible between him and his assassins. He could hear screams coming from different places on his ship and he felt a strange sadness for his crew and what they must be witnessing. Another bullet slammed into his left shoulder, spinning him sideways and throwing him flat on his back, his momentum carrying him until he was looking back at the two Customs agents. They both stared at him with weapons drawn. The blonde bimbo hadn't moved since she hit the deck, a stream of blood oozing from her gashed forehead. Captain Foster stared at Dexter who was a few feet closer to him than Alonso, and he recoiled in horror as Dexter raised his pistol and pointed it at him. Before the fatal shot was fired Alonso put the barrel of his pistol to the back of the unsuspecting Dexter's head and fired once sending Dexter crashing forward his blood splattering all over Captain Foster's starched white shirt. Alonso locked his eyes on Burt and time stopped for the Captain. The next round slammed into Burt's chest, throwing him back into the steel bulkhead, and he was dead before his body stopped moving.

If Captain Burt Foster had lived another thirty seconds he would have seen his murderer turn and casually walk to the side of his boat, step out of his uniform, revealing a thin wetsuit and with a graceful leap jump into the frigid waters of Washport Bay. But then if Captain Foster could have seen beyond the vale of death he also might have seen laying behind the closed, locked door in the supply room of the United States Custom office, the bodies of two murdered Customs agents.

Chapter 2

Less than seventy miles from Washington D.C. nestled on a picturesque horse farm, Lester Hollister sat at his desk, beads of sweat dripping from his forehead even though the air conditioner was working fine. His right hand was nervously drawing little circles on a legal size notebook that sat before him as he listened to the voice on the speaker phone. He felt terrible, waves of adrenaline coursed through his veins as he listened with acute attention. At the mention of the dead man's name he closed his eyes and thought he was going to get physically sick.

"This is confirmed . . . I assume," he managed to say, knowing the question was stupid but at a loss for anything else to say.

"Jesus, Lester, you think we'd be having this conversation if it wasn't confirmed? It happened this morning in some little piece of shit town called Washport Bay. Lester, this was definitely professional, done with inside information, places, times and dates."

"Inside is a terrible concept."

"You're damn right it is, it's terrifying."

Lester scribbled for a few seconds wondering what question to ask next as so many ran through his mind.

"Containment?" he finally asked.

"Hardly, where do we start? Seven people dead, one bimbo witness alive and secure but for how long? We can't hold her really. You got a boat load of crew who witnessed the killings, a small town sheriff that is already at his wits end with our people in Seattle, plus don't forget that two of the murdered were Federal agents." The voice stopped as if to give Lester time for it all to sink in then he continued, "Jesus, Lester, this is big."

Lester didn't need anybody to tell him that.

"How is she doing?"

"She's pretty much clueless."

"How the hell could Flynn have been so stupid?"

There was a long pause and Lester knew his question was almost as stupid as Flynn's behavior.

"Okay," he said, not waiting for an answer, "God what a fucking disaster."

"That's putting it mildly."

"Who else knows?"

"Right now it's in house, but it can't stay here, an hour maybe two then its going up the food chain. Once it leaves here, Lester, it's going to be a short time before the Director is briefed."

Lester's mind ran back through the conversation as he thought over the last few minutes, leaving the caller to wait patiently.

"Inside," he finally said for the second time.

"Yes Lester, inside."

"Alright, all calls secure lines only. Run a scan before using them, and this doesn't go beyond the two of us right now."

"Right, anything else?"

"Yeah, head for the hills."

"Thanks," and the phone went dead.

Lester leaned back in his chair, exhaled a deep breath, and wiped his still sweaty forehead with the back of his arm. He sat for a few minutes doing nothing, trying to grasp the reality of the conversation that he just had. Finally he reached to his right and slid out the top drawer of his desk. He thumbed through a small group of files before grabbing a thick manila envelope, pulling it out and setting it on his lap. Written in small letters on the top right of the file was a case number Z4878E21. Only he knew that some of the information in this file had been gained by people dying. In the last year two of his undercover agents had disappeared and he feared that this operation was compromised. Somewhere somebody was passing information on to the Balero family and that information was causing his people to end up dead. At least now there was no longer any doubt. It definitely was a blown case. The assassination of Joey "brighteyes" De Silva and two of his body guards this morning confirmed that. Also there was little doubt in his mind that they killed Flynn and the ship's captain just to make a point.

"Back off," he whispered, knowing full well that that was the intended message.

He pushed himself away from his desk, stood up still holding the file and walked to the small antique table that sat underneath a large portrait of his great grandfather. He grabbed the top drawer handle and swung the entire table away from the wall, revealing a wall safe. He crouched down and spun the dial before carefully opening the safe door. Reaching to his left behind the large potted houseplant that his wife had given him years ago he gently pushed the GFI reset button on the wall outlet. This normal looking switch had nothing to do with the house electrical system and everything to do with the alarm that was programmed to activate thirty seconds after the safe was opened unless the reset button was pushed.

Lester put the file in the safe, locked it and replaced the pivoting table back in place. He felt like getting in his convertible Mercedes and driving through the countryside, top down, air swirling around his face, pretending he didn't have a care in the world. But he knew he couldn't. He was facing a disaster, a totally blown case. Two years, untold amounts of money, two dead undercover agents and now this, and they still didn't have enough on the Balero's to even get an appointment with the Grand Jury.

That damn Joey DeSilva had played him and his people like a card game, he thought as he stood there not sure what to do next. DeSilva always wanted more money, stringing them on, yeah maybe he would testify, then the next damn week he'd get cold feet, change his story. Why Lester even remembered Joey once telling him that he was so worried about never being able to come home and see his poor old mother that he didn't know if he could go to court, what a bunch of shit. In some ways even though the sky was falling around him Lester was almost glad that Joey got aced. At least that asshole was out of his life.

Flynn was a different story, the two of them knowing each other for over eighteen years and he considered him a very good friend. They had met in the F.B.I academy in Quantico, spent their rookie years together in D.C. fighting organized crime, and they put more than a few bad guys away. Even two congressmen and one senator decided to not seek re-election and quietly disappeared from the political arena when confronted with information the two of them and their teams had gathered.

Flynn was smarter than he was and so charismatic that Lester had told him once that he could have made more money being a televangelist. Flynn climbed the Bureau's version of the corporate ladder a lot quicker than Lester did. Yet their friendship remained.

"So what were you doing, Joe?" he said to himself, knowing he would never get the truth.

Finally because he knew he had to get moving he walked into the kitchen, grabbed a diet Pepsi out of the fridge and walked to the large patio overlooking the riding arena. He sat down trying to enjoy the beauty of his farm, the peacefulness of rolling green acres crisscrossed with gleaming white fences that shined in the afternoon sun. He felt none of the joy that he usually did when he was home. "Inside" was too terrifying of a concept. Just how inside is it, he forced himself to ask? Does it extend to people who know where he lives, who his wife is, who his two daughters are? Do they know that his daughters attend Whitmore University? Christ, he thought as a surge of fear raced toward his heart and brain creating a panic attack that almost took his breath away, where does "inside" end?

Taking a few deep breaths he closed his eyes and fought the fear, concentrating as he pictured a wave of peace engulfing him, rising over him and washing the fear away, but it didn't help. He opened his eyes, took two more deep breaths, and with a clear understanding realized that his family could easily be in danger and he knew he had to go outside his people for help. Nothing else mattered at this moment but the safety of his family. He finished his Pepsi and realized it was time to pull an ace out of his sleeve and he knew right where he was.

Chapter 3

The telephone rang breaking the peace and quiet of the still morning. Jimmy McBain rolled over and blindly reached around the floor next to his bed. He finally found a pillow and pulled it over his head trying to drown out any noise but the sound of the gentle surf that filled his small beach bungalow twenty-four hours a day. He didn't even bother to look at the clock. There was no way he was going to talk to anybody this morning regardless of what time it was or who was calling. The only thing he knew for sure as he listened to that phone ringing and ringing was he had too much fun last night and he was going to pay for it all day.

Right now he wished he owned a lousy answering machine but he never liked leaving messages and he liked answering them even less, still, at this moment he wished to hell he had one.

"Hang up asshole," he muttered, his head still under the pillow his right arm wrapped over it pulling it tight. After about twenty rings he reached over, grabbed the phone and with a strong jerk pulled the cord right out of the wall before letting it fall from his hand and crashing on the bamboo mat next to his bed. Now only his head was ringing.

He staggered out of bed and stumbled into the bathroom hitting his toe on the plastic laundry hamper, cussing to himself as he poured two large glasses of water and forced himself to finish them along with two aspirin. He retreated back to bed and hopefully to a few more hours of oblivion before he would have to start paying the full price for a late night once again.

"Haven't I learned a goddamn thing?" he muttered to himself as he curled into a fetal position with the pillow once again over his head.

Learning from his mistakes had never been an easy lesson for Jimmy McBain. Some people have the knack of learning from other people's screw ups, some people learn from their own, and then some people never quite seem to figure out what keeps messing up their lives. It's as if the hand of fate just keeps dealing the same bad cards and the only way Jimmy could think to fix it was to pray for a reshuffle. But at least now he was smart enough to know there wasn't anybody else to blame but himself, not anymore, and that was a huge turning point in his life. It took him two failed marriages, and thirty-one years of his life just to get this far. The way Jimmy figured it there simply wasn't enough time in one short life span to ever come close to getting his shit together. Hell, he thought as he rolled over, trying to turn his brain off but not being able to, he'd been fighting something or someone or some institution his whole damn life. School, the cops, his ex-wives, bosses, everything was a struggle except one thing, and that one thing had become his salvation. At the early age of fourteen out of pure desperation his poor mother had enrolled him in a local karate class being taught at the YMCA. She could hardly afford the three month tuition and the cost of the karate suit but she was at her wits end with Jimmy and sending him to his father was about all that was left. Well, despite her misgivings Jimmy flourished. The exhausting physical workouts, the demanding schedule, the friends, the respect, all of these reasons and more, some Jimmy never understood himself, pulled him into a passion for the art. Part of it was Master Riddock, his no nonsense, no excuses, I don't want any shit from you instructor who helped Jimmy discover his gift for martial arts. By the time he was seventeen he had earned his black belt in Taekwondo. Yet that milestone just encouraged him to push himself harder. Soon he was studying

Thai kick boxing, Kempo and even Brazilian Jujitsu. By twenty he was teaching alongside Master Riddock three nights a week. By twenty-two he was winning tournaments around the country, and when he was twenty-three he came in second place in the world Taekwondo federation tournament in New York City, barely losing to some guy named Norris who went to Hollywood, became a star and made millions. Through years of training and effort Jimmy had become a martial arts warrior.

But his life was full of ups and downs. He'd been married and divorced, had a falling out with Master Riddock, then got a lucky break and spent three years teaching martial arts at the FBI academy at Quantico, Virginia. Those three years were the best and ultimately the worst of his life. He trained many of the FBI's best agents, made friends with some and gained the respect of most. During those three years he remarried, then found his wife was less than faithful. If there ever was a straw that broke the spirit of Jimmy McBain it was his second wife and the only thing worse than her betrayal was how he reacted to it. He beat the man almost to death. All the years he had spent in training, the discipline and self control that had enabled him to become one of the best martial art fighters in the country disappeared in a blinding fury at finding his wife in bed with another man. In that moment of uncontrollable anger he lost all but his skills. It was amazing that he didn't kill the man, but the damage was quickly done. Punch after punch smashed his wife's lover into a crumpled heap on the floor, unconscious, blood pouring mixed with the smell of sweat and feces, the man's left eye hanging by a few sinews of skin and muscle. It wasn't until Jimmy pulled the unconscious man up off the floor ready to strike again that he noticed his wife was pointing a pistol at him, shaking with fear, her face geisha girl white, her other hand on the phone as she desperately called 911. He had never seen such fear and it stopped him in his tracks. He dropped her lover to the floor, walked downstairs, sat down on the sofa and waited for the police to arrive.

The next year was a disaster for him. His wife filed for divorce, he lost his job at the academy and he spent four months in jail and he knew he was lucky he didn't have to do big time. By age twenty-eight he didn't have a thing except a son who if his first wife had her way he would never see and a record. Not just a criminal record but a reputation throughout the martial arts world as someone who went over the line.

Life does indeed take strange turns for all of us and Jimmy's came one night a few months after he got out of jail. He was living in a cheap apartment and working as a bouncer in a fairly nice strip club when he was introduced to a group of mobsters who thought it would be healthy for them to have someone with his skills around. Jimmy didn't have a clue what he wanted to do next with his life but he knew one thing for certain and that was he didn't want a thing to do with assholes like these guys. Still, he knew it could be bad for one's health to piss people like them off and even though he had blown it once, he knew there was no way he would ever use his skills to protect people like them.

That night he went home, turned the lights off, lit a few candles, smoked a joint of some very high grade pot and put a few cd's in the player. One of the cd's was Jimmy Buffet's greatest hits. After Buffet's finished he played it again and then hit the repeat button. For the next three hours in the glow of the dimming candles and the vapors of more British Columbia prime homegrown bud Jimmy discovered his next life. The islands were calling and he was going.

Chapter 4

It was after two when Jimmy finally clambered out of bed, poured a glass of orange juice and with two aspirin in hand walked out to his deck overlooking Red Hook Harbor on the east end of St. Thomas in the United States Virgin Islands. It was a good thing he had the day off, he thought, as his mind wandered looking over the ferry terminal and St. John. As he stood there, staring off into the distance, he couldn't imagine having to go to work the way he felt this morning. It would have been almost impossible to take a boatload of tourists out for a daysail, feed them lunch at Johnny's on the beach, and mix up his famous rum concoction without losing it. He probably would have puked before he got out of the harbor. There was no doubt in his mind that he would have before the day was over if he was stuck on board with a bunch of state side candy asses who'd have told him over and over how lucky he was to live here and how his life was their dream.

"Yeah, the perfect life in the islands, just go sailing all day and party all night, my, what could be wrong with that?" he finished his orange juice in one long swallow, then continued his monologue, "I'll tell you what could be wrong with it," he said as if he really was having a serious discussion with somebody else, "how about my liver for one thing, and a few brain cells as well, plus damn killer hangovers, and that's just for starts."

Standing there, he had to ask himself that same question that had been running through his foggy mind a lot lately. Was he going crazy (it happens to white guys after being in the islands too long he knew) or hopefully, maybe he was just burned out, hung over, feeling extra miserable, and he wasn't quite sure why, but for damn sure the last six months in the Caribbean had taken a toll on him. At first the islands seemed like a good move on his part. He got away from his past leaving a lot of guilt and confusion behind but as most find out who flee a place to start anew the problems just tag along like extra baggage. Getting a job working on sailboats had been a blessing though. Jimmy loved casting those dock lines free and heading out, sails pulling, the boat heeling, the warm trade-winds blowing. The destination didn't really matter, as long as it included a warm sandy beach, and a beach bar where you could shuffle your feet under the sand and get a cold one or two. He made minimum wage as captain but at least he had learned how to sail, and tips were good. The biggest problem was that after a few beers on the beach it was the beginning of party time that usually lasted until the wee hours of the morning. He'd seen some beautiful sunrises that way but the day was normally shot to hell.

Making his way to the shower he let the water run longer than normal even though the cistern was going to have to be filled soon. In the warm soothing shower he started to focus on the rest of the day. He'd drop by the office, spend a little time with Sandy, then probably head down to the dock in the afternoon and see how the fishing charters made out. Then if he could stay out of the Red Hook Tavern, he'd hang out and wait until "Wet Dream" the forty-eight foot sailboat he ran, tied up to its mooring buoy and he'd help the guests climb out of the dingy when they were shuttled ashore. He liked seeing who he missed when he had a day off, it was fun trying to guess who was with whom, and why. Some of the couples made no sense to him.

He would usually spend a few minutes talking to the guests who were in fine spirits after a day of sailing, sunshine and rum. Jimmy tried to like everybody, which was one of the reasons he did so well with the charter guests, and therefore why he did so good getting tips. He even got tips on the dock, just telling people he was the other captain of "Wet Dream" and it was his day off.

He tried to find the guests interesting as he listened to their stories, where they were from, what they did for a living. But most people weren't. Most of them seemed to live boring, hum drum, run of the mill, worker bee existences. If Jimmy was hoping for a little guidance for his future he soon learned one thing, more than likely he wasn't going to find it on the dock.

Sandy was behind the desk talking on the phone when he entered the charter office later that afternoon. She looked up, smiled, rolled her eyes just a bit, a friendly roll he knew, then went back to her conversation. Hopefully it was somebody booking a trip. Jimmy walked around the counter back to the coffee pot which was on a small wood stand underneath a beautiful picture of "Wet Dream". He poured the cup half full not really sure why he even reached for the coffee then walked over to Sandy and looked over her shoulder.

"Morning sweetheart," he mouthed and gave her a kiss behind her ear.

Sandy almost fifty, had seen a lot of crew come and go in her years in the islands but Jimmy was one of her favorites. There was just something about him, something mysterious, maybe even dangerous, she wasn't sure, but Jimmy had a charm about him that made her want to sweep him up in her arms, take him home, and cook him dinner, forget the bedroom. Jimmy McBain needed a mother more than a lover, she thought.

She rolled her eyes again at him but couldn't keep her smile hidden.

"Morning," she mouth back exaggerated then glanced at the digital clock on her desk that flashed four p.m.

Jimmy smiled, gave her a wink, blew her a kiss before he finished his lousy coffee and walked out the door. He didn't get seventy-five feet before he heard his name.

"Jimmy," he knew it was Flip Magee, captain of the Annie May, one of the better fishing charter boats that sailed from Red Hook.

"Jimmy," Flip said again as he walked off the stern of Annie May, and wrapped his huge arms around him. Flip was so big Jimmy almost disappeared in his grasp.

"Flip, how goes it?"

"Jimmy, today was good, four dorado and a three hundred dollar tip. Not bad. I'll buy you a beer."

"Flip, you are one of my bad habits around here. This is a non-alcoholic day."

Flip smiled as he stood there, "I've heard that before Jimmy my boy."

"I'll take a rain check. Did you see "Wet Dream" today?"

Flip gave him another big smile, gleaming white teeth against black skin, three large gold chains radiating against his bare chest.

"She looked good, Jimmy. Had twenty knots today, yea she looked really good, bro."

"Flip, remember you owe me," Jimmy said with a laugh as he started down the walkway that led to the small float where the guests of "Wet Dream" would soon be arriving. Once at the dock Jimmy kicked his flip flops off and sat down swishing his feet in the clear warm Caribbean water. He pulled his baseball cap down tight on his head trying to keep the afternoon sun from hitting his face. Staring out to sea, fighting his hangover he thought to himself that sometimes the only way to win was to bite the dog that bit you and an ice cold beer would taste pretty damn good right about now.

Chapter 5

Cantelle Bay Resort with its high priced thatched roof cottages, luxurious pools and a five star restaurant was just the kind of place that Frankie Balero loved to visit. Nestled on Three Cove Island it sat on a beautiful half moon beach of white sand and coconut palm trees. This exclusive playground for the rich had intrigued him from the first time he stayed here. Then four years ago, after a spectacular year of "business" he made the owners an offer they simply couldn't refuse. Take his money, lots of it and find a new life or as he casually implied when the negotiations stalled, they might not have the luxury to take his offer at a later date. Now, as he sat in his bungalow, all four thousand square feet of it overlooking his resort, he felt pretty damn good about himself.

Coming down to his oasis in the Caribbean, leaving the dreaded Chicago winter behind was about the best thing he did since having Michael Bonsetti taken out. Yeah, he thought, bloody mary in hand, this was his little paradise, plus it even made him money. Just think he had told a friend once, down here dirty money gets washed white as the grains of sand on his beach, and it never even has to leave the states, what a miracle.

A few tourists already sat under large white umbrellas, feet nestled in the sand, colorful drinks sitting on the little glass tables next to each umbrella. Three hammocks stretched tight between palm trees were already taken this morning. Two fishing boats were bobbing in the small swell at the dock next to the large boathouse on the far left side of his "honeymoon beach." He started calling it that after visiting a small local's beach on St. Thomas that had the same name. The advertising agency that he hired to promote his resort loved the name as well. They used two pictures of the beach and in bold Caribbean yellow printed "honeymoon beach" across the top of the glossy color brochure that they created for him. His resort was now bringing in legal money, each bungalow renting in the high season for nine-hundred and fifty dollars a night and dinner wasn't even included. This was his little cash cow, a small one compared to "business" in Chicago but at least the money was clean, and he loved being down here.

Frankie Balero had grown up in Chicago and spent most of his life there. His father was murdered when he was eight and his older brother never lived to see twenty-one. By the time Frankie was eighteen he was working for Maxwell Carlinie, as a mule, a very trusted mule. He ran drugs, guns, money, women, whatever Max wanted all over Chicago. He was smart, strong and his cockiness, even though it did get him a few beatings in his early years, gained the respect of most that he met. He was a straight shooter who did what he was told and could be trusted, and even more important, Frankie was loyal. He worked for Max until he was twenty-three, even did a few hits for him as special favors, taking care of some of Max's bigger problems, but he never liked that part of the business. It wasn't that killing people bothered him. The problem was that when somebody got taken out their friends never seemed to forget and Frankie was smart enough to realize early that he didn't want anybody chasing his ass. When he was twenty-three a lot changed in one day. Max got wasted, down at the barbershop where he always went, had his throat cut right in the damn chair. Frankie never found out who was responsible, or why, and after a month of being hell bent on revenge he was taken aside at gunpoint one evening and told that maybe it was time to get over it. He remembered looking down that gun barrel and seeing two ways his life could go at that moment, get over Max, and listen to what he was hearing or a bullet somewhere was going to have his name on it.

What Frankie didn't understand at the time was that once he wasn't working for Max there wasn't anything stopping him from working for himself, but he soon figured that out. Only a few months after Max's demise Frankie was setting up a small core group of five trusted people including himself to start his own business adventures. He stepped into prostitution, then loan sharking, gambling and within two years he had so much cash that he bought his first legitimate business, a used car lot. In three years there were twelve people in "his family". Two enforcers, both loyal but dumb as baseball bats, guys who knew only how to intimidate, threaten and if necessary break a few bones. There was Mr. Domminio, a financial genius who could move money around the city almost by telepathy and keep track of it all down to the closest dollar, neat and orderly in ledgers that even Frankie could understand. Two ledgers, one for Frankie and one for anybody else that needed to know his business and that wasn't many people, mostly the cops and the IRS.

Only one of the family scared him a little, but each family had to have its own black sheep, and Joey Bones whose specialty was making people disappear was one crazy s.o.b. Frankie was sure that Joey would do his job for almost nothing just because he loved it and anybody like that was a scary dude. Joey lasted three years until he disappeared one evening and to this day nobody knows exactly what happened to him.

Frankie swirled his empty glass feeling the warm glow of a morning bloody mary and thought about all the years since those early humble beginnings. The decades had rolled by at an incredible pace. Getting married, kids, school, colleges, women, lots of women and the years just went. Now he had three grandkids from his son and two from his oldest daughter, his youngest daughter never got married and lived out in California somewhere. God, he thought, by twenty-eight she should have settled down and had a few kids, and he feared she liked women better than men.

Now close to sixty-two Frankie figured it was time to leave most of his business dealings to the next generation. Let the young bloods fill in and run with the enterprises that he had developed over the years. His legal businesses and there were eight of them made him so much money he knew he could never spend it even if he tried. He understood that by getting himself out and turning things over to those that he had cultivated for the job, he was creating the best life insurance policy he could have. Still before he could live "down island" full time as he liked to call his Caribbean paradise, he had a few small details to deal with and one big problem. The stinking FBI was becoming a big thorn in his side. Getting them to back off and letting him settle into retirement was his last big to-do. Those damn Feds were putting pressure on his people and he couldn't figure out why. His business dealings were pretty clean compared to most, and he thought he had an understanding with the powers that be about staying under the radar, paying those he needed to and not leaving too many corpses behind. But now he was on someone's shit list headed by that damn Lester Hollister and these guys were out to bust his chops and he was tired of it. He was tired enough that he had spent a year and over a hundred thousand dollars just to get a reliable source inside Lester's team. Well, he thought as he stood up, if last weeks message didn't get through to Lester and his people then Lester was going to have to buy a new black suit to wear at his daughters funerals, because he was sick of dickin' around.

Chapter 6

Loud music echoed through the Red Hook tavern, some calypso reggae tune that Jimmy hadn't heard before. The sun was just setting and he was on his third beer, feeling that wonderful buzz that if he could learn to slow down might last most of the evening. Another full beer already sat on the bar counter before him, bought by Flip who was in great spirits after a three hundred dollar tip. Jimmy glanced out the open window of the "Hook" as the tavern was called by the locals and watched that last of the golden orb settle below the horizon.

"No green flash today," Flip said sitting next to Jimmy staring at the same beautiful sunset out the window.

"Yeah, well another beer then. One day we're going to see it. You and me, just sittin' right here in the Hook, staring out over the Caribbean and we're gonna see that green flash. I know it."

"Jimmy, you don't know shit," Flip laughed and Jimmy started laughing with him.

"Flip you're right about that."

Flip stood up and headed off for the bathroom and as soon as he was out of sight Jimmy motioned to Megan, the cute as hell twenty something bartender that he wanted her attention. She walked over, leaned her elbows on the bar, and gave him a cute smile as she brought her face close to his

"Yes," she said in her best phony English accent, "you called luv?"

"Megan, darling, do you remember the last time I called you," he paused giving her a chance to say something but she didn't so he kept talking.

"Why you know it was the most wonderful evening of my life."

"Jimmy did you call me all the way over here to remind me of a past indiscretion or do you want to buy something," the humor in her voice was unmistakable.

"Oh Megan darling, I'm weak in the knees."

"Better cut you off then," she laughed.

"No don't do that, tell you what, let me buy Flip a beer, but don't tell him it's from me or he'll insist on repaying my kindness and I'll never go home."

"Coming right up," she said with a smile and Jimmy's thoughts turned to lust on the beach.

"Jimmy," Flip said a few minutes later as he sat down next to him, "where'd this beer come from? I know you're too cheap to ever buy me one," he laughed then got Jimmy in a head lock and damn near suffocated him.

The evening continued, and the sun was long gone before Jimmy and Flip finally walked out the door. Flip gave him one more hug and headed toward Annie May as Jimmy started walking to his small bungalow overlooking Red Hook. Jimmy was preoccupied, fixating may be a better word, thinking about Megan and their one night together. He only stumbled once before reaching his front door, that same drop off in the side walk that he had tripped on last week.

Slamming his door closed behind him, he walked to the fridge grabbed a beer and headed for the living room to turn on some lights and some tunes.

"Hello Jimmy," somebody said in the darkness. Instinctively he spun towards the voice, dropped his beer, hands instantly in front of him ready to block. His front leg cocked, his back leg slightly behind him, his weight supported evenly over his body, the perfect fighting stance. His adrenaline raced through him and he was the fighting machine that he had spent so many years developing.

"Easy, Jimmy, did I startle you?" Lester Hollister said as he flipped on a small table lamp that was next to the chair he sat in.

"Jesus, Lester, what the hell?" his body trying to relax as he reached down, grabbed the spilled beer bottle and sat down on the sofa facing Lester.

"Jesus Christ, Lester," he said after taking a long drink of foamy beer, some dripping down his chin which he wiped with the back of his hand.

"It's been a while, Jimmy. I've been keeping my eye on you so to speak ever since you left the academy."

"Lester, you could keep your eye on the Pope in Rome and he'd never know you were there. What's up, besides you scared the shit out of me?"

Lester Laughed, "well you still got the moves, working out anymore?"

"Not really, not unless you count lifting beer bottles to my lips as working out. Shit, Lester, you probably know all my stuff, so tell me what are you doing here, and oh by the way it's good to see you . . . I think."

Jimmy and Lester were once very good friends, even though Lester was at least ten years older than him, and they had nothing in common. They met in a refresher self defense class that Jimmy was teaching and for some unexplainable reason they just hit it off, but not at first. Lester was a dyed in the wool republican, which drove Jimmy nuts. One day in practice Jimmy had enough of Lester's political views and told him if he ever uttered the name Rush in his class again he was going to have to do two-hundred push ups on the spot. Lester laughed it off but they quit talking politics, and religion, and after that their friendship started to grow. Jimmy got to know Lester's wife and lovely daughters very well. He spent time on the farm, often coming for dinner and ending up spending the night on the couch, after an evening of food, drinks and Canasta.

When Jimmy had his melt down Lester was one of the few academy friends who kept in touch after he left. But that was all in the past and Jimmy figured that part of his life was over and he and Lester had just drifted apart and he thought he'd never see him again.

Lester laughed again and studied Jimmy for a few seconds.

"You look pretty good, Jimmy. I thought you'd go to hell living down here."

"Well I might be getting close, but you want to tell me the reason for this surprise visit?"

"I guess I was in the neighborhood won't cut it?"

"Lester, how many miles am I from Washington? Christ, this ain't no social visit that much I'm sure of."

Lester was silent for a minute gathering his thoughts and Jimmy just sat there, looking at him, fearing that his life was about to take a major turn whether he liked it or not.

"Jimmy, I've got a problem and it's big. I've got a blown organized crime investigation, dead key witnesses, and a leak somewhere that I can't even discuss with my people. I'm about to get hung out to dry on this one and that isn't the worst of it," he paused trying to keep his emotions out of his voice before he continued, "I think my family is at risk."

"Shit, Lester," Jimmy swore as he pictured Sarah and Amy, Lester's twin daughters, and his lovely wife Margaret, in his mind's eye.

"I just don't know, Jimmy. I don't yet know how deep the leak is. Somewhere there is a traitor in my close circle."

"That's the shits, Lester, but that still doesn't tell me why you're here. I didn't think any of you Fed's remembered Jimmy McBain. Why I'm surprised you do, but then, really, I guess nothing about you would surprise me, Lester. So you're scared for your family, but I don't see what I can do. Jesus, Lester, what the hell!"

"I know, Jimmy, but listen I've given this a lot of thought. The girls have a two week college break coming soon. We were planning on a nice quiet family time on the farm but I can't do that now. There is just no way I can be certain of security."

"Lester, don't tell me you're thinking what I think your thinking."

"Jimmy, you love Sarah and Amy, they're like sisters to you. Think about it, its just two weeks. This is the perfect place for them, no passports are needed. I can get them down here without anybody knowing and it's just kick back time for the three of you."

"Lester, no."

"Wait a minute, just let me finish. I want to charter you three a sailboat to cruise around the Islands in. You'll love it and it gives me time to focus on what I am going to do next. Jimmy it's a piece of cake. Plus there's a few bucks for you."

"Lester, look at me. This will not be a piece of cake. Even though I love Sarah and Amy this has disaster written all over it."

"Why?"

"Why, because . . . because this is some secret FBI bullshit that is bound to blow up in my face."

Lester sat there looking at Jimmy, slightly shaking his head before he cast his eyes downward and exhaled a deep sigh of defeat.

"Don't give me that shit Lester, you know this won't work."

"No Jimmy this is the best thing I can do for my family. Margaret will be fine, she's going out of town to see her sister and she will keep a low profile, but the girls, I don't have a plan B Jimmy, I really don't."

Jimmy McBain finished his warm beer with one swallow and pictured Sarah and Amy again. They were the closest things to sisters he ever had.

"Lester," he said slowly and watched as his friend raised his eyes to look at him, "I don't want some piece of shit boat."

Chapter 7

Two weeks later on an afternoon flight from Charleston Amy and Sarah arrived at St. Thomas International airport. It didn't take them long to grab their bags and walk outside into the heat and humidity. Jimmy was leaning against a concrete wall at the far end of the terminal watching them as they looked around for him. God, he forgot how absolutely gorgeous they were and he knew right then he'd be keeping a close watch on these two. If it wasn't such a hassle, and illegal, he ought to make his life a lot easier and buy a shotgun right now just to keep the riff raff away. He laughed as he thought that he might also make a nine o'clock curfew that wouldn't be a bad idea either.

The girls stood on the walkway looking lost and soon a swarm of cab drivers descended on them, each trying to grab their luggage, trying to get the twins to follow after them. Jimmy watched the nervousness grow on their faces until he figured they had enough and he walked out of the shade.

"Jimmy," they both screeched, dropped their bags and ran down the concrete walkway and into his arms, kissing his cheeks and jumping up and down like Mexican jumping beans on steroids.

He loved it, and even though he tried to keep a straight face, he couldn't and he busted out laughing.

"Jimmy we can't believe it, here we are in paradise."

Jimmy thought it was Sarah but because they were identical twins it was going to take a while before he could figure out who was who.

"We're sooo . . . excited," the other one said.

"Okay you two, which one of you is Amy?"

The twins looked at each other and then at Jimmy before they both gave him a who- me- helpless- look, that he didn't buy for one second.

"Alright, you two, don't be messin' with an old man."

They burst into laughter again, still hugging him and jumping up and down like a winning game show contestant.

"Jimmy, I'm Amy, you can tell because I'll be wearing this small golden necklace and I'll have gold earrings on," Amy said reaching down and holding up a small gold necklace that hung between her more than voluptuous breasts, "Sarah will be wearing silver, besides you used to be able to tell us apart."

"That was before you two became so damn beautiful. Now let me grab your bags and we'll take a local bus to the boat."

He grabbed their bags and they followed him out of the airport past the rows of taxis and out to the street. The twins continued jabbering non-stop, and fortunately they didn't have long to wait before an open sided, twenty-five passenger Safari bus pulled over and they climbed onboard. They were the only white people on the bus.

"Good afternoon," Jimmy said as he sat down next to a heavy black woman who perspired in the heat and wore too much gold around her neck.

"Good afternoon," about ten people replied.

It was a short bus ride before they climbed off in Frenchtown, walked three blocks and found themselves at Deep Sea Yacht Charters. Walking into the small air conditioned office, Jimmy dropped the bags and looked around an empty lobby. Then he walked up and knocked once on the glass counter. He stood for another minute before a dark skinned woman in her early forties with long tight braids that Jimmy thought must have hurt like hell when they were made walked out from around a corner. She looked at the three of them, her smile vanished then a moment later she forced it back but Jimmy knew it wasn't real.

"Hello, may I help you?"

"Yes, I have a two week charter, Jimmy McBain. I'm here to pick up the boat."

She glanced over Jimmy's shoulder and gave the twins a stare that lasted longer than was comfortable.

"That's McBain" Jimmy interrupted, sensing that something was going on.

The lady seemed to snap back to reality, the phony smile reappeared, and soon Jimmy was signing release forms, looking over pages of provisioning and signing more pages full of disclosures and disclaimers.

After the pile of paper work was completed the lady who by now had become somewhat friendly called on a cell phone and a few minutes later in walked a young black man, his smile so big his face looked deformed.

"Mr. Dozer, this is Mr. McBain and his guests. They will be taking Sea Horse out, and I'm sure everything is ready for them."

"Sea Horse, now that is a fine boat," he replied never losing his smile, and Jimmy could see he meant it.

"This way please," he said, then he grabbed their bags and disappeared out the door without a second glance. Jimmy and the girls followed him and soon they were walking down a long dock, boats tied on each side.

"That lady was weird don't you think?" Jimmy asked looking at the twins, "I don't get it because most people are so friendly down here."

The twins looked at each other then started laughing.

"What?" he said knowing already that it was going to be a long two weeks with these two.

"What?" Sarah, he thought it was her, replied with a laugh,

"Jimmy think about it. That poor lady knows you're going sailing with the both of us for two weeks. She doesn't know we are practically family. Besides she's probably a good Catholic girl, get it now?"

Jimmy did and right then he realized that he was at a significant mental disadvantage with the twins.

Mr. Dozer stopped at the end of the dock, put the bags down, then gracefully pointed to Sea Horse. Jimmy's mouth dropped open as he stared at her. She was beautiful, not the normal, fiberglass boats that he was used to seeing in the charter business. No. He was looking at an Alden 54 and he knew that it was top of the line.

Mr. Dozer could tell by Jimmy's expression that he was pleased.

"She's a beauty," he said then stepped out of the way to let them walk past him and climb aboard.

Mr. Dozer spent an hour with Jimmy going over the boat's systems, showing him pumps, gauges, fuel filters, water separators, generators, and a ton of other boat stuff. The girls were busy putting things away and before Jimmy knew it they were ready to go. Mr. Dozer stood on the dock waving goodbye as Jimmy backed Sea Horse out of the slip and headed down West Gregoire Channel. The wind was blowing fifteen knots behind them and as soon as he could Jimmy spun Sea Horse into the wind, raised the mainsail, then tacked back, rolled out the headsail, and killed the motor. The wind grabbed the sails and off they went heading almost downwind, the warm Caribbean breeze blowing Sea Horse to one of the most beautiful beaches in the Caribbean that Jimmy knew, Drift's Bay on Iguana Island.

Sea Horse sailed like a dream as the wind picked up and soon she was racing down the channel. They passed Lion's anchorage, a place where many cruising boats anchored out for free, then after thirty minutes of awesome sailing, Jimmy turned hard to port, easing around a large rock outcropping, and pulled into Drift's Bay. Amy rolled the headsail up, then Jimmy brought the boat to a stop fifty yards from a beautiful white sand beach which was surrounded by coconut palm trees swaying gracefully in the breeze. He walked up to the bow, dropped the anchor in twenty-five feet of water, laid out a hundred feet of chain then walked back to the helm and backed down setting the anchor before turning the engine off.

"Once I get the mainsail down it's miller time," he said looking at the twins as they lay comfortably stretched out on the soft cockpit cushions.

"Jimmy, it's so beautiful," Amy said and by now he was once again starting to be able to pick out the small nuance that separated the sisters from each other.

"Well, the waters about eighty-two degrees and there aint' no sharks, except on shore, remember that, so you two ought to go swimming, while me, I'll be kicking back with a cold one," then he headed to the mast and started lowering the mainsail.

"We're going swimming alright," Sarah said, then they both disappeared below.

After securing the main, he grabbed a cold beer out of the galley then sat in the shade of the bimini dodger thinking about the twins and how they often spoke for each other like they were the same person, as if somehow they shared one well connected brain but had two individual, simply beautiful bodies.

In a few minutes the girls climbed back on deck wearing incredibly skimpy bikinis. If it wasn't the twins Jimmy would have started drooling the moment they appeared, but he couldn't.

"What is this? This isn't a nudist colony, you two! You're trouble, you know it. Get downstairs and get some clothes on . . . my god, you two," he said with a laugh choking on his beer.

"Jimmy don't be like dad, come on, it's a new millennium, besides nothing really shows," one of them said and Jimmy couldn't tell who it was because everything he associated with the twins being different from each other just disappeared before his eyes.

"Alright you two, now here is the law, no boys, no boys, no boys, and that goes for dirty old men as well, understand?"

They both giggled, giving him that who me innocent look again and he knew right then that he should have bought that shotgun. Then they both dove into the crystal clear water and started swimming for the beach.

Chapter 8

The sunset was incredible. A huge swath of red and gold raced across the western sky silhouetted against the tall clouds on the far horizon. It was all so magical as Jimmy sat there working on his fourth beer, but he knew a lot of things started to seem like magic around four beers. The twins were still on shore and he was starting to worry about them because the last time he had seen the girls they were heading toward the far corner of the beach, right to Joey's Beach Bar. The bar was just a shack built on the back of a flatbed truck so they could get past the zoning laws that forbid any permanent structures from being built on the beach. He could faintly hear some Caribbean music drifting from the direction of Joey's, and some vague laughter, but the surf made it hard to tell exactly what he was hearing. Jesus, he thought, if nothing else they should be back by now because they must be freezing seeing as both their swimsuits combined wouldn't cover a gnat's ass.

Jimmy was feeling mellow and lazy but he was also worrying more and more so he finally forced himself to move. He stood up, finished his beer, threw the empty can in the cockpit, climbed into the inflatable and raced off for the far corner of Driff's Bay. He had to go around the designated swimming area which was partitioned off with large red and white floats so he decided to swing out a little more into the anchorage and drive by a large yacht that had anchored about an hour ago. The yacht's anchor had barely touched down before four or five guys had hopped into a large dinghy and headed right for Joeys. Those damn twins were going to make him a nervous wreck before this trip was over and that would be getting off easy, he thought.

Pulling into shallow water just before shore he killed the engine then raised the outboard motor and coasted to a stop on the sandy beach. He climbed out, tied the long dinghy rope to a pole sticking in the sand that had a few other dinghies tied to it and headed for the bar. Ten short steps later he could see the twins and they were enjoying themselves immensely. They were surrounded by a group of testosterone filled young guys, all laughing and moving to the rhythm of a Caribbean beat. Five guys hung over the twins like flies on . . . well. Shit, Jimmy thought as he walked up to the bar. The girls had their backs to him so they didn't see him coming. He sat down on the edge of a bar stool which was occupied by some big fat guy who was drooling over Amy or Sarah, he couldn't tell which and as he sat down he swung his hips knocking the guy off the stool onto the sand.

"Hi girls," he said, looking at them shaking his head, as they spun around with very surprised, then embarrassed looks on their faces, "did you forget about your dear old dad? You know I was worried about you two," Jimmy said keeping his focus on the twins not the guys all around them.

The guy he pushed off the seat came up swearing as his friends all stopped whatever they were doing for a few seconds of awkward silence before they all burst into drunken laughter.

"Son of a bitch man, why'd you do that?" the drunken fat guy said standing right in front of Jimmy his breath smelling like a brewery and an ash tray.

"Shut up," Jimmy replied then continued in a jovial, let's us be friends voice, "you dudes know these two sweethearts are my daughters, right? I know you find that hard to believe, seeing as how we are almost the same age, but take my word for it, they're my girls, and I am a very protective father."

The twins were laughing so hard they had to hang on to each other to keep from falling off the bar stools they sat on. The guys standing around looked at each other and none of them knew what to make of Jimmy, but they all knew they hadn't invited this guy and they knew he was about to spoil their party and none of them wanted him to stick around.

Another one of the guys, a big one as well walked over to Jimmy, got right in his face and gave him a stare that was meant to put the fear of god in him.

Jimmy just shook his head.

"Let me tell you boys something. You've been so nice to my girls I want to buy you all a drink," he turned to the woman bartender, who just stood there with her mouth open, not knowing what to think.

"A round for my friends."

"We ain't your friends, pops. We don't even want you here, so why don't you split," the big guy said still sticking his face right in Jimmy's.

"Look, bozo, be smart, take my offer, have a free drink then go home."

The twins by now had suddenly stopped laughing and were painfully aware of the explosive situation that was brewing around them.

The big guy smiled an evil smirk then suddenly reached out and tried to push Jimmy off the bar stool. Jimmy simply leaned back out of the way, grabbed his right arm, and, using the big guy's momentum pulled him forward just enough causing him to lose his balance and he banged into the bar and fell on the ground. Jimmy put his right foot on the guy as he tried to get to his knees and pushed him back into the sand.

"Boys, please, I understand your frustration at the moment, but let's be civil," Jimmy said keeping his eyes focused on the guys around him.

"Civil hell," another one of them said as he suddenly came at Jimmy with a round house punch. Jimmy jumped to his feet, kicked the guy who was still struggling to get, then twisted away from the oncoming blow. Grabbing the punch as it went by his face Jimmy locked it in his grip then spun the guys arm high in the air as he kicked his attackers feet out from underneath him and the poor guy slammed into the sand landing on his back. Still holding the wrist Jimmy grabbed his elbow with his left hand and stepping over him flipped him on his stomach then started corkscrewing the arm, twisting it and driving it through his shoulder blade causing an incredible scream of anguish to explode from his attackers lips. His friends all froze, each one a second away from attacking.

Jimmy squeezed down on the arm once more and the guy screamed again. Jimmy was standing upright, his knees slightly bent, his left foot wedged tight in the poor guys armpit as he rotated the big guys arm behind him and slowly continued driving it out the other side of his body. Jimmy knew this guy wasn't going anywhere.

"Any of you assholes move and I'll rip his arm off and beat the hell out of you with it, got it?" he said staring at the young men standing around him, and then he gave another twist to the poor guy who screamed in agony yelling at his friends to back off.

"I don't want to hurt you dudes, so I think I'll take my daughters and head home. It's been fun but the fun is over."

Jimmy stood, dropped the guys arm, stepped over him and started reaching for the girls when out of the corner of his eye he saw a blur rushing at him. He spun to his right as somebody came racing in with fists flying. Jimmy didn't even think, just reacted, which if he had thought he probably wouldn't have kicked the guy as hard as he did. Jimmy's right foot caught the new attacker under the chin smashing him backward sending his feet flying off the sand and he crashed into the bar so hard that he almost knocked it off the flat bed truck before he crumpled in the sand.

Jimmy's adrenaline flowed and he was once again the martial arts warrior. He swung to the left where the remaining guys stood and screamed a kiaha as he whipped his left arm in front of him in a blocking motion. The entire group froze but only for a second before they turned almost as one, each operating on some sort of primitive self preservation instinct, and they took off running down the beach.

The twins were staring at Jimmy, with their mouths hanging open, neither of them were laughing any more. Jimmy turned to them, took a long deep breath trying to calm himself.

"Let's go," he said in a stern voice.

They drove the dinghy to Sea Horse without saying a word. The twins huddled together in the bow still drunk but sober enough to know they were in trouble and what they got themselves into was stupid. Once on board the girls went below and Jimmy sat on deck waiting. Soon the boys from the beach climbed into their inflatable and started back to their yacht. Jimmy watched as someone on board pointed out Sea Horse and every head on the dinghy turned his way, and somewhere in the back of Jimmy's mind was that little voice that told him this wasn't over, no not yet.

Chapter 9

It was after 8 p.m. and Lester was working on his computer. No other lights were on in his home office and the glow of the screen cast haunting shadows throughout the room. He had been working for the last three hours, staring at the screen, racking his brain, forcing himself to think through all the details, knowing that he couldn't afford to overlook anything. He finally stopped punching the keyboard and leaned back in his chair, scrunched his sore shoulders and pictured all ten members of his close knit team. He couldn't imagine any one of them selling out. All of his people had years with the agency and each of them had security clearances that would have shown any problems coming a long time ago. The leak could have come from further up the food chain. Maybe someone associated with Flynn and his people. But he was getting no answers there. The day after the murders everything associated with Flynn became classified beyond his clearance. Nobody was talking, and trying to open that door was impossible.

Focusing back to his people he thought that if it wasn't any of them then it could be somebody close, somebody who had access, a lover maybe, that was a good place to start, but thinking over his people he couldn't picture any of them being drawn into a compromising situation. All seven men and three women seemed happily married, and most had kids, Still, Lester knew sex happens, even twice in his twenty-eight years of marriage he'd had an affair, even though only once on each occasion. The problem with sex was that it didn't leave a paper trail, hotels bills paid with cash, no large money transfer to track down as when greed is the motivation. A discreet hour here or there, an overnight rendezvous, an out of town trip, hell it could be one of their house cleaners for all he knew. Christ, he'd need fifty people to watch his team and he knew that wouldn't work, talk about going the wrong direction. This was all about containment not expansion. Yet even if one of his people had a lover that wouldn't explain the breach of security, all of his people were professionals, nobody would scream out company business in the middle of an orgasm. He was at a complete loss, there was nothing more he could do at the moment, and that thought scared the hell out of him.

The GPS A-200 series tracking device, smaller than a quarter had been installed on every team member's car as well as their spouses. The beauty of the A-200 was that he was able to track each unit in live time or if he wanted he could see their movements for the last seventy-two hours by a simple click on his computer. He could even impose all ten units on the same screen, each transponder reflecting a different color.

He reached for the keyboard and closed out the file, then scrolled through his shortcuts on the menu page before hitting maintenance and opened up a simple ledger page showing costs for the last year. He ran the courser down the page and double clicked on lawn which opened up a half page of miscellaneous costs. He clicked on fertilizer and waited a few seconds before his computer brought up a screen showing a numbered list of eight items. He brought the curser down to where a ninth item would be listed and doubled click, bringing up a password bar. He typed in a seven letter password and waited until the screen showed a NOAA nautical chart of the Virgin Islands with three small dots, one blue, one green, the other red, all blinking at Iguana Island. He sat back and wondered what the twins were up to. Having an A-200 transponder sewed in the liner of both of their small daypacks was good insurance and having Flip hide another one aboard Sea Horse was easy. In his business he had learned years ago to protect those that you love and never underestimate what can possibly go wrong.

*

"My shoulder hurts like a son of a bitch," Tommy Olsen said as he held the ice pack tight to his right shoulder.

Tommy sat on the large sofa in the main living room of the yacht *Bunny Hut*, his four friends sitting around him and none of them was saying a word. Each of them felt like shit for letting their host get his ass kicked. Tommy was still drunk, pissed off and worse he felt like a fool.

"I bring you assholes down here to my uncle's resort, pay your fucking expenses, treat you better than you deserve, and you let some ninja asshole kick my butt. What a bunch of crap," Tommy said spitting the words out.

He stared at his friends sitting around him, his anger already starting to fade, but he wasn't quite ready to let any of them know it.

"Somebody get me a damn beer," he said to nobody in particular and all four of his buddies jumped up.

Mikey grabbed a cold one from the fridge, walked back and handed it to him.

"Sorry Tommy," he said his voice so apologetic that Tommy almost started laughing.

"Listen you guys, I ain't done with that guy on Sea Horse, far from it. I've got the captain listening to the radio and if that dude gets on it for anything we're going to be listening."

"Good thinking, Tommy," Billy said, holding an ice pack to his sore ribs. His right arm felt like it was broken even though he could move it a bit so he knew it wasn't. At least he had tried to take the ninja guy out, he thought. At least he did something.

Tommy stared at his friends one more time before he figured he'd given them a hard enough time. He started laughing as he looked around the room at the sullen expressions on their faces.

"Listen guys, it's our last night together before you shit heads fly home, so this party ain't over. Grab some beers, and put some tunes on. I got a great new porno flick. It'll take a while to get back to Three Cove Island so let's keep the party going."

Chapter 10

The first full day of sailing with the twins was perfect. The trade-winds were blowing twenty knots with seas only three to five feet. This simply was the best vacation Jimmy could ever dream of. They had departed Iguana Cay about ten-thirty and sailed a few hours to Sand Cay, a beautiful little island not thirty acres across with glistening white sandy beaches, surrounded with turquoise clear water. There were a few boats anchored there and Jimmy was impressed by a small French sailboat that had one guy and two women on board. The women spent most of the day in the nude sunbathing or swimming around the boat and Jimmy was having a hard time not being obnoxious. Finally around three he had enough, pulled up the anchor and they sailed to Salt Rock, where they went snorkeling for a while before they swam ashore and walked for an hour on another gorgeous Caribbean beach.

Throughout the day the twins had kept lathering themselves with gobs of sunscreen smearing white streaks of it everywhere and Jimmy thought about offering to apply some of that sun protection himself but he didn't because he just couldn't open that door, Christ, not with the twins, regardless of how beautiful they looked. But between the French girls and the twins his hormones were definitely starting to affect his thinking process.

That evening they tucked Sea Horse into a little cove called Loreen Bay which had no other boats. The twins helped cook dinner, two Cornish game hens that Jimmy had pulled out of the freezer early in the afternoon. They sat in the cockpit drinking fine Merlot and feasting on provisions that Lester had paid for. Jimmy opened a second bottle after dinner and poured the three of them another round.

There was another reason besides the beauty of this place that had caused Jimmy to pick this quiet little anchorage although he didn't mention it to the girls. There wasn't a beach bar at Lorreen Bay, as a matter of fact there was nothing on shore, no resorts, nothing, the entire Island was a national park and there wasn't a place the twins could go and get into trouble, not tonight anyway.

Jimmy was leaning back against the cockpit coaming, with a large cushion wedged between himself and the fiberglass, his legs stretched out and felt like he was in heaven. Amy was sitting with his feet on her lap and she was rubbing them with one hand while holding her wine glass in the other. Sarah was standing at the wheel turning it back and forth, a silly look on her face as she made loud swishing noise as if she was steering through huge seas.

"This is so much fun Jimmy. I just can't believe it," Sarah said still spinning the wheel leaning her body left then right as if she was being thrown around by battering waves.

"Sarah, darling, don't fall over the side. I doubt we could do a man . . . I mean a woman overboard rescue at the moment," he laughed, "not in these dangerous conditions, why . . . you might not make it back alive."

"Jimmy, you'd rescue me no matter what, I know it," she said still turning the wheel, smiling then she blew Jimmy a kiss.

Jimmy couldn't believe the situation that he found himself in at the moment, the twins, the boat, the quiet anchorage, the on going foot massage, the stars twinkling on and off in the sky, the merlot, it was just too perfect.

"Tell me, you two, do either of you have a boyfriend?"

Sarah and Amy glanced at each other and both smiled at the same time.

"Why, Jimmy," Amy said, as she twisted his foot backward a bit, "don't you know boys are trouble?"

"Yeah," Sarah blurted out, "they all just want one thing."

Jimmy almost choked on his Merlot, "What," he stammered, completely surprised at Sarah's unexpected answer.

Another look at the twins, each wearing that innocent look on their faces and Jimmy just started laughing and then suddenly he did started choking on his half swallowed sip of wine and couldn't stop, which made the girls start laughing and pretty soon all three of them were in hysterics laughing so hard that Sarah fell down on the cockpit floor which made everybody laugh even more. By the time they regained themselves everybody had tears running down their faces.

"That was not the answer I expected!" he finally managed to say, brushing tears from his cheeks.

"Well it's true and you know it. Why, I watched you today at the anchorage looking at that French boat," Amy said squeezing his foot again.

"Okay, okay I'm guilty as charged."

"Do you have a girlfriend?" Sarah asked.

"Maybe," he said smugly.

"Can we meet her?" they both said at the same time, again.

"Which one?"

"Jimmy," Amy twisted his foot again, "you're a jerk."

"No I'm not, just teasing, maybe I'll let you two meet her, if you promise to be nice," although Jimmy wasn't sure if he even had a girlfriend or not, but he started thinking about Megan the moment Sarah asked.

"Jimmy, I bet you have hundreds of girl friends down here. You're trouble. You're a heartache waiting to happen," Amy said and Jimmy pulled his foot away before she could twist it again.

Soon the conversation became a little more serious and the three of them ended up talking for hours. As the evening continued Jimmy became more impressed by the twins. What wonderful, caring young women they had become. He opened his heart to them, told them about his second wife and even told them the story of beating her lover and going to jail. The twins told him about past boyfriends, about trouble in school, about trouble with their parents. The closeness that the three of them felt as the night went on was so real, and it was after midnight when the twins excused themselves and climbed down into their own little private cabins in the forward split v-berth.

Jimmy lingered, watching the stars, feeling the gentle motion of Sea Horse as she gently bobbed in the small protected anchorage. As he stared at the starry night he couldn't believe the peace, the serenity, the joy that he felt at this very moment. This magical night would stay with him forever. Life was as good as it gets and he hoped that for the next thirteen days it was going to stay this way.

After what seemed like an hour but was only twenty minutes he climbed down the companionway steps and walked back into his aft cabin. He grabbed his cell phone, walked out on deck and called the "Hook". After three rings somebody answered and he could hear the party in full swing.

"Listen, this is Jimmy, is Megan working?"

He had a hard time even hearing the guy over the music that blared in the background but he thought the guy said yeah and hold on. Jimmy stood there staring out over the serenity of the anchorage, thinking that he sure liked it better here than at the bar when Megan came on the line.

"Hello."

"Megan darling, it's your long lost boyfriend."

"Which one?" but she had that smile in her voice and he knew she was messin' with him.

"Which one? Why, I'm shocked. I'll give you a clue. It's your boyfriend who is anchored this moment as we speak in Loreen Bay, on a fifty-four foot Alden, staring at the heavens and who misses you dearly. Does that help?"

"Jimmy, you're pulling my leg!"

"Never, listen, I'm babysitting two of my nieces for a few weeks and their rich daddy chartered us this boat. He had some business dealing or something back in the states . . . anyway, I'm here gazing at such a beautiful sky that it made me think of you."

"You're full of it."

"I might be but I never tell a lie. Listen, Megan why don't you come aboard and we'll go sailing for a few days."

"I don't know if I could trust you . . . you know you can be irresistible at times."

"Megan darling, this boat has four cabins. Why, I never dreamt that we would share a bunk, this is strictly platonic, just because I enjoy your company so much."

"Platonic, then forget it."

"Okay, maybe not completely platonic, what do you say?"

"Jimmy, oh Jimmy, what is a poor girl to do? Besides I'm at work. I've got drunk customers demanding more. Call me tomorrow."

"Absolutely."

He clicked off the phone and felt weak in the knees. Boy, he thought this could get really interesting if Megan climbed aboard.

Chapter 11

Tommy Olsen found himself on the sofa right where he had passed out last night sometime after three in the morning. Two of the boys, Butch and Sunny, looking like they were dead, were sleeping on the other small sofas their feet scrunched up underneath them. Tommy had a fleeting thought about alcohol poisoning and wondered if they really might be dead before he sat up. Mikey and Billy were no place to be seen and must have crawled off to their cabins. Tommy leaned over and looked at the clock in the galley, it was almost noon.

He felt sick, his head was spinning, the boat was rocking and he knew the only way to make it through today was to start with a bloody mary and not stop. Damn hangovers were getting worse the older he got and at thirty-four years old he had drunk enough to put most sensible people in an AA program.

Stumbling over to the stereo he hit play and headed for the galley as ZZ Top came on rockin'. Hell with his sleeping bud's, he thought, its time for their lazy asses to face the day.

He made some coffee then walked up into the pilot house hoping to see the captain but he wasn't around. Dropping himself down into the pilot seat he gazed over Cantelle Bay, looking at his uncle's resort. It really was beautiful down here. Lots of chicks, strutting around half naked, and the way he figured it most of them were just waiting for him to come calling. Plus his uncle owned the damn place and that helped impress the ladies. He'd been able to give more than a few willing foxes the inside tour of the resort and that tour usually ended in his bungalow. Damn, he really did love it down here he thought sipping his coffee.

He reached over, grabbed the radio microphone and clicked to channel 68, which the resort monitored.

"Cantelle Bay resort this is *Bunny Hut*."

Whoever answered the radio must have known that *Bunny Hut* was tied up at the dock but they answered politely anyway, "good morning, may we help you?"

"Yes, as a matter of fact, you can. I need five bloody marys delivered asap!"

"That's five bloody marys?"

"Roger. And if possible make them doubles."

"Yes sir," the lady on the radio said with a smile in her voice and clicked off.

Tommy walked back down to the galley where Billy was sitting with an ice pack held tight to his ribs.

"Still hurtin?" Tommy asked.

"Yep, my ribs, my back, my arm but mostly my damn head."

Tommy sat down beside him with a laugh.

"Billy, I got bloody marys on the way. That'll take some of the sting away. You know, dude, I'm proud of you the way you went after that guy on the beach."

Billy beamed with the compliment.

"You guys are out of here today but I tell you what just between you and me, I'm gonna hit that ninja asshole a couple of extra times for you, alright?" Tommy said then put an arm around his friend.

Billy laughed, "Tommy, you're so damn thoughtful."

*

"Jimmy, that breakfast was wonderful," Amy said as she finished putting the dishes in the sink, "you know you are starting to impress me, you cook, you communicate, at least last night you did, why I bet you can even clean. You know that's the way to a woman's heart, the three c's, cook, clean, communicate?"

"Amy, I'm a jerk. Remember, last night ? That's what you called me."

Sarah butted in, "she was only kidding. Besides that's not important, what is important is when do we get to meet your girlfriend?"

"Who said you're going to meet my girlfriend" he said looking up from the nautical chart he was studying.

"Well, you have one, don't you, or maybe you have three or four and you don't want us to meet any of them." Sarah continued.

"Three or four, you two are nuts? If, and I said if I allow you to meet my present girlfriend," he was suddenly sounding so sophisticated the twins looked at each other and rolled their eyes, "you must promise me you will be on your best behavior."

"We promise, really, we do," they said together.

"Alright. My favorite girlfriend of the day is Megan. I called her last night and she might be able to get away for a few days and come sailing with us. Does that sound alright with you two?"

"Absolutely," they said at the same time, and he thought about one brain and two beautiful bodies.

"Okay," he said as he stood up," let's go sailing. I know a great place to go this morning and if we like it we can spend the night."

"Aye, aye Captain," Sarah said following him up the companionway steps.

Soon Sea Horse was once again in her element, the trade winds blowing fifteen to twenty knots, the seas calm, only a few feet of long ocean swell, all the sails set and pulling hard. Jimmy sat on the side of the cockpit with his right foot on the wheel and his back leaning against the lifelines. He was feeling about as relaxed as he could ever remember. The twins were already lathered up, each wearing a skimpy bikini, trying to keep the sun off of their faces with broad rim straw hats, and both were peering out through expensive sunglasses. The twins could have been in a commercial, they looked spectacular, and this was just about as perfect as it gets. About the only thing that could make this moment any better would be if Megan was onboard wearing a copy of the twin's bikini. Ah, Jimmy thought with a smile, the trials and tribulations of life.

An hour later the anchor bit down off of a small beach on Goat Island. Jimmy killed the engine, walked over and sat down next to the twins.

"This is a great snorkeling spot. I've seen turtles and sting rays here and twice I've seen moray eels, but they won't bother you."

"What about sharks?" Amy asked sitting up.

"Remember, girls, the only sharks around here travel on two legs." They both laughed.

"Jimmy, call your girlfriend," Sarah said.

"Why are you two so damn interested in my girlfriend?"

"Because," Amy said.

"Because why?"

"Just because."

"Lets go snorkeling. I'll call her later."

Jimmy dug three sets of snorkeling gear out, adjusted the fins and masks to fit everybody, then into the warm eighty-degree water they went. An hour later they came back on board for a lunch break and then it was back in the water for the girls.

Jimmy held off getting in the water, he told them he had something to do and he would be back in as soon as he could. Once the girls were snorkeling he walked down to the chart table grabbed his cell phone and walked back on deck.

"Megan honey, good afternoon."

"Why, Jimmy, just a minute, let me kick Fred out of my bed," she laughed.

"Megan, you're terrible."

"I know. What's up?" she sounded so innocent and naïve.

"What's up? Did you forget my call last night?"

"Oh that was you?"

"Megan, you're breaking my heart. I have a serious question."

"Serious, my . . . you're not proposing are you?"

"In a way yes, I want you to know that all marriages aboard my yacht are valid for the duration of the voyage."

"I've heard that line before."

"You haven't from me."

"Jimmy are we going sailing or what?"

"Megan, absolutely when can you get away?"

"I called my boss this morning, I got four days off. Think you can put up with me that long?"

Jimmy paused as if thinking through such a difficult question

"Maybe?" he laughed.

"Now you're the one who's being terrible."

"Megan I'll meet you at the dock in Red Hook around eleven tomorrow morning."

"I'll be there, what should I bring?"

"Do you have a skimpy bikini?"

Chapter 12

Jimmy couldn't tell who was more excited as Sea Horse pulled into Red Hook, him or the twins. They had been pestering him all morning about Megan. What color was her hair, where was she from, did he love her, on and on it went until Jimmy couldn't stand their grilling and he hit the throttle full speed ahead getting every mile per hour out of his boat that he could.

Megan was standing on the dock, a small canvas bag at her feet. She wasn't bringing much and Jimmy thought that was a good sign. He backed off the throttle, spun Sea Horse into a slip, hit reverse and the yacht came to a stand still right in front of her. It looked like he had done it a thousand times.

"Good job, Jimmy," Megan said as she grabbed the mid-ship spring line and cleated it off.

"Megan, my dear, meet the twins, Amy and Sarah."

Megan glanced up from tying off the spring line and just about fell over. She was expecting ten or twelve year olds, not twenty-one year old women, and certainly not the way these two looked.

The twins both smiled shyly and Jimmy didn't know what to say.

"These are your nieces? You expect me to believe that? What kind of kinky trip is this going to be, Jimmy McBain?" she said half serious.

"Well," he said with a laugh, "they're more like sisters from different parents if you know what I mean?"

He unhooked the life-line, extended his hand down to Megan who handed him her small bag, then he pulled her on board.

"Sisters from different parents, that's original," she said as she gave him a hug then walked to Amy and held out her hand for a warm handshake before walking to Sarah and greeting her the same way.

"Somehow I don't want to know this story," Megan said sitting down under the bimini shade cover.

"Really it is quite simple. I've known the twins and their folks for years and we really are like family," Jimmy said as he sat down next to her.

A warm smile grew on Megan's face, "If you two have known Jimmy for years and you still," she emphasized still as she looked at the twins, "like him then I think we'll get along fine."

"Oh I know we will," Amy said.

"Why don't you two bring Megan downstairs and show her cabin number four. That's her private cabin," Jimmy said, with a shrug.

The twins both gave him a funny look and so did Megan before all three of them climbed down the companionway steps and disappeared.

Fifteen minutes later Sea Horse was once again racing across a turquoise Caribbean Sea, rail down, an occasional wave flying over the bow. Megan was at the helm, steering with both hands while Jimmy was standing right behind her with their bodies tight against each other as he pointed out some sailing tips, which they both knew she didn't need because she'd been sailing down here for years. The twins were sitting under the bimini cover all lathered with white sunscreen watching the two of them.

Jimmy leaned his head close to Megan's ear and whispered, "I think were being watched."

"I told them I need a chaperone. Hope you don't mind."

"Funny, that's what I told them, too."

She laughed, stepped back standing on his right foot and gently ground her heel on it.

"Jimmy I'm so glad you invited me, I really am."

"Megan," he reached down and kissed her left ear, "I'm delighted you could fit me into your busy schedule."

Megan steered for the next few hours, not sure where she was going but trusting Jimmy as he told her to change course and tack every once in a while. He had a special destination in mind for this evening and he wanted to keep it a secret as long as possible. Somewhere during the late afternoon it must have become obvious to Megan that they were heading for Peter Island but she didn't say anything. The twins were happy as ever and Sea Horse raced on, rail still down, and Jimmy just couldn't believe the wonderful situation that he found himself in.

Soon Jolly Man Resort came into view. They kept sailing until they were only a few hundred yards away from the entrance to the small marina.

"Time to head into the wind, Megan," he said as he blew her a kiss and headed for the mast. Megan luffed Sea Horse into the wind spilling the air from the sails.

"Amy, Sarah, help Megan roll in the headsail will you?" he said as he took the mainsail halyard off the self tailing winch and let the sail drop.

Jimmy climbed around Sea Horse like he was born to the sea. Soon the mainsail was neatly stowed, wrapped with colorful red strips of nylon, the headsail was rolled up perfectly.

"What a crew. I'd take this scurvy lot anywhere," he said in a pirate accent as he gave the girls a wink.

Jimmy grabbed the wheel from Megan and then reached for the cockpit VHF radio, and dialed channel 68 which most resorts monitored.

"Jolly Man Resort, this is Sea Horse, over."

There was a minute delay before a cheerful native talking with a Jamaican accent came back on the radio.

"Sea Horse, this is Jolly Man Resort. Good afternoon. How may we help you?"

"Jolly Man, good afternoon, I'm the 54 foot sailboat just off your dock I'd like a slip for tonight."

"No problem, captain. Come on in and use slip number three, it's a starboard tie."

"Roger that."

"Megan, would you please dig some fenders out of the port locker, and tie them on starboard? I have the dock lines in there as well."

"Yes Captain," she said in a sexy voice and Jimmy momentarily forgot what he was going to say next.

"Sarah and Amy, please help her with the lines," he stammered a moment later.

"Yes, Captain," they both mimicked Megan's sexy voice.

Once everything was ready Jimmy eased Sea Horse into her slip and turned the motor off.

"Job well done, Captain," Megan said as she walked back to him standing at the wheel and gave him a long kiss, a kiss that left him momentarily speechless, again.

"Why, I'll dock this boat all day long for a kiss like that," he finally managed to say after catching his breath.

"I bet you would," she replied with a grin.

"Beverage time," Jimmy said.

The rum punch came out, poured into glasses full of ice, and down in the islands ice was more of a luxury than rum. Amy cut little slices of kiwi and orange and decorated each drink with fruit slivers. The twins finished their first drink like it was water and Jimmy and Megan weren't far behind. After three drinks apiece they wandered up the dock and found a table overlooking the beach at the Jolly Man restaurant. Looking over the menu Jimmy almost gagged at the prices but he kept the shock to himself. This night was his treat and he wasn't going to spoil it by being a tight ass.

More drinks went around, the food came and it was all simply fabulous. Calypso music floated through the bar where they went after dinner for one more drink.

The twins were hammered by the time they all climbed aboard Sea Horse and it didn't take them long to pass out in their cabins, which is exactly what Jimmy was hoping would happen.

The moon had yet to appear and a million stars glowed in the heavens as the Calypso music continued to drift over the calm waters filling their cockpit with a soft rhythm that seemed to carry the soul of the Caribbean with it. Megan was sitting on a cushion leaning back against the rail as Jimmy climbed up from below after checking to make sure the twins were out.

"How's your nieces?" Megan asked.

Jimmy walked in front of her, reached down and gently brought her face up to his. He drew her lips close, looked into her beautiful eyes and kissed her with a passion that had been building for way too long.

Megan wrapped her arms around his head pulling him into the kiss, her tongue exploring deep into the softness of his mouth.

"Megan oh Megan."

"Jimmy," she whispered in his ear so softly that he almost didn't hear.

"What?" he said kissing her ear then running his tongue down her neck.

"Shut up and kiss me."

Chapter 13

The next morning was a slow start for everybody. The twins didn't make a sound until almost eleven and Jimmy and Megan were in no hurry to climb out of their little aft cabin. The hatches were all open and a gentle breeze blew caressing them as they lay naked. Megan's back was tucked against Jimmy's chest, their hips tight together like spoons in a drawer. Jimmy's left hand gently rubbed her neck, his right tenderly played with her small love handles.

"Oh Jimmy," she purred softly, her voice so sultry.

"Oh Megan."

Megan turned in his arms, faced him, brought her lips to his and kissed him gently. Then she kicked the sheet off that they were lying under and climbed on top of him, sitting on his muscular stomach. She put her arms on his chest and looked down with a smile on her face.

"You're very nice to wake up to, you know."

"So I've been told."

"Wrong answer," she said, then pushed his head sideways and brought her lips down and gently kissed his neck before bringing her lips to his ear and whispering, "that answer will get you nowhere."

"I knew it was wrong from the moment it escaped my lips, how about I've never woken up to a more beautiful woman in my bed than you in my entire short life."

"Close, but not good enough."
"Good enough for what?"
"Time's running out."
"How about kiss me you fool?"

Megan didn't say a word as she leaned over and brought her lips down hard on Jimmy's. Slowly she started rubbing her hips back and forth, her eyes closed. Jimmy reached up, pulled her face to his and gave her another passionate kiss. She moaned softly as he thrust his hips upwards matching her rhythm. With eyes still closed she pushed herself out of his arms, her hands back on his chest leaning over him. Jimmy gently ran his hands up and over her head, pushing long strands of hair behind her ear before bringing his hands down to the small of her back. She was now rocking harder against him, breathing deeper, soft moans of pleasure escaping on every breath she exhaled. Jimmy couldn't believe how beautiful she looked. He grabbed the small folds of skin on her sides and forcefully arched his back thrusting himself upward, all the while entranced by the passionate beauty on her face. With a deep sigh Megan pushed down harder forcing his body into hers and they melted into one, bodies entwined, dancing to the tempo of desire and passion, pushing, pulling, rocking, Jimmy holding her tightly, Megan digging her fingernails into his chest tugging, creating jolts of pain and pleasure as they moved together, hearts pounding as one. Cries of ecstasy filled the small aft cabin spilling over into the rest of the boat but neither cared. They made love until they were exhausted, then crumpled into each others arms. Jimmy held her tight feeling her hot sweaty body against his. Her breathing coming in uncontrolled gasps that blew against the side of his face and down his neck. He couldn't catch his breath either, sweat poured from him, his stomach was wet and slippery as she hugged him tight.

Jimmy's mind was flooded with endorphins, his body glowed with the sweet release that only such passion can bring and as he lay there he knew he was falling in love and he didn't have a clue what to do next.

*

The captain of Bunny Hut walked over to the table that Tommy and his uncle were sitting at just as they were finishing breakfast.

"Good morning Mr. Balero, Tommy," he said, as he pulled out a chair and sat down.

Frankie and Tommy must have been having a serious discussion because both men looked at the captain but neither said a word.

"Sorry to disturb your breakfast, tried to find you last night, but you weren't around," the captain said as he stood back up, looking at Tommy, "one of my crew that I had listening to the radio, heard Sea Horse, the boat you were asking about last night, thought you might want to know."

"Damn right I do," Tommy said looking at the captain then at his uncle.

"Is that the guy you were just telling me about?" Frankie asked.

"Yep that's him."

Looking back at the captain Tommy asked, "where is he?"

"He pulled into Jolly Man Resort, got a slip. I haven't heard him this morning. Don't know if he checked out or not."

"Thanks," Tommy said as the captain started walking away.

"Yeah, thanks, Carl," Frankie said.

"Well, that's a nice bit of news. What are you going to do?" Frankie asked, hoping to see his nephew who he knew was more mouth then anything else, rise to the occasion.

"I think I'm going to beat the hell out of that guy."

"By yourself?'

"Hardly, no, He's pretty good with that ninja shit. I was thinking about a little surprise."

"Sounds like you've given this some thought, have you?"

"Your damn right I have. That guy kicked my ass in front of my best bud's and he is going to pay."

Frankie smiled and hoped to god that Tommy was going to follow through with his threats. It was time the boy started acting like a man, not just a braggadocios punk.

"Time to go," Tommy said as he pushed himself away from the table and headed for the boat house.

*

Tommy was in the twenty-two foot Sea Ray powered by two 135 Honda outboards and he was making a good twenty-five knots. The boat was crashing through the swells sending cascading water high into the air before it was blown away by the breeze. He had left his friends back at the resort knowing they could get to the airport without his help.

The radio was turned up loud, automatically switching between channel 16 and 68. Tommy knew that more than likely either of those channels would be the one Sea Horse would use. Peter Island was fourteen miles from Cantelle Bay and at this speed it wouldn't take him very long to get there.

Tommy had been thinking about the best way to handle this guy since he woke up with a hangover this morning. He figured the smartest thing to do would be to stay out of sight, watch him and see where he went. If he stayed at Jolly Man it would be impossible to have a boatload of Frankie's boys come over and beat the hell out of him. But if he took off sailing for the day, and found some little deserted anchorage somewhere for the night then it would be easy for him and the boys to crash this guy's party. Tommy also kept thinking about those two foxes that were on board, man they were hot and he got excited just thinking about those babes. He figured if his boys started beating the hell out of that ninja guy, those two sweethearts might not be too interested in him. His first thought was so what, but he didn't like the idea of rape, it really wasn't his style. Still, he thought, those two babes all alone in some deserted anchorage pleading with him to stop the beating and he smiled knowing that he might have a nice little bargaining tool and he knew exactly what he wanted.

Chapter 14

"Annie May fishing charters," Flip said with a smile in his voice that he didn't feel, not this damn early. He looked at the clock near his bed and was surprised to see it was only six in the morning. For Christ sakes, he thought, who the hell would call this early. Still business was business and he never wanted to miss a charter.

"Good morning, sleepy head," he heard when he picked the phone up.

"Lester, what the hell time is it there?"

"It's early. I've been up for a while"

"Well, I haven't."

"So how's my daughters and Jimmy doing?"

Flip sat up, scratched his head, picturing Lester as he tried to get his brain working, they'd been friends and "business" partners for years.

"Fine I guess?"

"You guess, come on Flip, its Amy and Sarah."

"Yeah, and they're with Jimmy so . . . don't worry."

"Worry is what I get paid to do. Have you been following them?"

"Only on the computer."

"You don't have anybody checking on them, come on Flip, don't get lazy on me."

"Jesus, Lester, they're out cruising, it's all good."

"How good?"

Flip laughed, "Come on, Lester, the twins and Jimmy are family. You got to trust them, besides they're adults."

"Trust is something I've been having difficulty with lately."

Flip knew there was a lot more to the statement than just a simple remark but he let it go.

"Jimmy brought his girlfriend on board yesterday."

"Oh yeah, is she nice?"

"Megan is her name. Yeah, she's real nice, everybody around her loves her. She's a real sweetheart, Lester."

"And she's with Jimmy?" he said with a laugh.

"Jimmy's good people, you know that. Down here we live and let live and he fits right in."

Lester leaned back in his chair feeling better by the second. His daughters were safe, and Jimmy had a girlfriend on board. He knew his fears were stupid but still a father always worries about his daughters, especially when they are as beautiful as his.

"Alright Flip, I'll let you go, but keep tabs on them will you?"

"Lester relax, what could possibly go wrong?"

"Right," and the phone clicked dead.

*

"Jimmy, let's stay here another night," Amy said as she lay by the pool, bloody-mary in hand.

"Drinking already, you're off to a bad start."

"We're in the Caribbean, Jimmy, its vacation time, plus . . . I had a little too much fun last night."

"We all did."

"How was your morning?" Amy said with a smile and a cute little mischievous look.

"Breathless," he answered back knowing two could play this little game.

"Come on Jimmy what do you say?" Sarah piped in lying next to her sister on a large cushion.

This place was definitely not in his budget, he had spent over four hundred dollars already between slip fees, dinner and drinks and they hadn't even been here a full day. Still, Megan was loving it, lounging by the pool looking absolutely beautiful and he figured if they couldn't stay another night they might as well enjoy the resort as long as possible.

"I don't think so but let's hang here as long as we can, remember down here we are living on Island Time."

"Alright, Captain," the twins both answered at the same time.

Jimmy walked over and sat down next to Megan, she glanced up from her book, lowered her sunglasses and gave him a smile.

"Hi handsome."

"Hello beautiful, you know something?"

"Probably . . . what?"

"I think we go good together."

"Like Bonny and Clyde?"

"No more like Fred and Ginger."

"Well I know one thing," she said with another smile, then rolled her eyes.

"Oh what's that?"

She leaned over, her lips inches from his right ear "you sure got some moves," she whispered then gave him a shove which sent him rolling over.

"Hey watch it, I'm fragile," Jimmy said sitting back up.

"Yeah, fragile. That's a good one."

"Let's go for a swim," he said standing up holding his hand out for her.

She reached out grabbed his hand and let herself be pulled up which brought her into his arms, tight against his hard body.

"Not in public," she whispered then took three steps away from him and dove into the pool.

Jimmy turned to follow her but out of the corner of his eye he caught the twins both staring at him.

"What?"

They both smiled but it was Amy who mimicked Megan "not in public," she said with a laugh as her sister reached over and elbowed her in the side.

"Yeah. Not in public," Sarah repeated, looking at Jimmy then they both started giggling like twelve year olds.

*

Tommy slowed the Sea Ray just outside the small marina that was part of Jolly Man resort. He had a broad brim hat on and dark sunglasses. He figured even if that ninja guy glanced at him he probably wouldn't recognize his face. At least that was what he was hoping. There were a few sailboats in the marina and it didn't take him long to find Sea Horse, her name in gold letters on her transom.

So far so good he thought as he reached the end of the boat slips next to the bar and restaurant then he swung his boat around and slowly started out the way he came. He glanced at his watch and wondered what time check out was. Tommy motored slowly past Sea Horse again looking to see if anybody was on board but the boat looked empty.

Once away from the marina he grabbed the vhf radio microphone.
"Jolly Man Resort."
"Yes, this is Jolly Man," some one came back a minute later.
"I want to find out about getting a slip for tonight."
"Good sir, how long are you, are you power or sail?"
Tommy didn't know what to say. He didn't know much about boats.
"I'm power, sixty feet. What time is check out?"
"Check out is at noon. Do you want to make a reservation for tonight?"
"No. I'll call you back."
He clicked the radio off and looked at his watch again. It was already twelve-thirty. Maybe Sea Horse was going to spend another night, which would wreck his plans, but he'd come this far so he figured he might as well stick around and see what they did.

Steering the Sea Ray to his right he left the resort behind him, following the shoreline, his depth sounder showing fifteen feet of water. Once around a large group of rocks and with Jolly Man out of sight he headed for a white sandy beach. He hit the kill button and raised the engines up as the bow gently brushed the sand and came to a stop. He grabbed a set of binoculars, hanging them around his neck, then grabbed a long coil of rope that was in a small locker back by the engines and walked to the bow. He tied the loose end of the rope to a deck cleat before jumping off and landing on the soft sand. Uncoiling the rope as he went he walked about thirty feet before coming to some large palm trees. Throwing a few wraps around a thick palm he tied the Sea Ray off then headed for a hill and some rocks that overlooked the resort.

After walking for ten minutes he found a good spot out of the sun and somewhat hidden, and sat down looking at Jolly Man Resort. It didn't take him long to find the twins laying by the pool wearing those little bikinis that he thought with a laugh started all of this trouble in the first place. God, what bodies they had. The ninja guy and some other cutie were in the pool hugging each other like a couple of kids in heat on spring break. He looked at his watch, then settled back into his little corner in the rocks and focused on the twins. They looked so good laying there and soon his perverted mind was creating a triple xxx fantasy that would have made most of his porn flicks look pretty damn tame.

Chapter 15

It was almost three in the afternoon when Sea Horse departed Jolly Man Resort. The twins were still moving slow and Jimmy was wondering how to handle this morning's passionate and noisy affair, and if he should say anything to the sisters about it. It would be embarrassing to bring it up, but it seemed equally awkward to pretend that nothing happened and just ignore it, but after some more thought he finally figured the best thing was to let it go.

The wind was blowing and soon the sails were set and once again Sea Horse was carving deep furrows in the blue Caribbean. Jimmy was feeling great, his hang-over long gone replaced with thoughts of Megan's beautiful glow, her warm, wonderful personality and her lovely body. He couldn't get over that she was on board with him, and that she must feel the same way about him as he did about her. Love was way too complicated of a word at the moment but as he sat there watching her at the helm, pushing Sea Horse close to her limits he knew he'd found the woman that he had been searching for, and he had been looking for a very long time.

Jimmy finally pulled his thoughts back to reality and wondered just were they should go. After last night he thought a peaceful, kicked back evening in a quiet, deserted anchorage would be best. A lazy dinner by candlelight in the cockpit sounded good, along with good conversation, good wine and then maybe another lovely evening in bed with Megan. It all started to sound beyond good to him. Maybe tonight he'd turn the stereo on before he and Megan retired for the evening, a little outside noise to drown out whatever sounds might escape from their little private aft cabin, yeah, he thought, what a lovely plan for a lovely day.

A few minutes later, with Megan still at the helm, he forced himself up and went below, using the overhead grab rails as he made his way to the chart table and sat down. Spreading the local chart out before him he started looking for a nice anchorage for the night. There were a lot of choices but he finally narrowed it down. It was a good place to snorkel, the beach was awesome, although getting inside the reef was tricky, it was out of the way, and most boats didn't go there. It was one of the few anchorages that he could expect to have all to himself.

He climbed out the hatch and was surprised to see Sarah at the wheel with Megan standing next to her.

"Look, Jimmy, I'm sailing," Sarah shouted a huge grin on her face.

"Right. You are sailing and I must say you're a fine looking wench."

"I guess that's good?" she laughed back.

"Why don't we head to Henry Island? It's named after the famous pirate Henry Morgan, why there's even treasure buried there somewhere," he said watching Sarah at the wheel, and she was doing a great job steering Sea Horse.

"Treasure," Amy said excitedly, "all we have to do is dig it up and we're rich, sounds great."

"Yeah, Jimmy, let's go there and get rich" Sarah said sailing Sea Horse as hard as Megan had.

"Alright, but we share the treasure, none of this greedy stuff. Also if we want there is an old fort at the top of the island that we can hike to."

"A fort?" Megan asked.

"Most people don't know about it. It was built near the end of the world war two. It's mostly underground, huge concrete chambers and walkways, it's pretty eerie. I spent a day there a while ago with a charter and we walked through part of it. It goes on for miles."

"Why did they build a fort?" Sarah asked.

"It was built to watch out for German warships and to protect

Puerto Rico and the Virgin Islands. The view is spectacular from up there."

"No beach bar?" Sarah asked.

"Nope."

"That's good," she said looking at her sister.

As they neared the anchorage on Henry Island Jimmy once again saw the small white powerboat about half a mile away from them bouncing in the swells. He had noticed it earlier but he didn't think much about it then, just one more boat out on the Caribbean. But now it was back and just sitting there bobbing up and down and he got a funny feeling that whoever was on board was watching him. He jumped down the companionway steps, grabbed a set of binoculars off the chart table, climbed back on deck and focused them trying to see the little boat better. He could make out one person onboard but they were to far away to see much else. Watching the boat that he knew was watching them gave him a bad feeling and his first thought was about drug runners looking for a boat to hijack. He had heard of that happening in the past, but it hadn't happened for years.

"We seem to have some company," he said pointing to the boat that now suddenly started moving away. The girls stopped whatever they were doing and looked out to sea.

"Trouble?" Megan asked.

"Probably not, but I might take a few extra precautions tonight, just to be safe."

The twins looked at him and Amy was about to say something but she didn't.

"You guys want to anchor here?" he asked bringing his focus away from the little boat that was now definitely heading out to sea, "or we can go someplace else if you like?"

The three girls looked at each other and all three shrugged their shoulders.

"We don't know, Jimmy," Megan said.

"Well, I think we'll like this place."

Jimmy turned the motor on, pulled the sails down, and they made their way through the reef and into a small bay. There wasn't another boat there. Once he found where he wanted Sea Horse to lay for the night he walked to the bow and kicked the anchor release and the anchor and chain fell with a splash then Jimmy walked to the helm, backed down, setting the anchor and turned the engine off.

"Ladies, let us enjoy this lovely spot!"

*

The rest of the day was just a kicked back affair. The twins lathered themselves as usual, went snorkeling a few times, laid around and read while Jimmy and Megan found time for a short afternoon nap. The four of them started cooking dinner, drinking more of Lester's expensive wine as they did. They all had fun working together, talking, bumping into each other, laughing and telling stories, some true, the best ones not. They were a bunch of kids just playing around on a half million dollar yacht in the Caribbean, enjoying life and each other.

Too much sun, fun, wine and food took it out of them and after dinner and a few hands of Zilch, a dice game, it was about time for all of them to go to bed.

Sarah and Amy were just excusing themselves for the night when Jimmy looked at them, then Megan and said, "let's have a little meeting . . . alright?"

"Meeting like what?" Megan said surprised, she thought maybe Jimmy was going to say something about their love life but she hoped she was wrong.

"I'm not paranoid but I do like to think things through, and I don't think it's anything because if I really did we wouldn't be anchored here tonight. But that little boat was kind of weird, so I'm going to get each of you a flashlight and I want you to keep it by your bed," he said then he stood up and walked to the chart table, unfolded a chart, then looked at them and said, "come look at this."

The three girls gathered around him as he pointed out the fort on the top of the hill.

"There is a little dirt road at the end of the beach, here," he pointed it out on the chart, "it leads up to the main entrance of the fort. There are two entrances really. The main one has two large steel doors, the last time I was here they were wide open and I doubt anybody could close them, they looked pretty rusted in place. The second entrance is about two hundred feet past those doors and it's cut into the hillside. There's a small foot path off of the dirt road and it's only wide enough for a person to walk through, no cars or trucks, so it's easy to miss."

The girls were watching his hands as he traced them over the chart.

"Why do you want us to know all this?" Megan asked, with a hint of concern in her voice.

"It's nothing really. I just want you to know it's there. If for some reason something happens just head for the fort."

"Head for the fort, if what happens?" Amy replied a little worried.

"Nothing is going to happen, alright, but this is part of being prepared, like the boy scouts, so just think like the cavalry, and head for the fort," he laughed trying to ease their fears.

"Jimmy, you're scaring us," Amy said looking at her sister and Megan.

"Now don't worry, you three. I'm just a paranoid old guy with three absolutely gorgeous young ladies on board who are too beautiful for their own good."

"Jimmy you're full of it," Amy said. Then she turned and headed for her cabin followed by her sister. Jimmy stood, walked to the engine compartment, swung the hinged door up and reached into where the tools and misc. supplies were. He pulled out four small flashlights and then as he was closing the engine compartment, almost as an after thought he grabbed a large pipe wrench, brought it out and set it at his feet.

"What's the wrench for?" Megan asked somewhat worried because she knew Jimmy was normally a real easy going guy.

"Persuasion, do me a favor, go hand the twins each a flashlight, then blow them a kiss and tell them not to worry."

"Fine, but who is going to blow me a kiss tonight?"

"I'll find somebody," he said and he felt his knees go weak once again.

Chapter 16

I t was late, that was all Jimmy knew. Even in his sleep he felt the first little bump and it jolted him awake. Lying in the darkness he felt another bump and he knew at least two boats were tying up to Sea Horse. He rolled over, cupped his hand over Megan's mouth and shook her. She awoke with a start but he held her still.

"Shhh," he whispered in her ear.

He climbed over her, stood up, put a pair of cutoffs and a tee shirt on then grabbed the pipe wrench in his right hand. He stopped, listened, and now he was sure there was somebody already onboard. He could hear footsteps on the back transom ladder and then a slight bang as somebody hit the wheel with their foot. Jimmy ran to the companionway steps then climbed on the kitchen counter which brought his height up to the top of the hatch. He had two boards in place and the hatch was closed so nobody could climb down below without sliding the hatch open. His heart raced with fear as he heard more people climbing aboard. He waited knowing that once the attack started he would have the element of surprise for only a second, and if they had guns it was hopeless. Now he could hear people in the cockpit, and slowly he watched as the hatch started to slide forward. Jimmy held his breath, waiting, watching the hatch as it opened. Suddenly a set of hands grabbed the rails and a large foot stepped onto the first rung of the ladder. Then a head appeared in the darkness. Jimmy stood, and swung the wrench with all of his strength hitting the guy right in the face. He fell backward and disappeared into the cockpit with a muffled moan.

"Everybody up!" Jimmy screamed.

Jimmy jumped into the cockpit and in the moonlight he saw the outline of another man rushing toward him. He swung the pipe wrench again smashing it into the man's face who screamed and dropped to his knees. The way it sounded he probably killed the guy but Jimmy didn't care.

"Girls, remember the cavalry!" he managed to say before somebody hit him out of the darkness. He swung the wrench again banging harmlessly on the side of the boat as another blow hit him in the stomach. He spun to his right, kicked out and felt his right foot crash into the belly of somebody who flew backward out of sight. Suddenly he heard the twins both scream. He spun, looked forward, and he could faintly see the sisters on the deck as they frantically backed toward the bow and away from the small cabin hatches that they had just climbed out of. Two men were climbing through the rigging after them.

Suddenly hands grabbed Jimmy and he swung the wrench again hitting somebody before he pulled himself free and jumped past the dodger, landing on the foredeck right behind the two dark figures. He hit one of them in the back of the head sending him crashing to the ground. The other turned, faced him and even in the darkness Jimmy was shocked at what a huge man he was.

"Jump," he said and the twins leaped off the boat as the man hit Jimmy in the stomach doubling him over as somebody grabbed him from behind. Jimmy kicked back knocking whoever was behind him into the mast but at that same moment the big man in front of him slammed his fist into Jimmy's belly again, knocking the wind from his lungs, then somewhere out of the darkness something solid smashed into the side of his head and he crumpled to the deck. The last thing he remembered hearing was a terrifying scream from Megan.

*

The twins hit the beach stumbling, climbing out of the water, crying and so afraid that they could hardly stand. They glanced behind them but they couldn't see anybody chasing them. Then they heard a terrifying scream from Megan and Amy fell to her knees on the wet sand, her fear so strong she couldn't stand.

"Quick. To the fort," Sarah said as she pulled her sister up.

"My god, what about them?"

"To the fort!" Sarah repeated then grabbed her sister's hand and they charged down the beach.

*

Pain raced through Jimmy's body as he slowly started to regain consciousness. He was sitting upright, hands tied behind him, and he was wedged in the corner of the settee. An over head light cast dim shadows and he could hear moaning from outside in the cockpit. His face was swollen and he could barely see out of his right eye, his left was a swollen mass that wouldn't even open. His ribs shot a burning jolt of pain as he tried to take a breath. Forcing his left eye open he felt a warm gush of liquid and he knew that blood was pouring down his face

"You son of a bitch!" he heard someone scream and he was suddenly grabbed and pulled to his feet. Through his one eye he looked into a face he remembered from the beach fight a few days ago.

"You asshole!" the face screamed again.

"Fuck you," Jimmy managed to spit back before he was backhanded across his face sending blood splattering on the wall as he flew back into the cushion.

"You really did it man, you really did it!"

The guy's voice was going in and out and Jimmy wasn't making much sense of it. Jimmy wasn't really hearing much at all, or at least he couldn't focus on what he was hearing, his body hurt too much to think about anything else.

Jimmy started to pass out again and he banged his head on the table as he went down. Before he hit the floor rough hands grabbed him and pulled him back from the brink of unconsciousness. Then he was dragged to his feet.

"Show em," he heard the same voice say and he felt strong hands pulling him up the companionway steps and then they dropped him into the cockpit. It was just the beginning of first light and through his swollen eye he could faintly see Megan sitting near the wheel, terror etched on her face. Her hands and feet were tied with a thin rope and she just stared at him with such a hopeless look on her face that he started to cry.

Jimmy could hear moaning around him and he looked away from Megan and tried to focus on what he was seeing around him. In the cockpit were two men lying in a heap, neither moving, their faces a bloody pulp where he had smashed them with the wrench. He looked away and saw another man sitting, his shirt saturated with blood, his jaw cocked at a very crooked angle, all of his front teeth missing.

Then suddenly the face from the beach came into his vision.

"You see this, asshole. You killed two people tonight," he grabbed Jimmy by his shirt and shook him hard, "that's right. You killed two of my uncles men, and another one is never going to be the same," he said then he got right in Jimmy's face; "this was just going to be a little payback for the beach fight, but now, now man this is a whole new thing."

He let Jimmy go and he fell to the cockpit floor unable to hold himself up.

"Jaskee, you and Tony take the little boat. Go get the two girls that jumped overboard. Take them back to the resort."

Neither of them moved. They were too shocked at the carnage that had happened so quickly.

"Now!" he screamed and the two black men jumped up, and climbed into one of the two power boats that was rafted next to Sea Horse. They untied and paddled away in the growing light until they hit the beach. Jaskee pulled the boat up into some scrubby bushes trying to hide it then they started toward the far side of the beach right where the twins had fled.

Jimmy was laying on the cockpit floor, slumped over when he was grabbed, dragged to his feet and thrown into another boat that was tied along side Sea Horse. He looked up to see Megan as she was thrown in the boat and she landed next to him with a crash.

"I love you," he managed to say but he wasn't sure if she heard him. Then he heard the engine of Sea Horse start followed by the sound of the windlass pulling in chain and the anchor. The boat that he and Megan lay in was untied from Sea Horse, and they started out the channel. Jimmy pictured the boats going through the reef and out into deepwater. Then both boats stopped and in the glowing light of morning Jimmy could see Megan once again, still tied up, her fear still etched on her face. A few minutes later somebody climbed back onboard the powerboat and they started racing away. It took all of his strength but slowly Jimmy raised himself from the floor and looked behind him only to see Sea Horse slowly disappearing beneath the waves.

Chapter 17

"You did what?" Frankie screamed at Tommy, "are you insane?" Frankie was so mad Tommy thought he was going to hit him. Frankie's face was beet red, the veins in his neck pulsating, sweat dripping from his forehead, his eyes so wide with anger that Tommy thought his uncle's head might explode.

"You dumb shit!" Frankie screamed unable to keep his anger under control.

Tommy sat in his uncle's small office and he had never seen him so mad. Frankie was pacing the small room, his hands moving wildly in the air as he yelled. Occasionally he looked at his nephew but at the moment he couldn't even stand to see his dumb-shit face.

He had been pissed from the moment Tommy had woken him up and started telling him what had happened on Henry Island. When Tommy got to the part about two of his men being killed Frankie had jumped out of bed swearing like a banshee. When Tommy got to the part about kidnapping two people and sinking Sea Horse, he went completely ballistic.

After twenty minutes of uncontrollable rage Frankie finally sat down, exhausted, exhaled a deep breath, put his head in his hands and tried to regain some composure before he looked at his nephew again.

"What are you going to do now idiot? Have you thought this through? This is your shit, not mine. You created this and you are going to fix it."

Tommy felt so stupid he couldn't say anything so he just sat there.

"Do you have any idea what you have done? It's called piracy and down here it's frowned upon. There'll be so many cops, Coast Guard, maybe even Feds snooping around," he wiped his forehead with his hand before flinging beads of sweat on the floor.

"You know there's only one thing you can do now, don't you?"

Tommy slowly nodded his head.

"Can you do it? Can you take those two people you have tied up in the Sea Ray, connect them to an anchor and throw them overboard, because, asshole, I can't think of another alternative."

Frankie couldn't believe that he was even involved in this stupid shit. This was not his problem and he had a fleeting thought that maybe he should just call the cops, turn his nephew in and wash his hands of this entire nightmare. But that was impossible and he knew it. There would definitely be investigations, background checks, the cops would run this thing into the ground, there would be so much shit flying, and he knew a lot of it would land on him and his little paradise. He needed to keep his life in Chicago and life in the islands as far apart as possible.

He sat in his chair looking at his dumb shit nephew rethinking the story he had just heard and he started to get the feeling that something was missing and he wasn't sure what. All the pieces didn't quite add up. He started thinking about yesterdays conversation with Tommy around the breakfast table before Carl had interrupted them. He replayed Tommy's story about the beach fight, getting his ass kicked and the two beautiful twins. Shit, he thought, that was it, what about the twins?

He forced himself out of the chair walked over and grabbed Tommy by his greasy hair and jerked his head back so he was looking right in his eyes.

"Tell me, is there anything else I need to know, anything at all?"

Slowly Tommy nodded his head, causing Frankie's hand to move up and down.

"What?" he screamed at him.

"Those twins got away."

"Oh shit. Those babes, you mean there are four people involved in this shit?"

Tommy just continued nodding his head then dropped his face in his hands when his uncle let go of his hair.

"Where are they?"

"On Henry Island, I had Jaskee and Tony go after them. They should be bringing them here soon."

Frankie staggered back to his chair and slumped back down. He couldn't believe this and he thought once again about just calling the cops. His nephew had been a screw up his entire life and he really should just let the kid go down with this one. In the back of his mind he knew that and if it was anybody else besides his little sisters only child he would have.

"Okay, you idiot," he finally said knowing that it was up to him to fix this entire disaster, "there's two ways out of this. You say we have three beauties and one ninja guy, and they all have to disappear, right? Well . . . that ninja guys going to become fish food that's all there is to it, but those women now, here's something to think about. They can become fish food as well or," and for the first time since he climbed out of bed this morning a little smile appeared on his face, "or I know a crazy son of a bitch that will pay a lot of money for those three."

*

The twins huddled at the entrance to the fort to afraid to go in. It looked like a gapping mouth with twelve foot high concrete walls that led into the dark interior. The thick roof of concrete jutted out two feet over the entrance, and large drops of water continually dripped down, splashing, forming puddles that snaked away and ran down the hillside into the scraggly brush and trees that surrounded the pathway.

Amy pointed her flashlight into the darkness but the little beam was swallowed by the size of the tunnel. They were both still shaking, mostly with fear but also from the cold morning air. Each had on just a large tee shirt and panties. That was all they had been sleeping in.

In the early light of dawn as they had scrambled up the trail they watched as somebody had motored Sea Horse out from the bay. When their yacht slowly started to sink they stopped in their tracks disbelieving at first, then shocked and that led to panic bringing them to the point of hysteria once again. As Sea Horse slowly disappeared out of sight they were hugging each other, tears streaming down their faces, not really able to understand what was happening. All they knew and each of them understood this without having to say a word was that their lives were in danger and help wasn't coming. Their panic really set in a few minutes later when they saw two men climbing up the small trail that they had followed not to long ago. That forced them to move and now they stood inside the shadows of the concrete wall that was the beginning of the underground passage.

"We have to hide," Sarah said looking at her sister.

Amy just nodded in agreement and together, arms still around each other, they turned and slowly stepped into the darkness, the beam of one little flashlight disappearing into the void only a few feet ahead of them.

At first Sarah kept shining the light all over the place as they walked, the ceiling, the walls, behind them, in front of them but soon she started focusing on the floor placing the small glow of light where their next step was going.

Twice in the first fifty feet or so they passed openings on their right that led somewhere. They could feel a slight cool breeze as they momentarily stood in the entranceway, the beam of their light showing nothing but darkness. After a few minutes of indecision they turned and continued further into the fort. By now the entrance behind them was just a small glow of light and the perception of distance was becoming very difficult for them to grasp. Occasionally they would slosh through small puddles of standing water, and the air was heavy with a musty, rotten smell. The tunnel was slowly making a turn to the right and soon they lost sight of the opening. They stopped and leaned against the cold damp concrete wall, the darkness engulfing them.

"I am so scared," Sarah said.

"Me too," Amy replied, her voice almost breaking.

Then Amy wrapped her arms around her sister and they just stood there, shoulders against cold concrete, fear racing through their hearts and minds and neither of them knew what to do next.

Chapter 18

Jaskee was a large man, at least two hundred and thirty pounds, dark skinned and thirty-one years old. Tony was over forty, fat and out of shape. They both stood at the entrance to the fort staring into the darkness and neither of them wanted to go in. Tony was huffing and puffing trying to get his breath as he sucked on a cigarette. Jaskee was scared shitless because he knew they had no choice but to go in the fort and find the girls. There was no way he was going to go back to Cantelle Bay and face Tommy without those two.

Tony looked at Jaskee's face, "I ain't go'in in there, man."

"You damn well are and I'll kick your ass if you give me any shit."

"It's pitch black, you can't see ten feet, once you're in there man you won't be able to see your pecker in front of you."

"Maybe I'll make you go first."

"What difference will that make? You heard about the blind leading the blind, we need a flashlight or a torch or something."

Jaskee had been thinking the very same thing. A torch was their only hope.

"You're right about that. Let's find some palm trees. I've seen my dad weave a torch out of dried leaves before."

Both men set off into the surrounding brush walking through stickers, tripping over low bushes and rocks, getting jabbed with thorns, searching for palm trees. They finally found a small group of stunted palms about eighty feet from the entrance to the fort, and all around the base of the trees were piles of dead leaves.

"Take your belt off," Jaskee told Tony, who did and handed it to him.

Together they started grabbing handfuls of dead leaves. They must have gathered at least thirty dry leaves before they started weaving them around a thick branch that had fallen from a near by bougainvillea bush. Jaskee took his tee shirt off and ripped it into long strips and started weaving the cloth through the palm leaves, pulling the palm fronds tight as Tony added more to the pile. Taking the last of his tee shirt he wrapped it tight around the wood handle and tied off the end of the branches. Then he took Tony's belt and wrapped it around the palm leaves half way between the top and the bottom, pulling the belt as tight as he could. Now he held a torch that was three feet high, wove tight and held in place by his ripped tee-shirt and Tony's belt.

"Piss on it," Jaskee said putting the torch on the ground at his feet.

"What?"

"You heard me. Piss on it. Otherwise it will burn to fast."

They both pissed on the dried palm leaves and his ripped tee-shirt drenching it. Jaskee picked up the dry handle and they walked back to the entrance of the fort.

"Give me your lighter," Janksee demanded.

Taking the lighter Janksee flicked it once and held it underneath the torch and the leaves started to smoke before a small flame appeared. The flame was weak, it sizzled against the wet urine but slowly it started to grow. Jaskee held the torch down and the flames burned brighter, sizzling, stinking, flickering but it continued to burn. When the top six inches were burning Jaskee turned the torch upright which caused the flames to die down, but not go out. He looked at Tony then grabbed him by the shoulder, pushed him in front of him and without a word they started into the darkness.

*

The twins were now really cold, their teeth were chattering and they knew they needed to move. Sarah had turned the flashlight off to save the batteries and it was absolutely pitch black. How long they had stood there they couldn't tell, but it felt like hours. Only when they saw a flicker of light casting long shadows on the concrete walls at the far end of the tunnel did they finally move.

Sarah turned the flashlight on and held it in front of her hoping that no light could be seen from behind then slowly they started walking deeper into the fort. They passed another room on the right but this time they stepped inside and looked closer. There were a few old tables and chairs heaped in a corner but the back of the room was lost in the darkness. Sarah shined the light over the floor looking for anything that could be used as a weapon, a stick, a piece of pipe, but she couldn't find a thing.

"Let's keep going," Amy whispered and they backed out into the main corridor and continued walking, following the thin beam of the light only a few feet in front of them.

The floor was now broken uneven ground, mostly dirt and some packed gravel, they must have walked another forty feet or so when Sarah suddenly grabbed her sister's elbow and shined the light to her right. There almost hidden was a small notch in the wall with a ladder leading upwards. Sarah grabbed the ladder and gave it a good shake. Small pieces of concrete fell from above her and she felt the ladder pull free from the wall. Hesitantly she leaned the ladder back and stepped on the first rung, testing it with a slight bounce. Then she started climbing until her head was past the ceiling. She shined the light around her then pulled herself up stepping off the ladder onto more damp cold concrete. Sarah shined the light back at her sister then at her hands and motioned for Amy to follow her. Once her sister had climbed up Sarah put the flashlight in her mouth, grabbed the ladder and tried to lift it off of the floor. It was too heavy, she could only lift it a foot or so before it slipped out of her hands and landed with a bang.

"Help me," she tried to whisper but it was hard with the flashlight still stuck between her teeth.

Amy reached for a rung and together both girls pulled the ladder off the floor and slid it up until the base was past the ceiling then they laid it down as quietly as possible.

Sarah shinned the light around and saw that they were in a small room, but the wall directly across from them was lost in the darkness. Looking down into the small hole they had just climbed up they both could see the faint glow of light as the men continued to move closer to them. Sarah looked at her sister and then shined the light a few feet away from the opening and Amy quietly stepped back. Sarah did the same before she turned the flashlight off, casting them into complete blackness. Neither made a sound.

The flickering of light below them grew brighter, casting ghostly images on the tunnel floor and walls and soon they could hear muffled voices and the sound of feet scraping gravel and the occasional sound of splashing water. The light glowed brighter as the men came closer. The girls were terrified, they almost couldn't breathe. The light was now reaching upward into their hiding place revealing the small hole that they had climbed through. Now the men were only ten feet away, slowly moving, coming closer. The twin's room was now lit up enough that they could see a corridor leading from behind them before it disappeared into more darkness. The light suddenly stopped right under them. They could hear shuffling below them and suddenly the top of the torch was thrust up into their hiding place. Amy was so startled that without even thinking she stepped back away from the light, tripped over the ladder and with a scream tumbled backward into the darkness.

Chapter 19

The boat rolled awkwardly in the swell and Jimmy knew by the motion they were tied up at a dock. He was laying in the bottom of the Sea Ray, face down, his body numb with pain, his mind racing as he forced his head up and looked around. He saw that he was in a large boathouse, then another bolt of pain shot through him and he collapsed, but not before thinking about Megan. He vaguely remembered through the mind numbing pain that somebody had come back to the boat, climbed on board, kicked him once then grabbed Megan and dragged her away. There was nothing he could do to stop them and the terror on her face haunted him. He couldn't stop thinking about the twins either. All the way back from Henry Island he had thought about them, hoped against hope that they had made it to the fort, and that somehow they were safe. Lester had trusted his daughters to his care and he had failed.

His wrists were tied tight behind him and his legs were bound at the ankles. He was helpless and he knew he couldn't defend himself if his life depended on it and he had a terrible feeling that it would soon. Jimmy couldn't tell how long he had laid there, his mind bouncing back and forth between consciousness and some other far away place but it must have been a few hours at least. The two dead men were piled over each other next to him and they were already starting to stink.

Suddenly the boat leaned heavily toward the dock and somebody climbed on board. Jimmy rolled with the boat, lifted his head up and saw it was the white guy from the beach. He had a pistol tucked in his waist. He glanced at Jimmy then stepped near him and gave him a kick to the stomach that sent more pain racing through his body. The motors started and the Sea Ray backed out of the boathouse, then spun around and they went racing away from shore.

Tommy drove like a wild man, slamming into the waves, water flying over the bow, the two dead guys slowly bouncing away from each other toward Jimmy who lay in the back of the boat. Soon their bloody, stinking bodies were both resting against him, and Jimmy knew he wasn't going to live much longer.

Pain continued to shoot through his body as the boat slammed, but Jimmy was glad for it. He focused on the pain, used it to bring his body and mind back from the twilight world that the beatings had left him in. The pain meant he was still alive but he doubted for much longer. Twisting his hands he tried to find any slack in the ropes but he couldn't and his ankles were just as tight. A dreaded hopelessness overcame him as he lay there in the bottom of the boat and he couldn't get Megan's horror filled face out of his mind. He had to find a way to stay alive for her, and the twins.

They raced for a good fifteen or twenty minutes, best as Jimmy could figure, before suddenly the motors were cut back to idle and the boat coasted to a stop. Jimmy twisted, then painfully turned over and watched as the driver stood up from his seat, grabbed one of the bodies and started to lift it up. The guy struggled as he dragged the dead man toward the edge of the boat. The Sea Ray rocked in the swells and the rail took a dangerous dip as Tommy finally managed to prop the body against the side of the boat. He rested for a minute before once again struggling with the big black dead man before he finally wrestled the body overboard. What Jimmy saw next put the fear of god in him. The driver reached into his back pocket took out a large folding knife, flipped it open and made repeated stabbing motions that he could only guess were directed into the dead man's body. Jimmy knew he was bleeding the guy out and that meant the sharks were on their way. The driver finally pulled himself back from the edge of the boat, set the knife near the engine controls, his hands and arms covered with blood and he sat down on the seat. He looked exhausted and Jimmy hoped that somehow he could use the guy's weakness against him.

A few minutes later Tommy grabbed the second dead body and after another struggle managed to throw it over the side as well.

Jimmy knew he was next. He was about to be murdered by this asshole, and there wasn't anything he could do to stop him and he also knew that time was running out. The sharks were already thrashing around, and he could feel them banging into the boat in their feeding frenzy. He had to do something. He only had minutes left to live.

While the guy was still looking over the side Jimmy twisted his body again so now his feet were facing forward. He scrunched his knees up to his chest, held them tight, like a coiled spring just waiting for his one chance.

Tommy turned and looked at him, just stared for a minute without saying a word then he pulled his gun out and pointed it at Jimmy.

"You pull that trigger and you'll shoot a hole right through your boat, think about it man, you want to be sinking with those sharks out there?"

A confused look grew on Tommy's face and for a second or two he looked at Jimmy as if trying to figure out what he should do. Finally he put the pistol back in his waistband then he turned and climbed into the small forward cabin. Jimmy watched as a few life jackets were thrown out of the doorway before the guy emerged carrying an anchor, chain and some rope. Tommy grunted as he dragged the anchor and then dropped it at Jimmy's feet. The moment he turned his back reaching to grab the chain Jimmy unleashed his kick. The shock slammed the unsuspecting Tommy forward, smashing him into the steering console before be bounced back. Jimmy was ready and he fired another kick connecting with Tommy once again. The second kick slammed Tommy back into the steering wheel, and the dashboard, and he started to collapse but not before grabbing the pistol. Jimmy was too far away to reach him with another kick and Tommy now held the pistol in his hand as he started to turn and face Jimmy. Tommy was still trying to steady himself against the motion of the boat when suddenly his feet slipped on the blood of the dead men and they started to slide out from underneath him. Tommy reached out with his left hand trying to grab the side of the boat, his right fiercely clinging to the pistol. His feet continued to slide and in a panic he fired two rounds each slamming into the bottom of the boat near Jimmy's head. Still struggling to gain his equilibrium against the rolling boat he took two steps foreword trying desperately to get his body over his feet and regain some control. He was off balance, his head and chest angled toward the rear of the boat. It was now or never and Jimmy lashed out with everything he had, one last desperate kick that connected with the still struggling Tommy. The force of his kick snapped Tommy's head back, spinning him into the side of the boat just as the Sea Ray took a heavy roll dipping her rail and with a terrifying scream Tommy flipped over the side. In the next instant his right hand now empty of the gun grabbed the rail and he frantically tried to pull himself back on board. Then using two hands he pulled himself high enough that his chest was leaning over the rail, his terror filled eyes locked on Jimmy as he struggled to pull himself inside. Suddenly with a terrifying scream he was jerked backward and disappeared into the ocean. Only once did Jimmy hear him surface, and that was with a scream that he knew he would never forget for the rest of his life, then Tommy disappeared into a pool of bloody water and circling sharks. Jimmy lay there exhausted, trying to think when he suddenly became aware of water splashing on his head. He looked behind him and saltwater stung his eyes. Two fountains each a foot high cascaded the warm Caribbean Sea into the boat where the bullets had smashed through the fiberglass bottom. The Sea Ray was filling fast, it was only minutes away from sinking, and the sharks were still hungry.

Chapter 20

In the early morning light, with a cup of coffee in hand Lester sat down in his office and turned on his computer. He sipped his coffee once then blew on it as the laptop booted up and a small log-in box appeared. He entered the password then scrolled down to maintenance and waited. He typed in a second password and took another sip of coffee as the NOAA Virgin Island chart appeared. It took him a few seconds to realize that what he was looking at wasn't what he had been expecting. There were no colored dots flashing anywhere. Each of the three GPS units should have been sending out a signal, like they had last night when he had checked. A sickening feeling overcame him and he knew without a doubt that all three units didn't quit working at the same time.

He slid back in his chair, ran his fingers through his gray hair and forced himself to think. Not with emotions because that would lead to panic, but with clarity, with focus. What could cause all three units to quit working at the same time? One thought instantly entered his mind but he shut it out, then it came back again, and he knew he had to consider it. All it would take for all three units to stop working was for Sea Horse to sink to the bottom of the ocean.

For the next few minutes he just sat, forced himself to think of any other possibilities, anything, but he couldn't. Somewhere deep inside he knew that something terrible had happened down in the islands. Finally he stood up, went to the safe under his great grandfather's picture and opened it. He reached in and pulled out a cd then returned to his computer and inserted it.

The computer whirled and the screen scrolled through different nature pictures before he hit the enter button on a Rocky Mountain river scene. Lester moved the cursor until it rested on a small rock in the river and he hit enter. Another password bar opened and he typed in a seven digit code then waited as a map of the world appeared. Running the cursor down to the Caribbean he right clicked once and waited until the screen split in two, the islands of the Caribbean on the left and a row of numbers starting with 101 and ending with 104 appearing on the right.

"Four people," Lester said to himself, "only four people" he repeated in a soft muttered voice.

The numbers were codes for special people, and none of them were federal agents. This was his personal list, friends, trusted acquaintances, people he had worked with in the past. Flip was number three he knew, but the others he would have to look up. Sitting there staring at the screen he had a terrible feeling that if his fears were accurate he would need a lot more than four, he might need an army.

*

Flip was looking out the window of his small office in Red Hook at the charter boats bobbing in the gentle swell. The sky was bright red and he thought about the old sailor's saying" red sky in morning sailors take warning". He was feeling restless and he wasn't sure why. He hadn't slept good last night, bad dreams or something, he couldn't really remember. The weather forecast was for twenty knot trades with occasional showers throughout the day, not bad for this time of year. To bad he didn't have a fishing charter. He wondered how Jimmy and the girls were doing. He pictured them anchored some place quiet and peaceful, relaxing, getting a slow start on the day. That Jimmy, Flip thought with a laugh, sailing a fifty-four foot Alden with three beautiful women on board.

Flip turned back from staring out the window as the phone rang. Maybe he was going to have a charter after all.

"Annie May Charters."

"Flip, its Lester."

Instantly just by the tone in his voice Flip knew something was wrong.

"What's wrong, Lester?"

"They disappeared from the screen that's what, none of the GPS units are transmitting."

"None?" he said even though he had heard him clearly.

"That's right . . . blank."

"Technical problems?"

"I doubt it."

"Yeah so do I, so what do you think?"

"I could see the backpacks screwing up, they get left in the dinghy overnight and they get soaking wet, maybe they fall in the ocean, maybe a wave comes over the dingy and soaks everything in salt water, I don't know, but I could see something like that happening, but not with Sea Horse, that transponder should be working unless . . ." he stopped to afraid to verbalize what was going through his mind.

"Yeah I know . . . unless she's sunk. But, Lester, nobody knows your girls are down here, right?"

"Right, you, me, a trusted travel agent who booked them that's about all."

"Shit, Lester, I'll start searching. I've got a buddy that's a pilot we can be up in the air in less than an hour."

"Alright, keep me posted."

"Don't worry, Lester," and he hung up.

Flip grabbed his vhf radio and dialed channel 16, "Sea Horse, Sea Horse, Sea Horse, this is Annie May over," he waited a long time without any response before calling again, but only silence, a haunting evil silence that made his skin crawl, and he finally turned the radio off.

"Where the hell are you, Jimmy McBain?" he said to himself.

*

An hour later Flip was in the air, binoculars resting on his lap as he scanned the horizon. There were a few sailboats out on the water and they did a close fly-by of each of them as he tried to match the picture of Sea Horse he had downloaded off of the internet. He had the pilot circle St. Thomas twice, fly over Water Island and the anchorages there before heading to St. John, flying low over Coral Bay and Hurricane Hole. Shit, he thought they could be a lot of places.

Grabbing his handheld vhf radio he hit the transmit button.

"Sea Horse, Sea Horse, come in this is Annie May."

He waited for a minute then repeated the call, but there was no response.

"This is the charter boat Annie May requesting assistance in locating a fifty-four foot sailboat named Sea Horse, repeat I am looking for sailing vessel Sea Horse, any information regarding health and welfare of this vessel please come back to Annie May now."

The radio was quiet for thirty seconds before somebody got back to him.

"Annie May this is ChesterBlue, I heard them on the radio talking to Jolly Man resort yesterday."

"ChesterBlue do you have a time?"

"Not really, late afternoon I think."

"Rodger, Jolly Man resort. I'll call them. Thanks."

"Rodger that."

Flip switched to channel 68 knowing most of the marinas monitored that station.

"Jolly Man resort do you copy?"

"This is Jolly Man resort, over," a friendly voice came back moments later.

"I'm trying to locate a friend of mine, the boat is Sea Horse."

"Rodger that, Sea Horse checked out yesterday afternoon, late if I remember, why?"

"Just trying to find them."

"Well, it was late so they only had a few hours before it got dark and nobody sails around here at night."

"Jolly Man, where are you located?"

"We are on Peter Island."

"Rodger that, thank you."

Flip turned the radio off and grabbed a chart. He found Peter Island, then figured they had at best three hours of daylight after they left Jolly Man before they had to have the anchor down for the night. He drew a rough circle in pencil fifteen miles around Jolly Man resort. They had to be within that circle he knew, he just hoped to god they were above the water.

Chapter 21

Amy hit the cold concrete with her right shoulder slamming it hard then rolling on her back gasping for air. Sarah stood in complete shock as the torch was thrust higher into their hiding place. The twins could hear the two men shouting and cursing as the torch continued to cast its haunting shadows. Sarah flipped the flashlight on and pointed it at her sister. At least she was conscious. Amy was trying to sit up, the side of her face bloody, her right arm bleeding as well. Sarah knelt down beside her.

"We have to run," Sarah said.

The men below were still cursing and as Amy struggled to her feet a hand suddenly grabbed the ledge then one of the men stuck his head up.

Tony was standing on Jaskee's shoulders as the big man tried to keep himself steady under the small opening.

Both girls screamed as Tony struggled to keep his balance, yelling at Jaskee to stop moving. Sarah grabbed Amy's arm and they both stepped back. Sarah flashed the light down the corridor but the batteries were starting to get weak and the dim glow didn't show ten feet in front of them.

Still grabbing her sister's arm Sarah started to run.

"No," Amy shouted as Tony struggled to pull himself up. Amy reached behind her, grabbed the ladder and with all of her strength she threw it across the concrete floor, hitting Tony right in the face.

With a scream the back of Tony's head slammed into the edge of the concrete, blood exploding from his face where the ladder hit him before he disappeared back down the hole. He landed awkwardly on Jaskee and both men crashed to the ground.

"Run," Amy said and they turned and raced into the darkness.

The beam of the flashlight was so weak that it didn't show much, just a concrete floor, and they couldn't run fast because it was impossible to see very far ahead. Sarah had the flashlight out in front of her and her other hand had a death grip on her sister.

Tony's face was bleeding badly. His nose was broken and the back of his head was bleeding as well from slamming into the concrete but Jaskee didn't give a damn.

"Hurry, you asshole, on my shoulders, now!" he screamed knowing that they couldn't miss this opportunity.

Jaskee knelt down while Tony climbed on his back clinging tightly to the big man's shoulders as Jaskee stood up holding Tony's ankle and with a shove he threw him into the small opening. Tony fumbled around in the darkness until he found the ladder then he lowered it down and a second later Jaskee, still holding the torch, was charging up the ladder and they took off after the girls.

The darkness seemed to tighten around the twins as they tried to escape. The tunnel was much smaller than the main entrance, it had a low ceiling about six feet high and lots of turns, and it was impossible to see very far in front of them. But once again they could now see the flickering glow of the torch behind them. The beam of the twins' flashlight was fading with every step they took and it was getting harder by the minute to see. They raced on knowing that to stop or even slow down meant capture. The tunnel took another sharp turn to the right and suddenly in the distance they could see the faint glow of light come down from above. They took off going as fast as they dared, the light in the distance getting a little brighter with each charging step they took. They were running carelessly now, and suddenly Amy slipped on a damp slimy patch of concrete and her feet went out from underneath her. She crashed hard, skinning her knees, then her hands before slamming her hurt shoulder. Laying there she didn't think she could move and every second brought the glow of the torch closer.

"Amy get up!" her sister screamed and Amy forced herself to her feet but she could hardly walk let alone run. Another thirty painful steps and the girls were standing under a thin beam of light. They looked up into a small square opening in the ceiling and the sky about twenty feet over their head. There was a ladder leading up through the passageway, a small chimney built of concrete. The opening was about three feet square, only room for one of them at a time. Sarah grabbed the ladder without hesitating and up she went, praying that the rusty bolts that held the ladder in place wouldn't break. Hand over hand she climbed the flashlight laying where she dropped it. Amy started after her pulling herself up, pain shooting through her injured arm and shoulders, tears streaming down her face as she tried to fight her growing panic as the glow of the torch grew closer. Sarah reached the top and stuck her head out into daylight. It was blinding and she had to stop, she couldn't keep her eyes open and she didn't dare take another step. Amy was right behind her pushing Sarah's butt with her head trying to get her moving. The torch was now directly below them and they suddenly felt the ladder shake as one of the men charged up after them. Sarah had no choice, she pulled herself out of the chimney and fell landing on a small platform a few feet below her. Amy was right behind her and she climbed out of the chimney hesitating only a second before jumping and landing next to her sister. Together they scrambled off the platform, still half blind by the light and they hit the ground running at first not even caring what direction they went.

They both struggled to keep their eyes open, fighting the sudden brilliance of daylight knowing they had to find the best route to escape fast. They were at the top of a large hill, the blue Caribbean shining out all around them. In front of them thirty feet away they saw a dirt path, old and rutted, overgrown with weeds and bushes that led down the hillside and they raced to it. Sarah was in front, running using both hands to push away the bushes that had grown up in the path. Amy was right behind her, both charging down the hill. The path suddenly made a sharp turn to the left and Sarah slipped, her feet catching loose gravel and down she crashed before rolling off the path. Amy grabbed a small tree and tried to stop but her feet came out from underneath her as well and she landed on her butt, before rolling into a large bougainvillea bush, the sharp thorns gouging into her skin and she screamed. Both girls struggled to get up, both staring at the pathway behind them. Suddenly Jaskee came flying around the corner, the twins jumped to their feet but it was too late and with a flying leap Jaskee tackled Amy sending them both crashing to the ground. Sarah froze and in that instant another man came running into view took one look at her and even though he was running to fast to stop he swung his left arm out as he ran by her and slammed her in the stomach. With a scream she collapsed to the ground. Amy struggled but she couldn't do a thing against the huge man and as he pulled her up he slapped her once which sent her head snapping back and she would have collapsed if he wasn't holding tight. Sarah tried to pull herself up but she hurt so bad that she just rolled over. There was no more fight in her. Tony stopped himself by crashing into a large bush, hurting his left arm before he turned, raced back to Sarah, grabbed her by her hair and jerked her head up so she was looking right at him.

"You bitch," he screamed then collapsed next to her.

Chapter 22

The sharks were still slamming against the Sea Ray as Jimmy started crawling toward the steering wheel and the knife that Tommy had put down. The water was coming in fast and he knew he had minutes at best. He kicked the anchor out of the way then reached the bulkhead, spun around, and lifting with his feet he was able to slide himself up and stand. Looking over his right shoulder he grabbed for the knife just as the Sea Ray took another dip and he lost his balance and fell with a hard crash on the floor. Water was now a foot deep in the boat. Desperately he crawled back to the bulkhead and stood up again, but this time he wedged himself against the steering wheel. Reaching down he finally grabbed the knife, and praying that he could keep hold of it he started blindly sawing with the blade. He was cutting his hands as well because it was impossible to see what he was doing. Again and again he sliced the tough nylon rope that bound him before he was finally able to cut enough of it so he could break it with a strong pull. Then he leaned over and cut the rope around his ankles. Shaking the rope free he reached to his right and turned the engine keys on then hit the starter button and the two outboards roared to life. Throwing the throttles forward the boat slowly started moving. Jimmy knew that if it wasn't full of water the boat would already be up on a plane and racing away.

He had to get away from the sharks. That was his main concern right now, nothing else mattered. He was a great swimmer and he knew he could last for hours in the warm water but with these sharks in a feeding frenzy, if he sunk now he wouldn't last a minute. The Sea Ray was moving slowly maybe five miles an hour the engines screaming at full power.

He needed to get the water out of the boat, but glancing around he couldn't see anything that he could use to bail with. He pulled the throttles back then ran into the little foreword cabin, looked but found nothing he could use. He pulled the foam mattress off a bunk revealing a small locker underneath it that must have been used for storage. Flipping the plywood lid he looked inside then reached and started grabbing what ever he could find. There wasn't anything that he could use. He turned and looked around fighting the panic that was setting in. In two steps he reached the small ice box and flung the lid off. There were a few six packs of beer and bottle or two of rum then he saw a plastic gallon jug full of something. He grabbed the jug, pulled it out of the ice box, ripped the lid off and turned it upside down spilling its contents as he ran back outside. Grabbing the knife he sliced the bottom off at an angle leaving the handle and he started scooping water overboard as fast as he could. He threw the throttles into full speed then knelt down and started bailing like a mad man, the jug in his right hand, his left grabbing the steering wheel partially for support but also because the Sea Ray instantly started going in circles the moment he let go of the wheel. He was hunched over, flinging water overboard, trying to keep the boat going in a direction away from the sharks, all the time looking back trying to guess if he was getting more water out of the boat than was coming in.

In the next few minutes it became obvious he would have to do more or the boat would sink. The water wasn't going down. He pulled the throttles to neutral and the boat came to a sudden stop, water almost to his knees, then turning around he got down on his belly and started for the back of the boat. The waves were causing the Sea Ray to take deep rolls, the water inside sloshing from side to side making the chance of capsizing very real. Jimmy kept his weight low and almost swam until he could reach the motors. There had to be a drain plug in this boat he knew. This was his last desperate attempt, he couldn't think of anything else to do. He reached under the water with both hands, felt around then grabbed the large drain plug and with all of his strength he pulled it out then dropped it. Little water flowed in because so much was already inside the boat. Jimmy jumped to his feet, ran back to the steering wheel and slammed the throttles forward. Then he reached down, still having to keep one hand on the wheel and started throwing everything he could reach overboard. The anchor and chain went first, then whatever wasn't bolted down, he just kept throwing and slowly the boat started to gain speed, and the faster she went the higher the bow raised, the more water went to the stern and finally water started draining out of the drain plug. The sharks were being left behind, the blood stained ocean now becoming a distant crimson silhouette against the blue Caribbean.

For the first time Jimmy looked around trying to figure out where he was. Nothing looked familiar, but at the moment it didn't really matter as he spun the wheel and headed for the nearest island.

*

Flip was getting more worried all the time. The pilot had told him five minutes ago that they were running low on fuel and it was time to head back. He kept looking at the circle on the chart then out the window knowing that Sea Horse had to be close. He grabbed the vhf radio and once again hit transmit.

"Sea Horse, Sea Horse, this is Annie May over."

He listened for only a few seconds knowing that there would be no answer, Jimmy hadn't responded yet and he had been calling him all morning. Suddenly his radio crackled.

"Annie May this Is Jimmy, copy?"

"Jimmy for god sakes where are you?"

There was a momentary silence before Jimmy got back.

"I don't know, I'm in a little white speed boat, and I'm sinking fast, but I see an island up ahead. I don't know if I can make it!"

"Where's Sea Horse?" Flip asked his voice echoing with fear, "where's the girls, what happened, Jimmy?"

"Listen Flip, I can't talk much longer. I've got to keep bailing and keep my other hand on the wheel. We were attacked last night. Sea Horse is sunk. The twins I hope to god are still on Henry Island."

"Henry Island, repeat Henry Island," the radio static making it hard for Flip to hear.

Suddenly a new voice came in loud and clear over the radio.

"Break this is United States Coast Guard in St Thomas we are monitoring your conversation can we be of assistance?"

"Yes," Jimmy screamed, "get a chopper out to Henry Island. There are two, repeat two girls there that need help . . . now!"

Water was starting to flow back into the boat as Jimmy couldn't keep bailing and talking and steering at the same time.

"Coast Guard my vessel, Sea Horse is sunk just off the entrance reef of Henry Island near the bay. The girls jumped ashore, they're being chased, their lives are in danger, repeat their lives are in danger, over."

"Roger that, what is your location, and how many people aboard your vessel?"

Flip was hanging on every word.

"Only myself, the guy that brought me out here became shark food, and I don't have a clue where I'm at. I see an island probably three or four miles away. I'm trying to get there. Just send a chopper for the girls over."

'Alright sir, what is your name?"

"Jimmy McBain."

"What are the girl's names?"

"Sarah and Amy, just hurry."

"The chopper is already scrambling sir."

"I can't talk any more I've got to start bailing. I see some masts if I can get to those boats I'll call you with my location over."

"Jimmy, I'm on the radio, man what ever it takes make it," Flip said.

"Jimmy, we will be listening, good luck," then the radio operator changed her tone of voice and sounded almost like a recording when she said, "this is United States Coast Guard standing by."

"I'm signing off," Jimmy said then he reached down and started bailing, wondering why the hell he never thought of calling on the radio.

The Sea Ray almost made it to the island but not quite and it sunk in about a thousand feet of water half a mile from shore. It took Jimmy a long time before he was able to swim to the nearest anchored sailboat, the name Flying Fish painted on its transom and he started pounding on the hull.

"What the hell, goddamn," he heard cussing from inside the boat before a suntanned old man with white hair, and a scruffy gray beard stuck his head over the side. He was shocked to see Jimmy swimming there.

Jimmy looked up, tired from the long swim and said,

"Sorry to bother you, but my boat just sank and I could sure use a hand."

Chapter 23

Jaskee and Tony dragged the twins down the hillside and threw them into the front of the rigid bottom inflatable, then took off at a fast clip. Amy and Sarah were lying underneath a heavy tarp wedged tight up in the bow. They were too terrified to do anything but cling to each other and stay right where they were told to stay.

Both girls were a mess. The right side of Amy's face was covered with dried, caked blood and her shoulders and arms were scraped raw, full of cuts and bruises. She also had painful jabs all over from landing in the bougainvillea bush. Sarah wasn't much better. She didn't have as much blood on her but her legs were scraped raw and she had long cuts running up her back from when she slipped charging down the hillside and her stomach felt like it had been hit by a truck.

By the time the United States Coast Guard helicopter landed on Henry Island and the eight man special forces assault team hit the beach the twins were almost back in Cantelle Bay.

Jaskee and Tony didn't say a word to each other the entire trip back. Both men were wondering how the hell they got themselves into something like this and how the hell it was all going to play out. Jaskee kept thinking about that damn Tommy and how he had told him it was going to be a piece of cake. All they were going to do was break into some guy's boat, scare the hell out of him, maybe hit him a few times then drive away. Well, Jaskee thought that dumb shit Tommy sure was wrong. Two of his buddies were dead, and one was going to need a good plastic surgeon and an even better dentist. Plus they had sunk a boat, kidnapped a couple from the yacht and he figured as Cantelle Bay came into view, he and Tony had just kidnapped another two. There was no way this was going to end pretty, he knew, no way at all.

He slowed the boat down then coasted into the boathouse, killed the engine and tied up. The girls were still under the canvas and he hadn't seen anybody on the beach.

"Stay here and don't let them make a sound," he said looking at Tony before he jumped up on the wooden dock and headed for Mr. Balero's office.

He knocked twice on the closed door then walked in before Frankie said a word. Normally he would never do such a thing, but this morning was far from normal. Frankie Balero was sitting at a small desk where he had all of his electronic equipment, a ham radio, two vhf radios, plus his computers, printers and fax machines. He looked up at Jaskee and his face was almost white as a ghost. Frankie motioned with a jerk of his head to a couch near by and Jaskee dropped down then just sat.

The Coast Guard was on the radio signing off telling somebody that they would be standing by. Mr. Balero clicked the radio off then slid his chair back from his desk turned, and looked at Jaskee.

"You look like shit, boss," he was surprised he said it but it was true.

Frankie uttered a short laugh but there was nothing funny about the expression on his face, and Jaskee felt a rush of fear. If his boss was sweating this then he sure as hell had better be too.

"You get those twins?" Frankie said turning back to his desk.

"Yeah we got them, they're in the dinghy in the boathouse. Nobody saw us, there wasn't anybody on the beach."

Frankie just nodded his head slightly and Jaskee knew his thoughts were a million miles away.

"Where's Tommy?" Jaskee asked, his voice a mix of fear and anger.

Frankie slowly turned his head and looked at Jaskee then said, "He's not coming back."

Jaskee's first thought was the damn kid had already grabbed a plane and was long gone on his way home, but then looking at Mr. Balero he suddenly had an entirely different thought.

'Were did he go?"

"He's fucking dead, I think . . . that bastard idiot."

"Shit boss."

"Damn right, how the hell did we get into this?"

Jaskee didn't reply. If Tommy was dead . . . man he thought, this was getting worse by the second.

Both men sat for over five minutes, Frankie lost in thought, formulating his moves, like a chess master thinking ahead, pondering all the different possibilities, playing each scenario over and over, trying to figure a way to cover his ass. Jaskee just sat there knowing that this was way out of his league and he was going to shut up and do as he was told.

"This is pretty bad, boss," Jaskee finally said just because the silence was driving him nuts.

Frankie turned and looked at Jaskee, who had worked for him for the last three years. He was a good gardener, great maintenance man, pool cleaner and general handy guy but not somebody Frankie wanted as an accomplice to kidnapping, piracy and murder. Shit, Frankie thought, he'd be sweating this one if he was in Chicago surrounded by his people, but down here, with these guys, what a disaster.

"Listen, Jaskee," he said as he pulled his chair right in front of the big man and looked him deep in his eyes, "listen to what I'm telling you and if it ever leaves this room you are a dead man. Understand?"

Jaskee slowly nodded feeling the blood drain from his head.

"Okay. I need to clear the air with you. Let's just say that back home in Chicago I know a lot of guys with long Italian names, understand?"

Jaskee slowly shook his head sideways, feeling like a dummy, knowing that what he was listening to was going to change his life forever.

"Okay, back home I'm in organized crime, got it? You ever hear of the mafia?"

The big mans eyes grew wide as he shook his head up and down.

"Good, so that's my business and I make lots of money, and in my business trust is the most important thing there is, got it? Not brains, not talent, trust, do you follow me, Jaskee?"

"Yes, boss," he had a hard time getting the words out.

"Good, so we've ended up in this shit pile that neither of us created and we have to get out of it and I'm going to need your help," he stared at the large black man trying to get the message to sink in.

"I'm here for ya, boss."

"Good, listen, this might get a little ugly before it all settles down, but I want you to know something. You stand by me during this and I will change your life. I will bring you into my world of money, lots of money, but," he let the but hang out there like bait on a hook, "but I need something from you. I need your loyalty, unconditional. You do what I tell you to and you don't think twice. You keep your mouth shut and your ears open and once this is all behind us you will be a rich man for the rest of your life."

Jaskee was scared shitless but he was smart enough to know there was only one way out of this and that was to do whatever Frankie Balero told him to do.

"Boss, you can trust me."

Frankie smiled and slid his chair back.

"Good, now here is what we got to do. You go back to the boathouse and babysit those girls until tonight. Keep Tony there as well, he doesn't leave the boat house got it?"

"Got it, boss."

"Alright. Once it's late we'll bring the girls up here."

"Fine, boss," Jaskee started to get up but Frankie waved him back to the couch, then he slid his chair back over in front of him real close, his face inches from Jaskee.

"One last thing, Tony stays with you, all day, doesn't leave, not for one second."

"Jesus boss that might be hard, suppose he's got to take a shit or something?"

Frankie pulled his chair a little closer and whispered, "Dead men don't shit, Jaskee."

Chapter 24

By one in the afternoon Jimmy, showered, shaved and bandaged up, was sitting in a room at the United States Coast Guard station in St. Thomas. He had been picked up by a helicopter after contacting the Coast Guard by radio once he had been pulled aboard the Flying Fish. Flip had driven over from Red Hook and was waiting when he arrived. The two detectives from the St. Thomas Police Department, who thought this meeting should take place in their police station down town were there as well and they didn't like the idea of Flip being allowed in the meeting. But Jimmy looked in such bad shape that Commanding Officer Leboske finally overruled the two detectives and let Flip sit in as long as he promised not to say a word.

In front of Jimmy at a long table sat Commander Leboske, two other official looking Coast Guard officers, and the two detectives. Everybody had listened to Jimmy's story without interruption. A tape recorder was sitting on the desk in front of Leboske recording every word Jimmy said, but he didn't care, he wasn't making any of this up.

After telling his story twice the questioning started, courteous at first but soon the police detectives, one in particular started grilling him and it didn't take Jimmy long to realize that they didn't believe him and after ten minutes of grilling the two cops were openly hostile, doubting his story, trying to get him confused as to what he had already said. One of them was becoming a complete asshole and Jimmy was getting more pissed off by the minute. It never had entered Jimmy's mind when he sat down that they might consider his story a lie and it came as a complete shock when he realized that the detectives wanted to lay the disappearance of Sea Horse and three women at his feet.

"You have no idea where you were taken this morning, no idea of this guy's name or the name of his boat? Why you can't even tell us the name of the yacht that anchored next to you on Iguana Island. Then you want us to believe that some white guy leads an attack on your boat last night, kidnaps three women, beats you up, sinks your boat and then takes you out to feed the sharks and somehow you escaped. That somehow you were able to over power this guy, who had a gun and he ends up flying overboard and gets eaten. Then the speed boat you're on sinks before you can get to shore, and there's not one piece of evidence that we can see, nothing . . . Jesus kid," the cop was getting himself so worked up Jimmy hoped he would have a heart attack and drop dead, "this should be a fuckin' novel."

Jimmy finally lost it, "listen asshole, what do . . ."

Leboske cut him off, "there will be no hostilities here. That goes for both of you, do you understand Mr. Klein?" he said as he glanced from Jimmy to the lead detective who had been grilling him.

"Listen like I already told you," Jimmy continued trying to tone down his anger, "this is exactly what happened. The whole story is true, god, I can't believe this. This is not what I expected."

"Mr. McBain" Robert Ochee, the second detective said, his voice soft, playing the good cop, "what your describing is called piracy. It hasn't happened here in decades, not since the drug dealing days of the eighties, so why now, and why you?"

"I already told you guys, this started with a beach fight a few nights ago. Five guys were," Ochee cut him off, "five guys I don't remember you telling us about five guys. You expect us to believe that you beat up five guys," he said, leaning back in his chair with a smirk, thinking he had finally caught Jimmy in a lie.

"Right five guys only three of them got involved. Listen I used to teach martial arts. Look me up on the internet or something but just listen because this is true," then he told them the entire story over once again. Flip didn't say a word, he just sat in the back row finding it almost impossible to believe the story, and he knew Jimmy.

Once Jimmy finished, he slumped back in his chair, looking exhausted, he exhaled a deep sigh and ran his fingers through his hair. He had nothing more to tell them. There was a long silence before the commanding Coast Guard officer looked over at the lead detective who had been grilling him and asked, "Mr. Klein, any more questions before we release Mr. McBain?"

"Release him? I want him behind bars when he leaves this room!" Detective Klein shouted.

"What!" Jimmy exclaimed jumping out of his chair.

Everybody was taken by surprise at Jimmy's incredible speed. He stood there in front of them in absolute disbelief.

"Sir," he said looking at the commanding officer, "Megan is a woman that I am falling in love with. The two girls Amy and Sarah I have known for years. We're like family. Their father and I hate to tell you this is in the FBI, way up in the FBI, and you don't want him on your shit list. His name is Lester Hollister. I need to call him and tell him what happened. He told me to take care of his daughters and I couldn't," he was almost in tears, "and I know that he needs to be notified. Let me call him now. Then you can talk to him if you don't believe me."

The Coast Guard officers and the two detectives looked at each other before Mr. Klein spoke.

"Alright, Mr. McBain, you call Mr. Hollister, of course your conversation will be recorded, and while you are talking to him we will do a little homework. If your story pans out we'll let you go, fair enough?"

Jimmy wasn't even listening. He was trying to think of what he could possibly tell Lester.

"Good enough, Mr. McBain?" Detective Klein asked again.

"Good enough, sir, but I don't know his number."

"Don't worry, Lester Hollister near Washington D.C, we'll find it, and we'll dial it for you as well," one of the Coast Guard officers said as they all stood up.

Leboske led Jimmy and Flip out of the conference room, down a long corridor and then ushered Jimmy inside a small room asking Flip to wait in the lobby. Jimmy sat down at a desk, looked at the phone, and realized just how scared he was. How could he possibly explain to Lester what happened? What could he tell Lester when he asked him if his daughters were alright?

Jimmy knew the Coast Guard, police and a swat team had searched Henry Island for hours and found nothing. He sat there for what seemed like an eternity, staring at the phone, dreading what he was about to do. Suddenly the door swung open, and a young woman in a bright white Coast Guard uniform stuck her head inside, and gave him a quick smile.

"You can pick up the phone, the call is going through."

Jimmy reached over, grabbed the phone and brought it to his ear. He thought he was going to throw up as he listened to it ring, then Lester answered.

"Hello."

Jimmy didn't know where to start.

"Hello," Lester said again.

"Lester, its Jimmy, something terrible has happened."

Chapter 25

It was a very long day for Frankie Balero and he couldn't have been happier when the sun finally started to set on it. This day was a nightmare from the very beginning. He sat on his veranda watching the last of the sun disappear below the horizon, sipping a gin and tonic. He had made one call to Chicago, sent out one email and most important, he had made one long distance contact on the ham radio and now he needed to sit back and wait. Time to chill out he kept telling himself but it wasn't working. He had one lady, he didn't even know her name, locked downstairs in the hurricane safe room, two girls in the boathouse he hadn't even seen yet, one ninja warrior who more than likely had killed his nephew and made it to the cops, and then there was Jaskee, maintenance man turned killer, and lastly Tony who had his head caved in around three this afternoon with a lead pipe, that was a shit load for anybody's plate for one day. What happened to his peaceful little laid back Caribbean paradise he wondered as he took one long gulp and finished his drink.

He got up, walked to the bar and made another, the way he felt he could drink ten of them tonight but he knew he couldn't. Until all this was cleaned up he was going to have to be on top of everything, no room for error, not with what came down today.

The call to Chicago had been good, and two of his people were arriving tomorrow. One trusted security man and Bobby B Simponia, known to all as Bobby B and the B stood for brains. He was a genius and Frankie knew he needed both of them to get through this. At least he was going to have some of his people down here to wade through this crap, although he never wanted to invite any of them until now. That was the magic of this place it was so far removed from Chicago, and his other life.

The one call he hadn't made yet had bothered him all day. He had to deal with his sister, but how the hell could he call and tell her about Tommy? After a few more sips on his second gin and tonic he decided to let somebody in Chicago have that job.

He finished his second drink and knew it was about time to make his way down to the boat house and give Jaskee a break for a few minutes, and it was also time to meet the twins, who were the reason for this whole shit pile he found himself in. Tommy said they were beautiful, and he wondered if the Russian was going to think the same? That Russian was one guy who was too crazy even for him. Well, he thought standing up and heading for the boathouse, if the Russian liked em, he'd probably buy em.

*

Tigran, the Russian, liked beautiful women and he had enough money that there were always lots hanging around him. The collapse of the Soviet Union and with it the strong arm of Communism had been the best thing that ever happened to him. For most of his early years he had lived in East Berlin, and he had watched the fortunate ones, people with the right connections pass back and forth from his dismal world into the wealth of West Germany. Only in his wildest dreams could he imagine what it must be like on the other side, to have freedom and to be rich.

Yet before the fall of the Berlin Wall he was doing alright by East German standards. He was running a prostitution ring, that brought him money and it worked anywhere there were horny old men and hungry young women. From the sex trade to gambling, protection and even murder he was making a living, barely.

Twice he had been arrested by the police, and twice he had turned informer to save his life. That's how it worked back then, eat or be eaten. People feared him and in turn he feared others, that was life on the streets in East Germany. There was never much to go around but at least he had a part of it. The other thing Tigran had going for him was family. All his uncles, cousins, even his parents and in-laws were into crime. There wasn't anything else back then that had a better future. As disorganized as his early career had been when the Berlin Wall came down he was ready to go.

Drugs opened the world for him. From the very beginning he was ruthless, knowing that only a few could control the vast amounts of narcotics that flooded into East Germany. Early in his career he had been forced to make bold moves, risking it all, even his life at times. His first smuggling attempt involved crossing the Straight of Gibraltar from Morocco to the Spanish coast carrying a load of hashish on a leaky fishing boat. The load was small, only twenty pounds, because he didn't have the money to buy more. But soon the money started rolling in. The first thousand pound shipment of hashish made him a quarter of a million dollars in one night. Next he was dealing opium and heroin from Afghanistan, then home grown marijuana from Spain, Portugal and France. Two years after the collapse of the wall he was bringing small freighters across the Atlantic, his drug cargo easily hidden in sacks of coffee. From Jamaica, Columbia, Mexico and even Cuba, which turned out to be his most profitable country once he started paying the right people, his tramp freighters carried his drugs across the ocean. In Cuba he was able to buy high grade marijuana for five dollars a kilo and sold it by the ton in Germany for six hundred dollars a pound.

Money poured into his life and he spent it without any regard for the future. He bought his Villa on Lake Como in Italy, then his beach house in Colliure, France. The world was his, whatever he wanted, money was no longer a consideration.

Then things started to go wrong, it was inevitable, his world started to collapse and he simply went crazy. He got so strung out on cocaine that after three months of continual use he was forced to have nasal surgery to repair the damage. But the real damage was to his mind, he became unreasonable, demanding, dangerous, paranoid, stupid, and eventually very careless and it couldn't continue.

*

It was his family that finally rescued him. They had him kidnapped from his Villa in Lake Como and smuggled into Switzerland to start involuntary treatment. For a month he was locked away from his world and at first he fought everybody. The doctors, nurses, his family, even the prostitutes that were there for him, he hated them all. But slowly the poisons started to lose their hold and he started to realize how out of control he had become. One day he woke up and knew he could never do drugs again. He had tasted their power, tasted the rush of their pleasure, tasted the euphoric surge that had overwhelmed and engulfed him every time he did cocaine, but he knew he could never experience it again.

Sex became his next drug of choice and by the time he was out of the hospital he was almost as addicted to it as he had been to drugs. In some strange way his cocaine addiction had re-wired his brain and any pleasure now became addiction. In the weeks that followed his release he went from sex with beautiful women to group sex, to kinky sex, to watching the most perverted sex that his warped mind could imagine, but nothing satisfied him. It wasn't until he discovered bondage that his sex life was able to finally reach satisfaction. Women, sex and pain, what pleasure the three created for him.

Chapter 26

One small light bulb cast a dull glow on the far side of the boathouse and Frankie had a hard time seeing anything as he first stepped inside and softly closed the door behind him.

"Jaskee, it's Frankie," he whispered, his eyes trying to adjust to the dim light.

"Here, boss."

Frankie walked over to the inflatable and looked down inside it. The dock he was standing on was three feet above the water and he could faintly see the two girls huddled in the bow. They were clinging tightly to each other, shaking, one of them was crying softly, their heads resting against each other and their eyes locked on him. He felt a rush of excitement just looking at them, and he had a sudden sickening thought that maybe he understood more than he wanted to about that crazy Russian.

He sat down then kicked his bare feet over the dock and dangled his toes in the water. Taking a closer look at them he realized they needed a lot of cleaning up. Both girls looked like they had had a very hard day. Yet without a doubt he could tell they were beautiful. Long blonde hair, soft innocent faces, firm bodies, haunting eyes, yeah he thought with a smile, with a little clean up the Russian will love these two.

"Amy and Sarah, what a pleasure it is to meet you," he said but his voice held an edge to it that even surprised him, "sorry about keeping you two stuck in the boat all day, but I really can't afford for anyone to know you're here. It could complicate things, I'm sure you can understand. In a little bit we will go up to my house. I will have something for you to eat plus you can shower and I am sure I will be able to find something for you to wear. That is the best that I can offer at the moment."

He turned and looked at Jaskee then glanced past him and saw Tony laying in a pool of dried blood at the end of the dock.

"Jaskee, take a break, a short one, be back in ten minutes."

The big man stood up, nodded and went out the door.

Frankie turned his attention back to the girls. Deep down inside he was feeling guilty about what he planned to do with these two, and that surprised him. No one should have to endure what the Russian was capable of. Yet he was just as much a victim in all of this as they were. He just had to clean up Tommy's mess and unfortunately these two were part of it.

"Sorry about your friends, but I don't think you will be seeing them again," he said fighting the fact that some sick part of him was enjoying this more than he liked.

The girls looked up from the bottom of the boat shaking with fear.

"Can't you let us go?" Sarah asked her voice trembling.

"Oh of course I will, but not until the Russian shows up," he said with a laugh that chilled the girls to their very soul.

For the next five minutes he just sat there dangling his toes in the water, watching the girls, trying to imagine what they would look like after a shower and some makeup. Maybe he would put them in a sexy tight dress if he could find one and force them to parade around for Tigran when he showed up. Then he had another thought, maybe he would have one dressed to the max while the other wore some flimsy revealing nighty or something, that way the crazy Russian could see both sides of the package so to speak. Yeah, he liked that idea, both sides of the package.

A few minutes later Jaskee came in, quietly closing the door and stood next to Frankie, breaking his train of thought. The big man didn't say a word, he was too ashamed to even look at the girls. He couldn't believe what he was doing.

Frankie stood up, smiled at the twins then looked at Jaskee.

"I'll be back in a few hours."

"Right, boss, we'll be here."

"I know," then Frankie walked out the door.

Frankie spent a few minutes enjoying the evening as he slowly walked to his house. Once inside he turned off all the lights, darkening the outside around his house as well. He walked out the back door, down the steps, around the corner of his house and walked another twenty feet until he stopped at a small doorway that gave him access to the hurricane safe room. He unlocked the door, stepped in and quietly closed it behind him. The room was small and was lit by one light bulb screwed into a ceiling socket. Most of the space under his house was taken up with a huge concrete cistern. The rest of the space except for the small entry way he stood in was his safe room. Ever since hurricane Hugo and then Marilyn destroyed much of the Virgin Islands people had been building rooms designed to survive the worst hurricanes. His survival room had a tiny separate bathroom off to one side and then the rest of it was just about big enough for a bed and a couch. In one corner was a tall closet that held some cans of food, three cases of wine, and some clothes. The room was heavily reinforced with concrete and steel, and it had a small four inch wide by eight inch high piece of thick safety glass installed in the door, which swung on huge hinges that were bolted into the concrete. Everything about this hurricane room was designed to survive the worst that nature could throw at him and it also just happened to make a perfect prison cell. He glanced in the small window and saw the young lady lying on the bed staring up at the ceiling. She didn't know he was there. He watched her for a few minutes, thinking that this really was a shame. The whole damn thing was, from Tommy getting wasted to all three of these girls having to disappear, what a damn waste. The girl just looked at the ceiling not moving and he couldn't imagine what was going through her head. Finally he turned away, locked the outside door behind him, walked upstairs and laid down on his bed. He was drained. He reached over and set the alarm clock for two a.m.

then pulled a pillow over his head. As he tried to fall asleep, one reoccurring thought raced through his mind, over and over, like an old record with a skip, and that thought was, there wasn't a damn thing he could do to change any of this and that was the biggest shame of this entire dirty deal.

Chapter 27

Frankie was already awake when the alarm went off. He was lying in bed staring out the window, seeing only the darkness that surrounded his resort. He had been wondering about Jaskee and if he had been able to stay awake, but somehow he knew he had, the big man was too terrified to screw anything up.

He hadn't slept much, most of the night he tossed and turned thinking about Tommy and the situation that he now found himself in. That damn kid, what a complete screw up, but there was also a part of him that was starting to feel sorry for Tommy as well. What a lousy way to go, even for a dumb shit like Tommy, he thought. Frankie had never liked Tommy, always thought his sister spoiled him when he was young and made him into a pansy. Still being eaten alive the way he was had given Frankie the creeps all night.

Throwing the thin sheet off he stepped into his flip-flops and headed to the boat house. The night was still, there wasn't a breath of wind and except for the loud croaking of the frogs it would have been hauntingly quiet. He had no need for a flashlight as he had walked this gravel pathway so many times he could have done it blindfolded. At the doorway of the boathouse he stopped, put his ear to the wood and listened, there wasn't a sound. He stood for a few more minutes thinking about this whole mess and wondering how it was all going to end. Would the cops come to Cantelle Bay and ask some questions? There was nothing that could tie him to all of this, nothing except his missing boat which fortunately he had heard the guy on the radio tell the Coast Guard had sunk in really deep water, and the fact that Tommy was definitely not going to make his scheduled return flight home early next week. Maybe he should have somebody from Chicago fly down here with fake I.D. and fly home in Tommy's place, he'd have to think about it.

Bringing his thoughts back to the present he opened the boathouse door, quietly walked in and closed the door behind him. His eyes were used to the darkness so it was easy to pick Jaskee out as he stood up. The big man looked at him but didn't say a word. Frankie walked over and looked into the dinghy and could see the girls huddled in the bow asleep. Pity, he thought to wake them up and bring them back into this nightmare. He walked to the work bench that was on the other side of the boathouse and opened the top drawer. After fumbling around for a minute, he pulled out a handful of thick plastic electrical ties that he used around the resort to support bundles of electrical wires, and he also grabbed a roll of duct tape. Tucking the ties into his pocket he walked back to the dinghy then motioned for Jaskee to come stand next to him. Ripping two pieces of duct tape off of the roll each about a foot long he handed one to Jaskee then he laid down on the dock, as close to the twins as he could get. The big man just stood there not knowing what to do and finally Frankie had to look over his right shoulder and motion with his head for him to get down on the dock beside him. He finally figured it out and laid down next to his boss. Frankie looked over at him and in an exaggerated motion mouthed one, two, three then at the same time they both forced the tape over the girl's lips and around the back of their heads. Instantly the twins awoke, and both tried to scream but the tape was already in place, their lips sealed, and nothing came out. Even in the dim light Frankie could see their eyes full of terror. The girls tried to scramble back away from him and Jaskee but there was no place to go. Frankie grabbed one of them by her hand and forcefully pulled her to her feet and then as he stood he yanked her out of the boat and up onto the dock next to him, Jaskee did the same. Reaching in his pocket Frankie pulled out a plastic tie and forcing Amy's hands behind her back he wrapped the tie around her wrist before pulling it tight. Amy could hardly stand she was so afraid. Turning to Sarah he grabbed her hands and holding them in front of her he bound them also.

"My we look pretty tonight," he whispered.

Before he moved he grabbed one more tie and ran it through Sarah's hands and then pushed her into her sister and ran the tie through Amy's hands and cinched it tight. The girls were locked tight to each other.

"Let's go," Frankie said as he grabbed Amy's arm and leading the girls, headed for the door.

In the darkness the girls stumbled toward his house, pulled by Frankie and pushed from behind by Jaskee. There was no way they could escape, no way they could scream, nobody could see them, they were completely helpless, and they knew it. They took one reluctant step after another their feet crunching on the gravel bringing them closer to a place they were sure they didn't want to go. Once they reached the front porch Frankie pushed Amy to his right and they started walking around the side of the house. A few more steps and Frankie jerked Amy to a stop, then he opened a small door that neither of the girls had noticed. Frankie swung the door open into a dimly lit room and started to push Amy inside. Amy fought against him with all of her strength, but it was futile. The men were too strong and Jaskee forced Sarah into her sister and they had no choice but to step inside. The room looked like a dungeon. Once the four of them were inside Frankie closed the door behind them.

"This way," Frankie said his voice sounding menacing as he led them to another door. Amy looked at the door and was shocked to see Megan looking back at her through the glass. Sarah saw her also, but there was no joy in any of their hearts, not with this reunion, there was still only fear.

"Get out of the way," Frankie said as he pushed the girls aside then pulled a key out of his pocket and unlocked the door. Megan took a few steps back as the door swung open and the twins were pushed into their new cell. Frankie didn't say a word at first just stared at the girls, slightly shaking his head before he pulled a small pocket knife out of his pants. He grabbed the twins and cut the plastic ties off of their wrists.

"I believe you know each other," he said almost politely, "I will bring some food down shortly along with some clothes. There is a shower in the bathroom, tear the duct tape off and clean yourselves up. And don't make a sound down here any of you," then he closed the door behind them and the girls could hear the heavy lock as it slammed shut.

They rushed into each others arms, tears flowing, all three hugging tightly, each terrified and wondering what could possibly happen next.

"Where's Jimmy?" Megan finally asked as she pulled herself away. She looked at the twins, hoping to see a ray of hope on their faces, but she only saw their terror. Megan took a step back and collapsed on the bed. Somehow, in her heart she knew Jimmy must be dead and she burst into tears.

Chapter 28

In a private office located in the Virgin Islands Police Department Detective Frederick Klein sat with his partner Robert Ochee and their boss Captain Desmond Boschulle. Each had a coffee cup in his hand trying to get going this morning. Desmond sat in silence, thumbing through the short three page preliminary report that his detectives had put together for him.

A large nautical chart showing Henry Island and the surrounding area sat on the table before Desmond.

Captain Boschulle finished reading the report and dropped it on his lap then looked at his detectives, "Mr. Hollister as you know does work for the FBI, this is confirmed and he has assured us that he has the deepest confidence in Mr. McBain. So what do we do with that?"

After a short silence Robert looked at his partner as if trying to get some advice then looked back at his boss and said, "there's really not much to go on, Desmond, not yet, but either Frederick or I will be heading out to Iguana Island this morning and over to Joey's Beach Bar. The bartender working that evening is a young lady named Heather Harding. We've already contacted her by phone, and she has agreed to meet with us, but over the phone she pretty much confirmed Mr. McBain's story."

"Alright what about McBain, do you believe him?" Desmond asked, his voice stern, almost angry, his eyes grilling his detectives'.

Both detectives nodded their heads up and down before Frederick said, "Yeah, we believe him. I got pretty rough with him at the

Coast Guard yesterday and, yeah . . . as much as we don't want to, we believe him."

"So we've got a case of piracy, kidnapping, and god forbid three murders. Well, that shit does not happen down here anymore," Desmond said, getting angrier with each word he spoke.

Frederick and Robert looked at each other and neither of them knew what to say. Neither of them wanted to be the one to tell Desmond that it sure sounded to them like this shit still happens.

"Is there any other way to look at this?" Desmond finally asked, breaking the awkward silence.

"Like how, boss?" Frederick asked, knowing it was a dumb question. He knew what his boss wanted to hear.

"I don't know. Use your imagination. One guy, three lovely women on a sea cruise, sex triangle goes bad, jealous rage, sex, drugs and guns, somebody shoots somebody, I don't know. Without bodies we really don't know if anybody is dead or not. I just want another angle, that's all."

"Another angle?" Robert said, "another angle, besides, piracy, kidnapping and murder, well Desmond I don't have one."

"Listen guys, we are going to pursue this case on all fronts. I've got to work with the Coast Guard, with the Feds, with my boss and finally with goddamn politicians, who are my bosses' boss and believe me those elected officials do not want this type of crime happening here, got it?"

"To be blunt as hell, Desmond, nobody does, but something happened to Sea Horse and her crew, so what do you want us to do, make shit up?" Frederick said, already pissed off by the direction his boss was leading this conversation.

Desmond knew he pushed it too far, too fast and he slumped back in his chair.

"Of course not, I just want to keep an open mind, no conclusions yet, every possibility on the table."

He reached over and grabbed a chart and slid it around in front of him.

"Henry Island," he said softly but both Frederick and Robert already understood the direction this investigation was heading, and they both knew it was bullshit.

*

Jimmy and Flip along with Lester, who had arrived early this morning sat around Jimmy's kitchen table with a chart of the Virgin Islands before them. Another chart which showed more of the surrounding area including the British Virgins was laying next to it. A dark circle was drawn on the Virgin Islands chart around Henry Island and an x was drawn where Jimmy figured Sea Horse went down. There were a few other circles and x's drawn in light pencil on the chart as well.

It was only ten a.m. and all three were exhausted. Jimmy and Flip had been up most of the night looking at charts, trying to form some strategy, forcing themselves to come up with something before Lester arrived. Lester hadn't slept at all. He was sick with worry and he had been feeling so helpless back home. Even now, sitting with two of his most trusted friends he felt that same hopelessness and that same fear that came crashing into his mind. It was impossible for him to keep it away. It ate at his very soul and deep down even though he refused to admit it he feared he would never see his girls again. Still, Lester forced his mind to think, forced the fear away enough to try and function. He had already accomplished one important task, he was able to reestablish contact with one of his people down here in the islands and she was available if he needed her. There was no way he could use Feds right now, he couldn't trust any of them.

"Listen Lester," Jimmy said as he grabbed the Virgin Islands chart and pulled it in front of them, "Flip and I figure the island that Megan and I were taken to has to be within this circle," he said and he pointed out a large circle in pencil on the chart. Lester looked at it then said, "but Jimmy that circle covers almost the entire chart. That's too large of an area. We need to narrow it down."

"I know but I can't tell how long Megan and I were in the boat before we landed. I think I passed out . . . so I don't have an accurate time reference. So what Flip and I did last night was to try and figure it backwards?"

"How's that?"

"Well, we know I swam ashore at Flamingo Bay, on Scrub Island, after the boat sank out from underneath me," he pointed Scrub Island out on the chart, "and the best I can tell I was somewhere between three and five miles away from it when I kicked the guy overboard, so that puts me in this circle," he pointed to another lightly drawn circle on the chart which was about ten miles wide around Scrub Island.

"Okay," Lester said following his thinking.

"Also I know I was to the east of Scrub Island so let's just figure I was in this half of the circle, and I'm guessing here," he said as he pointed to another small x on the chart, "so then Flip and I started thinking about what else we had to work with, and I figured that I spent about half an hour that morning tied up in the bottom of the boat once we left the boathouse before the guy stopped to throw me overboard."

"Okay good so far, I think this works," Lester said looking up at both of them before he looked back to the chart.

"So I can only guess how fast the Sea Ray was able to go, and I figure twenty to twenty-five knots. So that means the island and the boathouse can't be any further away from here," he pointed out the x again on the chart, "than ten to fifteen miles, but the real problem is we don't know what direction," he said slumping back in his chair.

All three men looked at the chart and nobody said a word for a few minutes.

It was Lester that came up with the next bright idea,

"Alright. That is still a huge area, there's a hundred islands or more and it could be any of them, but" he paused and looked up from the chart into his friends faces, "but how many of them have a dock with a boathouse?"

Chapter 29

The police boat stopped ten feet from the beach and Detective Ochee threw out a small anchor. He looked over the side, tried to guess how deep it was then jumped overboard. It was deeper than he thought and he swore when his feet hit the bottom and he was soaked to his fat belly. He struggled ashore and headed for Joey's beach bar.

This mornings meeting with Chief Boschulle had bothered him. It was obvious the direction this investigation was already going. Shit, he thought, it was just starting and it was already heading down the slippery, white-washed- no- media- frenzy, no negative publicity, peace in paradise at any cost, bullshit trail. What were he and Frederick supposed to do, ignore the facts? Just go through the motions, play detectives for a few more days, then throw their hands up in the air, and tell Desmond it had to be that Jimmy McBain kid, so let's go arrest him. That was what Boschulle wanted to hear and he and Frederick already knew that. He also agreed with his partner and he didn't think Jimmy was guilty. His story was weak, really weak, but that didn't mean he was guilty and he feared if he or Frederick didn't come up with something soon the pressure was going to start building to arrest somebody and Jimmy McBain was the only target on the radar screen. At times like this he wished he had taken another career path, even a taxi driver would be better than this shit.

Kicking his feet in the sand he finally reached Joey's. A young women mid-twenties was sitting on one of the few bar stools that surrounded the cutest little beach bar he had ever seen.

"Heather?" he asked.

"Yes," she said with an accent that he couldn't place.

"I'm detective Robert Ochee, thanks for meeting me this morning."

"You're welcome."

She was a little nervous, that was obvious and he wasn't sure why. He knew some people get that way whenever they have to talk to the police. Maybe a past offense, maybe an existing warrant, maybe criminal charges back home, hell there could be a ton of reasons. Some people when they come down to the islands have no intention of returning stateside for at least seven years which except for murder and a few other serious crimes is the statute of limitations.

"Just so you know," he said as he sat down on a stool next to her. They were the only people at the bar. It didn't open until noon, "this is about the beach fight. I know you've already told me what happened on the phone, but I want to go over it again."

She was still nervous, trying to hide it but not doing a very good job, and he suddenly had a thought, one of those clarifying moments that just happens in his business.

"Listen Heather," he said in a calming voice trying to ease her anxieties, "listen to me and trust what I'm telling you. This is not about you. It's about the twin girls, and the guys on the beach and the fight. I'm trying to put the pieces together and you may just tell me something, something that you think isn't important, but might help me," he paused looked her in the eye and gave her a wink, "you know I don't recognize your accent . . . and frankly I don't care if you're here legally or not, remember this isn't about you Heather, please trust me on this one, okay?"

She smiled a little and he could see her body relax a bit and he knew he hit the nail on the head.

"Okay," she said with a smile, and she did seem to relax a little more before she started talking, "I was serving drinks to the two cute twins. I don't think they were used to drinking much because after a few drinks apiece they were getting . . . well . . . hammered," she made a funny face like it was her fault they were getting drunk.

"Go on."

"So they were really cute together, laughing and telling me they were on a beautiful sailboat with this great guy that was their cousin or uncle, somebody I never really did figure it out. They kept telling me I needed to meet him, like he was the greatest guy on the planet. They were here maybe . . . I don't know, half an hour or so. They were my only guests and I was really enjoying them. It was fun. Then suddenly these five guys walked up from the beach and before I knew it they were buying the girls drinks left and right. Well, I've done this long enough to know that it was getting to be a bad situation fast and those two didn't have a clue. I was starting to worry for them, but what can I do? I don't even have a phone here. I started going light on the booze, making the girl's drinks almost virgins and I don't think they could even tell. Well . . . then, I don't know maybe a half hour later, something like that this guy walks up from the beach and sits down. I think he pushed one of the guys off of a stool, maybe the guy was drunk and fell, I'm not sure, but it was funny and everybody started laughing, at least at first. But I've seen lots of bar fights and it looked like the guys who had been slobbering all over the twins weren't going to let it go by.

"Then this guy that had just walked up from the beach blows my mind by telling the five guys that he's the girl's dad and he really appreciates them taking care of his daughters. He even offered to buy them all a drink. Well, hell, there couldn't have been ten years difference between him and the twins. I didn't know what to think."

She stopped talking and looked at Robert who had his elbows on the bar, his eyes closed listening, painting a picture with every word.

"Are you alright?"

He laughed, "I'm fine. Just putting your words into little pictures in my mind, go on."

"Okay, so like I said he offers to buy them all a drink and they start giving him some crap and one of them I don't remember his name gets up and tries to push the guy off of the bar stool and that's when it all started."

"What started?" he said even though he knew the answer.

"Well, the fight, that's what and it didn't last long. I was really afraid for the girl's dad, or cousin, whatever he was. I mean its five against one, right. But I couldn't believe it. Before I knew what happened he had one of the guys down on the ground, then another one attacks him and he is suddenly flat on his back or stomach I can't remember either, sorry, but the guy's screaming for his friends to back off. Then somebody else rushed him and he kicked him so hard that the guy slammed into the bar almost knocking it over, and I went flying, landing on my bum."

At that Robert opened his eyes, looked at the bar on the trailer and thought that it must have been one hell of a kick.

Heather had been watching his face as she told her story and she stopped when he opened his eyes and looked around.

"Should I keep going, there's not much left to tell."

"Please."

"Well, then, and I'll never forget this, the guy looks at whoever else was standing and gives this karate scream that made me almost pee my pants. I mean it was powerful and the guys just turned and ran away.

"Then the twins, and their cousin, uncle, I don't know . . . just left without saying a word to me. The other guys finally got up cussing their heads off and I just froze. I didn't look at them, I didn't even move. It took them a few minutes before they walked down the beach and disappeared. Boy I was glad that was over."

"That's it?" he asked.

"That's it. I don't remember anything else, really."

"Could you identify any of them?"

"Probably, I mean . . . I was really scared but I think I could."

Robert stood up grabbed his card out of his shirt pocket and handed it to Heather.

"Thanks Heather, please call me if you think of anything else," then he turned and started for the beach.

Heather held his card in her hand watching him go then suddenly she shouted, "Detective."

Robert stopped, turned around and looked at her, "what?"

"Are those girls alright?" she asked sounding worried.

"I really don't know."

Chapter 30

The United States Coast Guard had started their investigation of the disappearance of Sea Horse, thirty minutes after the initial radio contact with Jimmy McBain, and a day later Commander Leboske was still struggling trying to fit all the pieces together. Two Coast Guard officers had already interviewed the management of Deep Sea Charters, and that didn't turn up anything of a suspicious nature. According to a Mr. Dozer the three charter guests seemed extremely happy and as Mr. Dozer had told his officers, he'd been in this business for years and there was nothing about this group that gave him any reason for concern before they left the dock.

Sea Horse had already been found, lying in two hundred and fifty feet of water, in the approximate location Mr. McBain said it would be. The cutter Invincible had no trouble locating her using a side-scan submersible, which took photos as well as relayed echo graphics of the sunken yacht back to the Invincible.

Then there was yesterdays meeting with the only known survivor and therefore only suspect at the moment and it weighed heavy on Leboske's mind. He kept seeing the anguish that Mr. McBain suffered as he told his story over and over. How he broke down in tears more than once as he relived the events that led to the sinking of his boat and the disappearance of the three women he had on board.

The two asshole detectives from the Virgin Island Police Department hadn't accomplished much, he thought, sitting at his desk, drumming his fingers absentmindedly. The faxed copy of their initial investigation that he had received this morning from their boss Desmond Boschulle made him wonder if they had a brain between the three of them. Still the wheels were now in motion, the investigation up and running, but unfortunately he felt like it had already crashed into a solid brick wall. In less than twenty-four hours it seemed to him that all forward motion on this case had come to a complete halt.

Commander Leboske sat in his office holding a five page preliminary report that he and his team had put together, and it bothered him that there were no conclusions. There was no way at the moment that he could wrap the disappearance of Sea Horse and three people into a neat little gory bundle with a beginning, middle and ending. There was no ending, not now, not until they could figure out what happened to the three young women. There were no bodies to be found, which often is the case in boating accidents, but this didn't sound like much of an accident, not according to Mr. McBain. It sounded like piracy, and he feared maybe even something worse, human trafficking. The slave trade still exists in many parts of the world, and he had seen it first hand in the Caribbean. He had busted a lot of drug smugglers in the past, but the smugglers that carried people, they were the worst. He had seen desperate people crammed in all sorts of vessels from unbelievably overcrowded, leaky Haitian fishing boats to cargo ships full of people, he'd even discovered people locked inside containers, with no food and little water, with no bathroom, locked inside a damn metal box for days. That was beyond his comprehension to understand. How could anybody submit another human being to such conditions? It was all about money, he knew, smugglers could make a fortune delivering a boat load of illegal's into the United States, and for most of those poor souls there was only one way they could ever pay a debt that big. If they didn't have the money up front they were sold to the highest bidder in places like Miami, or New York. Sold into a life of toil, and sweat shop labor, that could last for years before their debts were paid. But young women had a much more unpleasant future. Slavery and prostitution went hand in hand, and for the women, even girls as young as ten, prostitution was often their only way out. Even if they refused they had little say in the end. There was just so much money to be made and such little risk. If the girls were busted they were too terrified to talk to the police so they were normally just sent home courtesy of Uncle Sam. But the real criminals, those who forced this unholy situation upon the unsuspecting girls were hardly ever caught. It was terrible. It made the war on drugs seem like a waste of time to him. His biggest fear in this case was that because the three missing women were young, white and he imagined beautiful he knew they could bring a fortune in the right situation. If those girls were alive he needed to find them now, and he doubted the Virgin Islands Police Department was going to be of much help. He could probably get the Feds down here but it could take a week and that was way to long. Every day that went by would make it ten times harder to ever find them, if it wasn't too late already. These girls were about to disappear from the face of the earth into a sexual nightmare and he had little time left to prevent it.

He slid his desk drawer open, grabbed the phone book and thumbed through it before he found the number. He picked his phone up and dialed, not sure exactly what he was going to say.

The phone rang a few times before it was answered.

"Hello."

"Jimmy McBain?"

"Yes, who is this?"

"Jimmy, this is Commanding Officer Leboske, United States Coast Guard, remember me?"

"Yes sir, don't believe I'll ever forget you either."

Leboske laughed.

"Well, son I want you to know that the United States Coast Guard wants to help. This is a terrible situation that has happened, terrible and I believe your story. I want you to know that."

"Thank you," Jimmy said not sure what Commanding Officer Leboske was thinking, but his timing wasn't bad.

"You really want to help us, sir?"

"Absolutely, why do you have a thought?"

"Yes as a matter of fact I do," Jimmy said, thinking fast, wondering, just maybe.

"Well son, spit it out, what can we do?"

"Put a chopper in the air and look for a boathouse."

"A boathouse, Jesus there's a lot of them!"

"I know, but this boathouse needs to be within a twenty mile radius of Scrub Island, that should narrow it down some."

"That helps, maybe, but Jesus, still that's a huge area. Tell you what Jimmy McBain, I think I might be able to arrange something like that, I'll call it a training drill or whatever I can come up with. So a boathouse within a twenty mile radius of Scrub Island, I'll call you and let you know what we find, alright?"

"Thank you."

Leboske hung up and sat drumming his fingers on his desk for a minute, thinking about this strange request and how he was going to go about it. Finally he called his secretary and gave her the information to begin the search for a boathouse. He had to repeat himself twice when she asked to confirm that the object of the search was a boathouse, not a boat.

"Yes, a boathouse, any boathouse I don't care what size it is as long as it is within a twenty mile radius of Scrub Island, got it?"

"Yes sir," she replied.

"Good, lets get the helicopter going asap," he hung up, then sat staring at the phone asking himself if this was the best idea he could possibly come up with and with a sickening feeling he realized that it was.

Chapter 31

A small float plane glided low over the Caribbean Sea. The pilot Kevin Lentnek was glad the sun was behind him as he cut the throttle and started his approach. It was always tricky coming into Cantelle Bay. He had to make sure he cleared the reef, didn't clip any sailboat mast in the narrow channel and still have enough room to land. Plus he always had to factor in the cross winds and some dumbshit tourist on a wind surfer, or a floater out there bobbing around on some cushion oblivious to everything around him, or her, but their rum punch.

The pontoons hit the water three hundred feet from the beach and the plane came to a slow crawl before Kevin felt the gentle grab of the shore and he turned his engine off.

"One moment please," he said looking at his two guests who hadn't said a thing the entire trip over from St. Thomas.

Kevin jumped down onto the port pontoon, lifted a small hatch and grabbed a coil of rope about twenty feet long that had some chain and a small anchor attached to it then he jumped on the sand. He tied the loose end of the rope to a hook welded in place on the pontoon then carried the anchor up the beach, and gave it a throw.

"Welcome to Cantelle Bay," Kevin said as he walked back to the plane, gave his passengers a smile and hoped that they tipped him.

He reached up and grabbed three small bags, thinking these two were traveling pretty light. He set the bags on the sand then helped the first guy out of the plane. He was a big man at least two hundred and forty pounds and over six feet tall. He had a scar running down his left check, and he hadn't smiled once the entire trip, and Kevin thought this guy wasn't somebody he wanted to get to know. His second passenger was about fifty Kevin figured and again there was something about the guy that gave him the creeps. These two didn't seem like normal tourists, and for the last eight years all he had been doing was flying people around the Caribbean. He couldn't put his finger on what it was about them that made him feel that way but something did. They didn't seem like a gay couple, no these two were just weird he finally thought.

He carried their bags up past the wet sand and dropped them on a picnic table.

"Thanks for flying with me," Kevin said as they walked up to where he was standing.

The short man reached his right hand out and Kevin thought he was going to shake his hand goodbye which would have been weird, seeing as how they hadn't said two words the entire flight. Instead the guy slipped him a hundred dollar bill, then the big guy grabbed the bags and they headed up the beach, without a backward glance.

Well, a hundred dollar tip wasn't bad Kevin thought as he walked up to the bar, pulled out a chair and ordered a beer. Yeah, he thought, it takes all kinds, but it's just that some are a lot weirder than others.

Bobby Simponia and his traveling companion Charlie Markenson walked into the air-conditioned lobby of Cantelle Bay Resort and were greeted with a big hug by Frankie Balero. The men had known each other for years, trusted family.

"Welcome to heaven, guys," Frankie said as he walked behind the counter and grabbed two keys.

"How come we ain't ever been invited here before?" Charlie asked.

Frankie smiled, thought he would let it pass, but then said, "because I never needed any dumb shit mobsters here before that's why."

"Okay," Charlie said and knew he should just shut up.

Bobby smiled and knew that Frankie was already setting Charlie in his place. Charlie was along as insurance, just in case they needed him, and if they did, it wouldn't be for his brains. But for now all he had to do was stay out of the way, keep his mouth shut, and everything should be fine. Charlie didn't have a clue as to the reason for this sudden trip and Frankie hoped it was going to stay that way.

Bobby on the other hand had given a lot of thought to Frankie's situation. He had been filled in on every detail, even the crazy Russian and he figured Frankie was on the right track.

"I've got your rooms ready guys, lunch around noon, dinner around six and cocktails whenever you feel the need. Just stay sharp . . . Charlie," he said looking at him with a smile, knowing that Charlie gave up drinking years ago.

"Right, Frankie, sharp," he repeated feeling dumb already.

Bobby and Charlie followed Frankie out of the office down a short walkway, past a few tourists and to a row of little cottages that overlooked the beach.

"Charlie, you're in the Sea Breeze cottage, enjoy it," Frankie pushed the door open and let the big man walk past him.

"Jesus, Frankie, this is pretty nice."

"Well, like I said, enjoy it. It usually brings me six hundred a night."

Charlie beamed when he heard the normal price, then he walked to the couch and dropped like a rock.

Bobby and Frankie left Charlie sitting on his ass and they continued down the little gravel footpath past three other cottages until they reached another bungalow that sat by itself perched on a little hill at the end of the path.

"You get the best, Bobby," Frankie said as he opened a door and they walked into a very large one room cottage with views of Honeymoon Beach and the Caribbean Sea out the big sliding glass doors that led to a large deck. Frankie walked into the kitchen, grabbed two ice cold beers from the fridge then headed outside. Bobby followed and they sat down on some comfortable deck chairs around a teak table. Frankie handed Bobby a cold one and they popped the caps and each enjoyed the first drink of the day.

Frankie didn't say anything for a while, just looked out over his beach and the Caribbean, drinking his beer, letting Bobby take it all in. Bobby was one of the few Chicago people he had thought about inviting down in the past but just never got around to it.

"Pretty nice, Frankie, you did good getting this place."

Frankie smiled "You're right, Bobby, it's pretty damn good down here. It's a great place to hang out, it cleans dirty money, and I really love it here. It's good for my nerves . . . at least it was until my dumb shit nephew and his friends showed up."

Bobbie laughed then said, "paradise ain't always perfect."

"Well we've got to get it back to perfect, you given my situation any thought?"

Bobby finished his beer as he kept looking out over the ocean thinking this really was spectacular.

"Yea, I've given your situation a lot of thought."

"Okay."

"Well I think you're on the right track. I got a feeling the Russian is a good way to wash your hands of this, but there are a few things to consider."

"You're right about that, I've got my list."

"The time factor seems number one. This needs to get cleaned up like right now. When do you expect him?"

"One of his boats is down island I think in Antigua, so it's maybe . . . I don't know, twenty-four hours from here."

"Where is the Russian?"

"That's a good question and I don't know the answer. I talked to one of his people on the ham radio and I told them to tell him I had his birthday presents ready, all three of them, ready and wrapped."

"Birthday presents?" Bobby said with a laugh as he glanced over at Frankie, then back out over the blue Caribbean.

"Yea, believe me he knows what I'm talking about. You see Bobby, this isn't the first time we've done a transaction like this."

"Not the first time?" Bobby said forcing his eyes from the Caribbean back to Frankie.

"No, not the first time . . . and let's just leave it at that," Frankie said.

Chapter 32

Sitting around a large dining table in a villa overlooking the Mediterranean Ocean Tigran, the Russian, and another man were eating breakfast. It was eleven in the morning and they were still in their robes and both were exhausted from their late night activities. Tigran sipped his tea, a deep smile on his face as he thought about the woman that they both had enjoyed last night. She had just left an hour ago, three thousand dollars richer. It had been difficult but he had lived up to his agreement with her pimp, which was simply that by ten o'clock this morning she would walk out of his villa un-aided on her own accord. It took some restraint on his part last night but all and all it was a wonderful evening and worth the cost.

He looked over at his lover, a young man whose perverted tastes equaled or exceeded his.

"Louis, she was nice yes?"

Louis smiled and ran the tip of his tongue over his lips as if he could still taste her then he inhaled deeply savoring the lingering odor of her sweat and fear.

"Yes Tigran delicious."

"What should we do today?"

"I haven't thought about it, but . . . there is always time for passion."

Tigran thought his lover meant perversion but he didn't say anything, and he turned his attention back to his breakfast. A few minutes later his cell phone rang and he reached into his robe pocket and pulled it out.

"Yes."

As he listened a slight smile grew on his face which caught his lover's attention and he put his fork down and watched Tigran. The Russian's head was nodding slightly up and down, the ends of his lips arching ever upwards and Louis suddenly felt a surge of excitement.

"When?" Tigran asked then listened in silence for another minute before he pulled the phone away from his head, closed it with a snap, and put it back in his pocket.

"What, Tigran?" Louis asked, his voice soft held back with restraint that he didn't feel at the moment.

The Russian didn't respond at first, he let his thoughts run, thinking about the possibility, and then the inconvenience of it all.

Louis kept looking at him, and Tigran could see the lust in his eyes, yet the Russian felt more tired than anything, and at the moment he wasn't sure if it would be worth the effort. But he thought back to some of the women he had owned in the past and he knew the prolonged joy that they could give. The last woman he bought he had enjoyed for six weeks before he had grown tired and discarded her.

"Please Tigran, you must tell me," Louis was having a hard time keeping his excitement in control.

"A friend has something for me, but it is far away and I don't think it is worth the effort."

"Something or someone?"

Tigran looked at his lover and felt a slight rush of excitement.

"Neither really, or I guess I should say three someone's, still they are a long way away and I know they will not be cheap."

"When have you worried about money, my love?"

Tigran knew he was right. Money was not a factor in his life any longer. He did what he chose to do, when he wanted to, there was no concern about cost.

He could see the passion in Louis's eyes awakening, and seeing his lover excited created passion in him as well.

"This is what I will do," he said as he grabbed his cell phone out of his pocket, flipped it open and dialed a number, calling one of his trusted people who worked in his care.

"Yes, I have just learned that I have something in the Caribbean. Frankie Balero has been kind to me. Yet, it does seem far to go. Please contact him and have him email me some photos. He will understand."

He closed the phone and gave his lover a smile and both men felt an ever growing rush of excitement.

*

The fax machine rang in his office and Frankie was surprised because not that many people used faxes any more, most reservations were made online. He was lucky he was in his office, having just stepped in to see if he had missed any calls after his meeting with Bobby. He grabbed the fax and looked at it, then smiled. This wasn't a reservation he quickly realized. No, this had the chance to be a lot more rewarding than just some damn tourist coming to his resort.

On the single page fax was written:

Rather tied up at the moment. Can you send photos, email them to me in Barcelona.

Frankie sat down and thought about it. If the Russian wasn't interested in the girls then he didn't have any other options but to kill them and that seemed such a waste. He reached over, opened his desk drawer and pulled out his digital camera. Standing he slid the drawer closed then started for the kitchen. It might take a while but he was going to make sure those three looked good before he took a few photos. It was time to dress up the merchandise because this was one sale he didn't want to lose.

*

The overhanging light had made it hard to sleep and all three of the girls were exhausted. Ever since Amy and Sarah were dragged into their new prison cell the girls had said little to each other. Finding Megan had lifted the twin's spirits at first, but as the three of them laid on the bed the seriousness of their situation continued to haunt them. They were locked in a prison cell somewhere by some creep who scared them to death, with no hope of rescue because even though nobody wanted to admit it they all knew that Jimmy must be dead by now.

When the man walked into their cell he tried to be nice, almost like a friend, which to say the least was confusing for all three of the girls. He asked how they slept, if they were cold, if they wanted anything, like he wasn't their jailer. None of the girls said a word, just watched him as he juggled a tray of food putting it on the bed without spilling anything.

"You need to eat," he said almost sounding like a father.

But then he just stood there, looking at them, not saying anything and it scared the girls even more because they couldn't imagine what was running through his mind. His face was expressionless, no hint of emotion, no way that any of them could guess what he was thinking.

Finally he shifted his feet and said "listen you three, this can be easy or it can be hard," and before any of them could react he grabbed Megan by her arm and pulled her to her feet. She struggled at first but it was hopeless.

"Stand right there," he said his voice suddenly full of venom and they couldn't believe it was the same guy who told them they needed to eat a few minutes ago.

Megan stood locked in place too afraid to take a step, thinking she would probably collapse if she tried to move. The creep took a few steps back, reached into his pocket and pulled out a camera. He took a picture of Megan, the flash blinding them all.

"Smile," he ordered and Megan thought he must be nuts but she forced a little smirk as he snapped another photo.

"Good, now sit down and you blondee, get up" he said looking at Amy, almost hissing his demand out.

He snapped a picture of her then motioned with the camera and Sarah got up and stood next to her sister.

"Right there baby," he said, as he snapped a few more pictures.

As soon as he was done Sarah slumped back down on the bed followed by Amy a moment later.

Frankie stood looking at the three, thinking to himself how nice it might be to sample some of this lovely merchandise himself before he turned them over to the Russian. But that would have to wait a bit, because this morning he needed to focus on selling his product and these girls had way too many clothes on for that. It was all about marketing he thought with a sick laugh.

Chapter 33

The call to the Virgin Islands Police department did nothing to make Lester feel any better. By the time he hung up he knew those idiots were not going to accomplish a thing. Captain Boschulle hadn't told him much, and when he pressed him Boschulle became pretty hostile, telling him the investigation was ongoing, that they already had a suspect and that was about all they could do at the moment. It was all bullshit, and Lester knew it. The cops had their eye on Jimmy and they were far less interested in finding his daughters and Megan than protecting the reputation of the Virgin Islands, and piracy was about the last thing Boschulle wanted splattered across the airwaves. A love triangle gone bad, or a charter boat sinks and people disappear, maybe sex, drugs, and even crazy tourists abducted by UFO's, all that would be acceptable, but not piracy. Lester understood all to well that a cover-up was already rolling. He could only guess but he figured in a few days at most, Jimmy was going to be arrested for kidnapping and murder and that damn Boschulle was going to do everything in his power to make a case of it.

Flip and Jimmy just sat looking at Lester. They could read his face and it wasn't promising.

"Not good?" Jimmy finally asked.

Lester glanced at his friends and slightly shook his head,

"No, not good."

"What did he say?" Flip asked his voice soft lost in thought.

"That basically they already have a suspect, which he didn't mention by name, but I'm sure it's you, Jimmy, and also that his detectives were on the case, that's about it."

"That's all! What about Sarah, Amy and Megan?" Jimmy shouted, but he was also thinking the same thing that Lester was thinking, they didn't have much time before the cops came knocking.

"That's what really scares me. He never even mentioned the girls by name, not once," Lester replied.

Flip and Jimmy both looked at him in astonishment.

"Didn't mention them, my god, what else is there?" Flip asked.

"There's covering their ass," Jimmy replied, fighting a panic that was making him physically sick.

The three sat around Jimmy's kitchen table for a long time, nobody saying anything, each lost in their own thoughts, but all focused on the same thing. Where were the girls right now, and what could they possibly do to find them?

"The Coast Guard might help," Lester finally said.

"Yeah, it's something," Flip replied half heartedly.

"Yeah, something," Jimmy agreed.

All three of them were feeling so helpless at the moment, the stark reality of the situation settling over them like dark clouds before a hurricane. The girls had vanished, and with each passing minute it was going to be harder to find them, and the police were worthless.

In a day from now the girl's could be anywhere in the world, Jimmy thought. He could almost see the missing posters of the girl's spread across billboards, on milk cartons, in post offices and police departments across the country. He remembered seeing computer enhanced aged photos of missing people, so they might still be recognized years later. Years later, echoed through Jimmy's mind.

"The boat house is a lead," Jimmy said forcing the posters and milk cartons out of his thoughts.

Flip and Lester both looked at Jimmy, everybody was grasping at straws, like drowning men reaching for anything that would float.

"I'm calling Leboske," Jimmy said and grabbed the phone and the phone book. He looked up the number then punched it in.

"Commander Leboske please, this is Jimmy McBain."

Flip and Lester eye's were glued to Jimmy.

"Commander Leboske, sir, good afternoon," he said moments later.

Jimmy didn't say a word for the next few minutes, just listened, his friends trying to read his expressions, trying to keep their fears in check, waiting for him to hang up from a phone call that could be their only hope.

"Thank You," Jimmy finally said gently and hung up.

"What did he say?" Lester and Flip both asked at the same time.

Jimmy looked at his friends, "They just finished searching for boathouses around Scrub Island. He was about to call me. There's twenty-one of them."

"Shit," Flip and Lester said, once again at the same time.

"That's too many," Lester said, looking at Jimmy, "and even if we found the right one, would you be able to identify it?"

At that moment the weight of the world descended on Jimmy's shoulders. Could he identify the boathouse? He certainly hadn't been able to see much lying in the bottom of the Sea Ray. Besides, how could he possibly get inside and look at twenty-one boathouses, there wasn't enough time.

"I don't know. Leboske is going to fax the GPS coordinates of the boathouses to me down at Wet Dream charters."

"Suppose we use a sea plane? Maybe some of them are resorts and we can just fly in unannounced like tourists and look around," Lester said.

"Suppose some of them are on private property?" Flip asked.

"I guess it's tough shit, they may chase us off . . . but I doubt they'll shoot first," Jimmy said thinking that trespassing didn't mean much at the moment.

"I don't know, whoever is behind this is going to be very paranoid right now. If we come flying in, land and check out his boathouse he is going to run so fast we'll never catch up," Lester said, trying to see through it all.

"What else is there?" Jimmy said softly, summing up each of their feelings.

"Call George Branch, see if he'll take us up," Flip said looking at Jimmy.

Jimmy dialed his number and waited for a long time before George answered.

"George, it's Jimmy."

"God, Jimmy, I can't believe it, I am so sorry. Can I help?"

"Yeah, George you can, is your seaplane running? We want to check some things out by air."

"Jimmy, its down, engine maintenance . . . Sorry, hey . . . call Kevin on St. John, tell him I told you to call him, he owes me and he's a good guy. Wait a second and I'll get his number."

Jimmy wrote his number down, hung up from George and called Kevin.

*

Twenty minutes later Lester, Flip and Jimmy were standing at the Red Hook dock waiting for a light green seaplane that would be arriving from St. John. Jimmy had the page of GPS coordinates that Leboske had faxed over to Wet Dream Charters folded up in his back pocket and a chart of the Virgin Islands in his right hand, which he had already marked with the location of each boathouse. That was about all they had going for them at the moment, but at least they were doing something.

Soon Kevin brought his plane in for a smooth landing and then jumped out and secured her to the floatplane dock.

"Hi guys, I'm Kevin, glad I can help," he said as he held the door open and they climbed in. A few minutes later they were airborne heading for the first of the boathouses marked on the chart. In less than ten minutes Jimmy knew it was going to be impossible to identify the correct boathouse from the air. Even if they flew right over the boathouse he was looking for without going inside he wouldn't be able to recognize it.

They flew by another four boathouses and Jimmy was feeling worse by the minute and he could imagine Flip and Lester sitting in the back seat feeling the same hopelessness that he felt.

It was loud in the plane and Kevin hadn't said much, just concentrated on flying and looking at the chart. Jimmy was looking out the window lost in his thoughts when Kevin nudged him with his elbow.

"Just what are you looking for in this boathouse? I mean . . . do you think you could recognize it from the air?"

Jimmy looked at him and shrugged his shoulders.

"I had hoped so, but now . . . I don't know. Maybe if I could get inside and see it I might, but from the air I think it's about impossible."

Kevin shook his head slightly and said, "sorry, Jimmy, I heard what happened, I'm really sorry, man."

Jimmy didn't say anything at first just continued looking out the window before he glanced back at Kevin.

"I just don't know what else to do. The boathouse is about our last straw. It's weird, but somehow I thought this would work out, but . . . I'm feeling so damn hopeless right now."

Kevin looked at Jimmy with a surprised look on his face.

"Weird, did you say weird, like weird, with a boathouse?"

Jimmy didn't follow, but said," yeah . . . why?"

Kevin smiled really big then glanced over his shoulder at Flip and Lester.

"Hang on, gents," he said as he banked the plane hard to his right, "if you want weird with a boathouse I just may have your spot."

Chapter 34

The dull rumble of the back up diesel generators purred as Detectives Klein and Ochee sat in Robert's small office, charts and papers spread on his desk. Damn WAPA anyway Frederick thought, can't the Water And Power Authority ever get their shit together? The power had been off for most of the morning, which in the islands was about as common as a rain squall in August.

The men were hoping Desmond wasn't going to come crash their meeting because neither of them liked the direction he was leading the investigation. If this wasn't going to turn into a white-washed, bullshit case, with little concern for the truth then it was up to them to figure it out and they knew they didn't have much time. Once McBain was arrested Desmond's ass would be riding on the case and that was a hell of a lot of pressure for Desmond to get a conviction, regardless.

"So that Heather lady on the beach what did you think?" Fredrick asked, his feet up on the table, fanning himself because on generator power the air-conditioning didn't work.

"Pretty much agreed with Mr. McBain's story."

"No inconsistencies?"

"Not really, I mean her version was a little different, all eye witness accounts are, but I believe her and the more I think about it I believe McBain as well."

Frederick was quiet for a minute stretching his legs out hoping to ease his back pains.

"Yeah so we both agree," Frederick continued, "the kid didn't do any of this, he's innocent, but we both know Desmond wants to pin it on him. It's all bullshit. So what else do we have to work with anyway?"

"That's the problem. There's not much. There's not one thing we can put our hands on as evidence. Not a goddamn thing."

"You're right. Not a damn thing. Which makes it pretty easy to start pointing fingers back toward Desmond's one and only suspect who we suspect is innocent."

"Right, confusing as hell and getting worse by the minute, I think," Ochee said shaking his head like he was trying to get water out of his ear.

"Where's Mr. McBain now?"

"I'm not sure, but you know, Frederick, I think it's important that he works with us, and that he knows we want to work with him. We need to have him trust us."

"I don't know, Robert, I grilled him at the Coast Guard pretty damn hard. I don't think he likes me."

Robert gave his partner a funny look, "When did you give a shit about that. Nobody likes you . . . you getting sensitive?"

"No, he laughed, "but how do we get him to trust us. We don't even trust our boss."

"Well, there isn't much we can do besides call him. I guess we could drag his ass in here and have a meeting which I think would be counterproductive, it'd just scare him."

"Yeah, you're right."

"So I think you should be the one to call, I mean I'm pretty much the bad cop already," Frederick said.

"Hell, Frederick, you've been a bad cop ever since you started."

"Don't give me no shit, just call him."

Robert opened the file on his desk and looked up Jimmy's number.

The phone rang and rang but after ten rings with no answer he hung up.

"No answering machine I guess."

"Nope, I guess not."

"Oh well, I wonder were Mr. McBain is?" Robert muttered under his breath.

*

The seaplane flew once over Cantelle Bay, then banked and came around again as Kevin backed off on the throttle and grabbed the radio.

"Cantelle Bay Resort requesting permission to land, this is Kevin Lentenk. I dropped some passengers off this morning in my seaplane, I think I left my wallet at the bar over."

"Roger, permission granted," a woman came back on the radio a few seconds later.

"Oh, by the way, I've got friends from the states with me. They would like to look around your resort, thinking of booking something for their wives next time they're down here, any problem looking around for a little bit?"

"No problem, feel free to pull onto the beach down by the dock, you'll be out of the way down there, and then enjoy Cantelle Bay Resort."

"Roger that."

Kevin put the radio microphone back in place and looked at Jimmy then Lester and Flip in the back.

"Alright guys, you heard her, lets check this place out."

*

Louis called Tigran from upstairs minutes after Frankie had emailed the photos. He was in his bedroom, and had been constantly checking the internet, his lust driven by his warped, perverted imagination.

"Tigran," he called again, as he stood up and walked to his doorway.

"Tigran, you must see these, oh they're so delicious," he said peering down the long winding stairway to the living room below. Tigran had been almost asleep and he resented being disturbed. But Louis was so excited that he overlooked his inconsiderateness and forced himself off the couch. He walked into the kitchen, grabbed a bottle of water, and climbed the stairs.

"Louis, don't be so excited," he said as he walked past his lover, and over to the computer.

"Tigran, look for yourself."

The Russian sat down and looked at the first photo on the screen. Louis stood behind him and gently starting rubbing Tigran's neck and shoulders. The picture was of a lovely young woman, dark hair, deep brown innocent eyes, and she had a very strange smirk on her face. Her smile, if that is what it was, intrigued Tigran.

"What could she possibly be thinking, Louis?"

"Oh Tigran, I can only guess, but I know she is terrified, just look at her."

"Does that excite you my love?"

Louis squeezed Tigran's neck then bent over and brought his lips close to his ear.

"You know fear excites us both, it is so powerful."

Tigran smiled knowing his lover was right, then he clicked the keyboard and watched as another photo slowly scrolled across the screen and stopped. This picture was of another beautiful young woman, with long blonde hair and deep blue eyes. He felt Louis squeeze his shoulders harder, his lover's small signal of approval. Tigran reached forward and pushed the slideshow button and sat back in his chair. The pictures slowly scrolled across the screen, and he smiled to himself as Louis continued to massage his neck and shoulders. But soon he became confused because he had been told there were three gifts not two. It wasn't until the last photo that he realized the woman with long blonde hair they had been looking at was actually two women. He reached and stopped the slide show and stared at the picture of two identical blondes standing next to each other.

"Identical twins," the Russian whispered.

"Oh, Tigran, that could be so enjoyable, so enjoyable. Just think of the possibilities."

"Yes my love, "Tigran said, knowing his lover was right, "just think of the possibilities," he repeated softly, with a soft laugh.

Tigran started the slide show again, the photos slowly dancing across the screen, and he felt his lover's excitement grow as they watched. After seeing the picture of the twins together once again he made his mind up. He reached into his robe, grabbed his cell phone, flipped it open and called his pilot. Suddenly the Caribbean didn't seem very far away.

Chapter 35

Kevin pulled the seaplane ashore fifty feet from the dock and a large boathouse. Jimmy's heart was beating so fast he thought he was going to throw up. They climbed out of the plane and stood on the sand while Kevin threw out the anchor.

"Let's not run to the boathouse, guys. Let's act like a bunch of tourists which probably down here means that first we head for the bar," Lester said knowing that everybody needed a drink especially him, regardless of what time it was.

"Good thinking, Lester, we need to think like tourists," Jimmy said although he did feel like running straight for the boathouse.

They walked up to the bar, sat down and ordered a round of beers. Jimmy kept watching the tourists walking around. This place must cost a fortune he thought. He looked at his friends and then at Kevin.

"Thanks Kevin, I don't know what is so weird about this place but this could be it. I'll know more if I can get to the boathouse."

"Well, let's just say that the guys I dropped off this morning were weird, right out of a gangster movie or something."

Lester perked up and looked at Kevin.

"Gangster movie?"

Kevin laughed, "Don't know for sure, but I dropped off two guys this morning and they definitely were weird, so that's the connection," he looked around the table, "weak I know," he said as if he suddenly needed to make an excuse as to why they were here.

"No, Kevin, it's a start," Jimmy said.

It took them only a few minutes to go through the first round and Jimmy had almost finished his second when he spied a young woman walking slowly down the beach, kicking the gentle waves and watching the water explode in the air. She was about thirty yards from the boathouse and getting closer with each step she took.

"Excuse me, gents," Jimmy said as he slid his chair back, stood up and started for the beach.

Three minutes later he was walking next to her.

"Lovely, isn't it?" he asked softly which caused her to turn and look at him. She smiled slightly then looked back out to the blue Caribbean.

"What do you mean?" she asked a few moments later as she stopped walking and looked at him.

"Well," Jimmy laughed, "I thought I meant the view but now I'm not so sure."

"So what could be more lovely than this?" she said spreading her hands open as if she was pointing to everything around them.

Jimmy smiled, "well, it would take a lot, that's for sure."

"I can't think of a thing."

"Well I can and at the risk of being totally rude, I think you are. My name is Jimmy McBain, I live down here," he extended his hand and after a slight hesitation she reached hers out and gave him a little squeeze.

"Lucky guy . . . live down here."

Jimmy slowly started walking hoping she would follow his lead and after a few steps she did still heading for the boathouse.

"Well, we all make choices, some of mine have been good, and a few, well, haven't."

"It's pretty nice down here . . . this is my first time in the islands. I'm from Seattle. Don't get this weather up there."

Jimmy glanced at her left hand. No wedding ring.

"And your name is?" he asked her.

She smiled, and he could tell she was wondering whether or not to play this little game. She looked out at the water again, then kicked a small wave before she turned back to Jimmy and with a smile said, "Bonnie Hilton."

"Hilton, like hotels, did I just strike it rich . . ." which brought a laugh from her before she replied, once again with that beautiful smile of hers.

"Hardly."

"Bonnie . . . I have to ask you something, it's personal, and I know we just met, but . . . I am a jerk for trying to meet you. I mean I can't imagine you're down here alone, un-chaperoned, not married, I mean do dreams come true for guys like me or what?"

She laughed again, "Yeah you're a jerk, but I think you're a nice one, I mean what guys aren't jerks at times, right? But I'm somewhat flattered that you walked all the way down the beach to ask me these silly questions, and yes I am, un-chaperoned, and currently not married . . . I'm with my sister."

"There really must be a god who loves me," Jimmy said knowing he was being stupid but it was fun and Bonnie seemed to be enjoying it.

They started walking again, talking, kicking the waves together, Jimmy focusing on the things that he thought were of interest to her. It was all about listening and tuning in he knew. Bonnie seemed like a real sweetheart the more they talked. She had a beautiful smile, a wonderful laugh and beautiful haunting hazel eyes. If his heart wasn't so heavy and he wasn't falling in love with Megan he just might . . . but that wasn't the case.

They walked, talked and kicked at the sea until they came to the dock that jutted out into the water for about thirty feet and ended next to a boathouse. It was almost too bad Jimmy thought and he stopped walking.

She stopped as well.

"Let's walk to the end of the dock?" he asked then reached out for her hand and held it as they walked to the end, sat down, and dangled their feet in the water.

Jimmy was feeling like a shit using her this way.

"I have to get back to my friends soon, Bonnie, I just want you to know that I'm really glad I was a jerk, took a chance and met you."

She laughed and looked at him, a nice smile on her face.

"Me too, Jimmy, I'll be around for a few more days if you're in the neighborhood."

"Bonnie you have no idea how nice that sounds but I won't be . . . sorry. I'm leaving in an hour."

"Well," she said then stood up and he could tell she was disappointed, "then see you around, maybe Jimmy McBain, and she started down the dock."

"Yeah, maybe Bonnie Hilton."

He watched her walk away until she stepped off the dock onto the sand, then she started kicking sand heading for the resort, she never looked back. He turned from watching her, took a deep breath, leaned forward and with an ungraceful belly flop landed in the warm Caribbean ocean.

Swimming under water he turned to his left and reached the boathouse on one breath. As soon as he hit the surface, and looked around he knew this was the right boathouse. There was no doubt in his mind. A flood of emotions raced through him as he treaded water and all of the fears he had felt here came crashing into his brain causing him to lose his breath. He lay on his back for a few seconds, trying to calm himself before he took another deep breath, swam down and away from the boathouse and slowly back to shore.

Pulling himself out of the water it took all of his self control to not charge up the beach to his friends. He didn't glance at the resort as he slowly walked down the beach, just kept looking at the ocean and every once in a while kicking some sand in the air. It took him almost ten minutes before he sat back down at the table with his friends. It may have seemed like a long ten minutes to him but for his friends it felt like hours.

"Another round of cold ones," he said as he glanced around the table and locked his eyes on each one of them, even Kevin's.

"You know guys, this is the place I've been looking for."

Chapter 36

Once back at Jimmy's everything was suddenly moving fast. The hours of frustration and hopelessness that they felt earlier were gone. Finally they had something to work with. Lester grabbed his briefcase the moment he walked in the door, pulled out his cell phone without saying a word and walked into Jimmy's room, closing the door behind him. Jimmy and Flip glanced at each other but said nothing as they both walked almost as if guided to the large nautical chart of the Virgins Islands that Jimmy had pinned to the wall in the living room.

"There it is Jimmy," Flip said as he pointed to Three Cove Island.

Jimmy pulled the map off the wall tearing small holes in the corners and laid it down on the table.

"How do we do this Flip?"

"Man, I'm not sure. This is like a movie, a really bad one."

Jimmy looked up from the chart and almost smiled but not quite, "A really bad one," he repeated softly.

The two stared at the chart and Three Cove Island for a few minutes, an awkward silence hanging in the room fueling their fears, each second ticking away like a bomb hidden in the closet.

"Jimmy we have to get on the island," Flip said knowing full well that he wasn't telling Jimmy anything he didn't already know.

Jimmy looked up from the chart, nodded slightly then walked to a small drawer near the phone, pulled it open and grabbed a pencil. Back at the chart he made four small circles on the island.

"These look like the best places to get ashore, maybe under the cover of darkness we can get a boat close and I can swim in. I don't see how we can pull a boat up on the beach, too obvious," Jimmy whispered as if talking out loud might give his plan away.

"I'm starting to feel like James Bond, Jimmy and its scaring the shit out of me."

"Scarin' both of us."

Then that awkward silence re-entered the room and each man was lost in his thoughts and fears. The penciled circles seemed to jump off the chart as Jimmy looked at them feeling a fear that engulfed him and made his knees weak. A roller coaster ride of emotions had stripped him down to his very core, had reduced him to a fear that he had never known, a fear that what he faced was beyond his abilities, beyond his training, beyond his skill, beyond even hope. He knew this fear would cripple him as quickly as getting run over by a semi truck and he couldn't allow it but, he wondered, could he stop it?

Still looking at the chart, he couldn't stop thinking about what the girls could be going through at this very moment? What fears, even terrors could they be experiencing. He forced his mind not to ponder the physical horrors that they could be going through, but his mind raced, unstoppable, driven by his fears. What if they were already gone, already taken from Three Cove Island, then what? The world was too big of a place. If they were gone from the Island, he suddenly realized with a fear that almost buckled his knees, they would be lost forever.

Lester finally walked out of the bedroom breaking the silence and sat down at the table.

"That's good," he said.

"What's good, Lester?" Flip asked, putting his own demons and fears on hold.

"I talked to somebody I know. He and his wife will be checking into Cantelle Bay tonight. He's good people, I've worked with him before and I trust him. I didn't go into much detail but I did mention that this is a missing person's case, three young women, wrapped around a drug deal gone bad. I think I used the word kidnapping once or twice, just so he'll be on the right track."

Lester looked at his friends who stood around the table looking like Napoleon after Waterloo, yet he was feeling more optimistic right now than he had since Jimmy's early morning call from the Coast Guard office. At least he had something to work with.

"What have you guys come up with?" Lester asked.

"Not much, Lester," Jimmy said, his words trailing off softly like he didn't have enough air to finish his sentence.

"Well, we figure we need to keep an eye on the resort and we need to be there to do that. What do you think, Lester, this is more up your alley than ours," Flip said.

"Well getting my people there is the first step. Then every move we make is calculated, nothing is left to chance. Also, without a doubt we don't make any mistakes and I know that none of us can waltz back in there and play tourist, not again."

"What about the cops?" Flip asked.

"That's a good question," Lester said looking at both of them then glancing back to Jimmy, "I don't want to talk to that Boschulle asshole that's for sure. He is not on my friendly list right now, but I don't know about the two detectives, that's your call, Jimmy."

"Jesus, Lester, I don't know but I agree with you about that Boschulle guy. Maybe right now we need to stay as far away from the cops as we can."

"We can always call em if we need em," Flip added.

"That's probably the right thing to do. I doubt the cops know as much as we do at the moment," Lester said.

"So it's up to us to stake out the resort. Lester do you think the girls could be there?" Jimmy asked looking at Lester, searching his face for a ray of hope.

"I don't know, Jimmy, I just don't know, but at least we have something to work with. So the first rule in my business is to make no mistakes. No Rambo bullshit allowed, alright. We stop, we think this through, and we bring people in as we need them," he looked around the table, then in a soft voice, almost a whisper he continued "and we hope."

"I don't think I can just sit here, Lester," Jimmy said nervously.

"Me neither," Flip agreed.

"Good. Because nobody is going to sit around here. But it's light for another hour or two and we need to start thinking this through. Believe me . . . the most important thing we can do is to think this through . . . and here is what I think."

*

It was after midnight, dark as a night can be, clouds blotting out a sliver of moon that was already close to the horizon and would be setting soon. Jimmy was three hundred feet from shore swimming naked with one hand above his head, carrying a small dry bag with clothes and a pair of tennis shoes, worrying about sharks. Jimmy had jumped overboard from a small dinghy that Flip had been driving a quarter of a mile from shore. As he swam into the darkness he turned and watched Flip slowly disappear, heading for a small bight of a cove a half mile away that they had circled on the chart earlier this evening. Where Lester was Jimmy didn't have a clue. They had left him on the powerboat when he and Flip had climbed into their dinghy, and Lester hadn't told either of them his plans.

Jimmy turned his glance back to shore and started thinking about what he had to do, and that he couldn't make any mistakes. Reach the boat house, change into his dry clothes then head to the resort, and keep his eyes and ears open.

Lester hadn't been able to tell him what to look for, just be careful, keep alert and don't get caught. If this got blown tonight the chances of ever finding the girls were about zero, Lester had told him, and he knew he was right.

Jimmy swam until he reached the boathouse then pulled himself up on the concrete dock and sat trying to get a grip on his nerves. It was now almost impossible to see, what little light the moon had given him earlier was blocked by the roof. He sat for five minutes, before he forced himself up and put on his dry clothes. Once dressed he slowly started putting one foot in front of the other with his hands out in front of him until he found the far wall of the boat house. He knelt down groping in the darkness until he found a large wooden crate. He pulled it out from the wall and stashed his bag behind it. Then ever so carefully he stood up, walked to the boathouse door twisted the handle open and peered out into the darkness.

Chapter 37

Flip was perched on a large hill at the end of Honeymoon Beach peering through his set of binoculars. He was three hundred feet from the closest cottage, wedged tight into a large group of rocks. He had been watching the boathouse ever since he arrived, hoping he might be able to see Jimmy swimming in but he couldn't. Either he got here to late or it was just too damn dark out on the water.

The resort looked very quiet. Flip couldn't see a soul anywhere, but that didn't mean there was no security milling around. People could be hidden anywhere, plus there could be cameras, and motion detectors. He scanned the resort with the binoculars seeing only shadows in the dim light. He studied the walkway along the beach, then up into the bar and restaurant, the main lobby and tourist information booth, trying to see anything that moved. Nothing did, only the shadows that played games with his mind.

Cantelle Bay resort looked strange in the darkness, almost sinister, and thinking about the girls he knew that this place held some dark secrets that no amount of beautiful beaches and cute cottages could ever cover up. He wondered who owned this place, and what kind of person could be involved in such evil. But most important he wondered about the girls.

It was going to be hard to sit here all night and just watch, he thought, as his back was already starting to bother him. The small hand held radio on his belt was the only way he had to communicate with Lester or Jimmy and that was only in an extreme emergency. Flip knew that his job was just as important as what Jimmy and Lester were doing, but it bothered him that he was just sitting on his ass. Yet he knew this was a team effort with only one goal, to rescue the girls. He was the eyes tonight. He was the eagle perched high, waiting, seeing all before him, alert for any problem that could affect the outcome of their strategies. He would be the first to call Lester or Jimmy and tell them trouble was heading their way.

He shifted his weight trying to ease a small cramp in his back, trying to settle into his little hiding place as best as he could. Glancing at his watch, he hit the glow button and saw it was almost twelve-thirty, it was going to be a long four hours. He and Jimmy were scheduled to meet Lester at four-thirty this morning. Lester's last words before he and Jimmy had climbed into the inflatable were simple and direct.

"Be careful and don't get caught."

Right, Flip thought now as he studied Cantelle Bay resort, don't get caught.

*

Jimmy walked quickly from the boathouse, across an exposed beach to a row of tall palm trees and stopped. Squatting down he took a few deep breaths fighting fear and looked around. He didn't move for a few minutes, just listened to every sound, trying to find anything that didn't fit. The resort was off to his left with the first buildings a hundred feet away. There was no moon now and darkness seemed to engulf him and his surroundings. But the darkness was also his friend at the moment, keeping him hidden, and that was all that mattered right now. After five minutes he stood and slowly continued away from the beach into more palm trees, using the few resort lights that he could see as a reference point.

The palms were growing further apart leaving him feeling more exposed with each step he took. Soon the palms ended and he was now walking around scrubby bushes and slender trees. Some of the bushes had long stickers and it was difficult to spread the foliage apart as he went without stabbing himself. Stopping for a few minutes, kneeling down again, hiding in the darkness he listened to the silence of the night. It was hauntingly still, not a breath of wind, not a cricket's call, nothing. A few minutes later his knees started to hurt and he stood up and still hearing nothing he turned to his left and started toward the resort.

He was coming in from the back of it, opposite the beach, having crossed over a small asphalted road that led away into the darkness to his right. Still struggling through dense brush he cautiously made his way until he was looking directly into a long building with a covered roof. There were a few cars parked in front and Jimmy once again hunched down to his knees and watched, not making a sound. After a few minutes he sat down, and looked at his watch, it was one-fifteen. He pulled a small pair of binoculars out of his pants pocket and started looking into the shadows and darkness. What he was looking for he wasn't sure but he knew one thing, he couldn't get caught. He thought about Lester, wondered what he was doing right now, and about Flip, but mostly he was thinking about the girls. Could they be here? What if they were? How could he possibly find them? Where would he start looking? Sitting there in the stillness of the night, the silence echoing off of his eardrums he knew this was going to be a very long evening.

*

Lester was hanging on to the steering wheel as the small powerboat rolled on the waves. He was a quarter of a mile from shore, looking through his high powered military issued night vision binoculars, Cantelle Bay resort shined a dull green. He was amazed at the clarity and how well he could see the resort long after the moon had disappeared. Damn military guys anyway, he thought, they always had the best toys.

He had followed Jimmy as he left the boathouse but lost him in the tall palm trees on the shore line. He didn't bother trying to find Flip. The resort was quiet and he hadn't seen anyone, and he didn't know if that was good or not. There had to be security somewhere.

Soon the rocking of the boat and staring through the night vision glasses combined to make him feel sick. It was slight at first, his mouth getting dry, his knees feeling weak as he became more and more lethargic. Then the nausea started and soon it was twisting his stomach inside out, his head spinning like a top, his guts churning, and his breathing getting shallower by the moment. There wasn't much he could do besides hang on and try to go with the motion of the boat. If he pulled the glasses away it helped but then what was he accomplishing out here. He had to keep watching, regardless of how it made him feel. After a few more minutes he let go of the wheel and putting a small boat cushion on a gas can he sat down, locking his elbows tight on the rail as he tried to steady the binoculars.

The boat motion was getting worse and finally knowing there was nothing else he could do, he leaned over the side and threw up.

Here he was sitting offshore a resort that may have his daughters captive, bobbing up and down like a cork in a washing machine, trying to keep the night vision glasses steady and getting more and more seasick by the minute. Yep he thought, as he leaned over the side and threw up again, it's going to be one hell of a long night.

Chapter 38

At dawn, two burly crew members on the 135 foot motor yacht, Bella Bella cast off her dock lines at the Catamaran Club Marina located in Falmouth Harbor, Antigua and the yacht slowly headed out of the harbor. In the early light the captain picked up the first channel marker and turned gently to starboard. A small swell pushed against a three knot current and it raised uneven waves that slapped at the bow, but the yacht easily cut through them. A young woman, the latest in a long procession of stewardesses that he had hired brought him a cup of coffee and stood by his side looking out to sea. Stews normally didn't last too long on board the captain thought, sipping his coffee, so it made little sense to try and get to know them. He had hired her for her looks, knowing the type of woman his boss liked having around, and so far he had enjoyed having her on Bela Bela. She was a good cook, easy to get along with and didn't mind the work, regardless if it was cooking or cleaning or washing and waxing. She was a pretty good sport he thought. But now that the owner and his damn boyfriend were on board he wondered how long she would last. Those two were something else the captain thought as he picked up the second channel marker, this one flashing red.

The captain had been thinking about finding another yacht to run for a while. There were always other jobs available for him, if he wanted, but it seemed every time he seriously started looking, his boss would offer him more money and so the golden ball and chain just grew stronger. It was weird, and he often thought that maybe Tigran had microphones hidden throughout the yacht and every time he talked on the phone that damn Russian would monitor every word he said. Hell, he didn't know, and he never would, but the job sure paid good.

"Laurie, are Tigran and Louis up?" he asked as he turned and looked at the stew with a smile.

"No, I haven't heard a thing."

"Well, they arrived pretty late last night, but once we turn the corner and we get out of this protected channel, the seas will build and I doubt they will stay below very long."

"Right, black tea for Tigran, a teaspoon of sugar and an espresso for Louis, right?"

"Right, and a smile . . . that seems to go pretty far for these two."

"A smile, right, skipper," she said with a little nervous laugh.

Laurie had never met Tigran, or Louis, but she had heard enough about them from others in the marina that she almost quit her job before she started just because of the rumors, but she needed the money and the Captain seemed nice. Oh well . . . she thought looking at the waves, she had always been able to take care of herself and she could again. If things got weird she would just walk off the boat. She wasn't going to take any shit from them and just because she worked on Bela Bela that didn't give anybody access to her pants.

The seas started building as they turned past the last bluffs and it wasn't long before Louis, wearing a small speedo swim suit and an open silk shirt, came up the companionway steps and sat down under the hard dodger of the fly bridge. Laurie gave him a few minutes before she walked next to him, and sat down.

"Good morning, I'm Laurie, the new stew. I haven't met you before. Are you Tigran?"

"Darling . . ." he drew the word out and Laurie instantly disliked him, "Tigran is still below, I'm Louis."

"Well, good morning, sir, would you like an espresso?"

"Please," then, ignoring her, he turned his attention back to the waves that continued to roll toward him as far as he could see.

Laurie was soon down below struggling to keep herself from flying around the galley as she pulled out the espresso machine and plugged it in. The bow was starting to slam and she could picture waves and white water flying. Cooking on a moving boat is always a dance but Laurie was pretty good and it wasn't very long before she had a steaming cup of espresso on a small plate. Carefully, making sure she didn't spill any, she made her way back to the fly bridge.

"Here you go, sir," she said, deciding to use the formal approach with her new boss until she was told otherwise.

"Thank you," Louis said and in that moment the boat lurched and the espresso slid off the plate just as Laurie was handing it to him and the scalding hot latte landed on his lap.

"You stupid bitch!" he screamed at her as he jumped up and frantically brushed the burning espresso off of his speedo.

Laurie couldn't believe how fast it had happened. In the next instant she turned, grabbed the captain's water bottle that was hanging on the helm chair and unscrewing the lid she poured it all over his crotch.

"Shit, shit, shit," he screamed, still jumping up and down, glaring at her with such utter contempt and with such evil eyes she felt her knees go weak, then he turned in disgust, still cussing and climbed down below, disappearing into the darkness his cussing slowly fading away.

Laurie was in shock, she sat down on the cushion, feeling like she was going to throw up.

The captain didn't say a word, and it was a long five minutes before she finally looked at him and said, "I can't believe it."

The captain had been trying to keep a straight face from the moment Louis started screaming, but he couldn't once he looked back at her. He softly started mimicking Louis as he mouthed shit-shit-shit. Laurie didn't know what to think but the look on the captain's face was too much for her and as hard as she tried she couldn't stop herself from laughing.

"Where are we off to, skipper?" she said a few minutes later once the laughter stopped.

"To the U.S. Virgin Islands, a little resort. Tigran knows the owner, its nice, you'll like it."

"You think? I got a feeling I'm fired already."

The captain gave her a reassuring smile then said, "I doubt it, but . . . we shall see."

"Right, "she said softly, thinking she should head down to her small cabin and just start packing her bags.

It was an hour later when Tigran came on deck, made his way to the fly bridge and stood next to the captain. Louis wasn't with him.

Laurie went below made his tea and a few minutes later very carefully handed it to him, no platter this time.

"Breakfast, sir?" she asked.

"That will be fine, thank you."

Tigran stared out to sea, silently sipping his tea, and the captain wondered just what the hell was going on. This trip was completely out of character for what he was used to. The early morning phone call yesterday from somebody he had never spoken to before telling him to get the boat ready, that Tigran and Louis were flying in and they wanted Bela Bela to depart at first light this morning. Usually he had a weeks notice before the yacht was going to be in use. It was a good thing he had already hired Laurie, but he had no idea how long she would last. If Louis had his way she would probably be overboard by now, that asshole. But he wasn't going to let that happen on his watch. If the two Russian crewmen that lived aboard full time went overboard he wouldn't even slow the yacht down. He never liked either of them, they were lazy, drank too much and always spoke in Russian, and the way he figured it they were probably calling him an asshole to his face. So the hell with them, whatever happened to those two he could care less, but he had hired Laurie and he was going to make sure nothing happened to her, nothing at all.

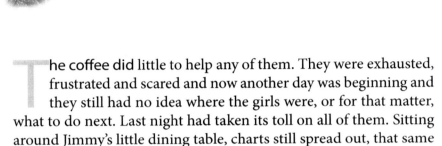

Chapter 39

The coffee did little to help any of them. They were exhausted, frustrated and scared and now another day was beginning and they still had no idea where the girls were, or for that matter, what to do next. Last night had taken its toll on all of them. Sitting around Jimmy's little dining table, charts still spread out, that same feeling of hopelessness once again ate at them all.

"Lester, I don't think I can sleep, no matter what," Jimmy said in response to Lester's statement a moment earlier about how bad they all needed to sleep.

"Well we got to. We'll start getting very sloppy if we don't. The best thing we can do is to sleep for a few hours."

"I'd need some knock out drugs or something Lester," Flip said his head perched on his hands

"Me too," Jimmy agreed.

"Well I've got some, so that's covered, they're FBI med's."

"That ought to work, but I still don't see how we can sleep. I mean suppose we miss something at the resort, suppose they move the girls, what if we're sound asleep and we miss our chance . . . whatever that might be. I mean how can we sleep?" Jimmy asked his eyes bloodshot, his words slurred from fatigue.

"Well, remember this . . . I have people at Cantelle Bay right now, so if anything happens which I doubt it will, not in the daylight, then someone is watching," Lester said in a reassuring voice, one that didn't express how he really felt.

After a minute of silence, everybody too exhausted to talk, Lester stood up, walked into the bedroom and came out with a small bottle of prescription medicine.

"Here. Take one," he said as he handed a small white pill to Flip.

"You sure?" Flip asked but his mind was confused already and he knew he needed to sleep.

"I'm sure."

Lester handed a pill to Jimmy then took one himself. They didn't even rinse it down with water.

"My phone will wake the dead," Lester said then walked over to the couch and laid down.

"Get some sleep, guys, it's going to be another very long night," Lester said relaxing into the sofa, "believe me, tonight is going to feel twice as long as last night, and if you don't sleep now, you will fall asleep tonight and that can't happen."

Flip finally forced himself up and headed out the door toward Annie May and Jimmy operating on auto pilot stood up and headed for his bedroom. None of them felt like sleeping, none of them could turn their minds off but hopefully Lester's little white pills were going to do the job or tonight they would all be worthless, and too much was at stake for that.

*

It was a beautiful morning, the sun crisp as it rose above the Caribbean Sea. Frankie sat on his veranda watching the small waves that lapped at his beach. Sitting next to him was Bobbie and they were both finishing up breakfast. Charlie was already strolling on the beach, wondering why they had invited him.

"Any more contact?" Bobby asked.

"Yeah, they left this morning. It's about a hundred and fifty miles, so they will probably arrive after sunset."

"Is that a problem?"

"Not at all. The yacht is too big to get inside the reef so they'll have to anchor offshore anyway. Then the way I see it, we simply show them the merchandise, name our price and after a few drinks and some negotiation we do the deal and the girls are whisked aboard his yacht and out of our life. Pretty simple really."

"Any trouble getting your price . . . what is your price anyway?"

"I'm not sure. But at least a hundred thousand."

"A piece?"

"Hell no, but remember a hundred grand is better than having to—" he paused not wanting to use the word murder, "a hundred grand and we get our hands clean of this whole Tommy mess, that's not bad."

"Frankie, it ain't bad at all."

After wiping his plate with the last of his toast Bobbie looked at Frankie again, who seemed to be lost in his thoughts as he looked out over Honeymoon Beach.

"Any regrets?

"Regrets, what?" Frankie said coming back from somewhere.

"Yea Frankie, any regrets, I mean what you're doing to these three women is pretty fucked."

Frankie looked at Bobby and didn't say anything for almost a minute, just looked over his beach.

"Yeah, I got regrets. I regret Tommy getting killed, I regret losing a few of my staff, I regret all of it and yeah I do feel like shit about these three . . . but what can I do Bobbie? I mean I don't see any other way out."

"I don't either but I just wanted to know . . . Do you have any info on these three, like names or anything? I mean, who the hell are they? Although maybe it doesn't matter seeing as how they have to disappear anyway from the face of the earth, but Jesus, Frankie."

"I know Bobbie, it's the shits, I know the two blondes are Amy and Sarah the other one I never even asked her name," he glanced at Bobby then said with a little smile, "I almost wish I was keeping that one for myself."

"Christ, Frankie, you can't do that shit."

"I know I can't, that's part of what makes me want to."

"You're a sick son of a bitch."

Frankie turned and looked at Bobby, seemed to focus on his last comment, then turned back to looking at the beach. There was a long pause before he replied softly, "you know, Bobby, you're right, I am a sick son of a bitch."

*

In the Virgin Island Police Department Frederick and Robert sat with their boss in his office and Desmond was pushing them hard.

"You don't see it that way . . . neither of you do?" Desmond asked almost glaring at his detectives, wishing these guys would understand the pressure that he was under. All these two had to do was follow his lead, back him up, and in the next day or so they would arrest a suspect, and turn this whole shitty case over to the court system and their job would be finished, at least for now. But Desmond knew they weren't biting . . . not yet, and he had to ratchet up the pressure.

"What do you want Desmond, you want a signed confession from McBain, good luck, you try and get it. I tell you that won't happen," Fredrick said, disgusted with his boss.

"It might after we arrest him and keep him in solitary for a few days, sleep deprivation, scare tactics . . . there's ways you know."

"Goddamit, Desmond. I think you're talking about torture. This ain't Iraq for Christ sake," Robert shouted as he stood up and walked around the small office.

"Listen, you two . . . here is the bottom line. This case is going to be major headline news across the goddamn USA. Front page shit . . . so it's going to get resolved very quickly, and I can resolve it with your help. Let the courts prove whether or not McBain is innocent. Shit. That's how the system works, right?

"Desmond, listen, neither of us think the kid is guilty of anything besides beating somebody up, and being in the wrong place at the wrong time. We need to be finding out who this guy is that became shark food, what his story is," Frederick paused then corrected himself, "was. I mean I know it's a dead end . . . right . . . but with a little time."

Desmond cut him off, "time, like what time . . . remember we already got the New York Times, probably every fucking newspaper there is plus I know CNN is going to handle it. Time is what I don't have. I need an arrest and closure."

"Even if he's innocent, Desmond?'

Desmond sat back in his chair and wiped his forehead. These assholes he thought. What don't they understand? They can come along for the ride or the way he felt right now he'd find some way to fire their asses. Maybe he'd even plant some drugs on them, set them up with something stolen from the evidence room and stash it in their houses, or their car, something. There were more than a few ways to make these two sorry they didn't see things his way.

He sat there looking at Robert and Frederick trying to figure out how the hell to let these two know just how serious this was. He couldn't threaten them . . . but maybe somebody else could. Something simple, like blowing up their mailboxes in the middle of the night or one of their kids doesn't come home from school on time, or maybe their dog is found hanging from a tree. Hell, he knew he could come up with something and he had plenty of people to do this shit for him so his hands never got dirty. That was the best part. His hands always stayed clean no matter what.

Chapter 40

The phone rang and rang and slowly Jimmy awoke from a drug induced sleep. Somewhere in his mind was a dream that he wasn't ready to let go of, not yet. He started to roll over away from the phone, trying to find his pillow when suddenly he knew he needed to answer it. Why he wasn't sure as he reached around trying to find the phone before he sat up, rolled to the far edge of his bed and grabbed it off of the small nightstand. He was too asleep to say anything. He just held it six inches from his ear trying to remember the last of his dream.

"McBain?" instantly he knew it was detective Ochee, as his dream slipped away into another world.

"McBain," he repeated," is this you?"

Slowly Jimmy brought the phone to his ear as he sat up then propped his back against the headboard. He took a few deep breaths trying to get his thoughts straight.

"This is me, detective."

"Good. You recognize my voice."

"Yep."

"Make detective out of you yet kid."

Jimmy didn't say a word. He scrunched his knees up tight to his chest and held the phone to his ear, waiting for Robert to continue. There was a long pause and Jimmy felt like hanging up but he knew he shouldn't.

"Alright, Jimmy, Frederick and I need to talk to you. It's

important, and I think we need to get together, so how about we meet someplace?"

Jimmy was half asleep but the other half of his brain was finally working.

"Why? So you can arrest me?"

Robert laughed, "kid, we can do that anytime, anyplace. No. That's not it, trust me on that one."

"Why then?"

Robert was silent and Jimmy figured he had asked a very good question.

"Well, because we think you're innocent in all of this, and we want to help."

"Good, is that it, or is there more . . . I mean you just told me I was innocent . . . so there's got to be more . . . right?"

"Listen Jimmy, in my business you either have people on your side or they're on the other side. There's little middle of the road in police work. Either we figure you're guilty and we do everything we can to bust your ass, or we think you're not and we try to keep you out of jail, got it?"

"Yeah."

"Okay so that's why this call is from a phone booth at Tickles Bar and not our office, and Frederick is standing right next to me listening to all of this."

"Okay," was about all Jimmy could think to say. At times like this he knew it was better to keep his mouth shut and listen, listen very closely.

"Let me put it this way," Robert continued, "there are three cops involved in this case. There's myself, Frederick and our boss, Desmond, and two out of the three think you're innocent and the third wants to arrest your ass today, understand?"

"Yeah, I think so."

"Good, so we are on the same team, Jimmy. You, me, and Frederick, we need to work together to keep your ass out of jail."

Jimmy was completely awake by now, as he kicked his legs off the bed, stood up and walked out into the living room. Somehow he wanted Lester to hear at least one side of this conversation. He sat down next to him and Lester slowly opened his eyes.

"What do you want from me?" Jimmy asked then cupped the phone to his chest and mouthed cops to Lester.

"Right now we just want you to know where things are at. Frederick and I want you to trust us, that's the only way we can help you."

"Okay, I believe you, trust you two I can do."

"Good, that's number one, now also I have a feeling that you, Lester and Flip and who knows who else you have helping, I mean I doubt you have been sitting around eating bon bon's so I got to ask . . . do you have anything for us?"

Jimmy didn't know what to think. Here were the cops asking him for information, that wasn't a good sign.

"Listen, Robert, We found the island that I was taken too, I'm sure of it. I was in the boat house yesterday and there's no doubt in my mind."

"Where?"

Jimmy paused, not sure what to say. He held the phone to his chest, looking at Lester, who had no idea what the conversation was, "Robert, trust me on this okay? I found the island and right now I don't want to tell you. It's not about trust it's about us figuring out what we are going to do next and I don't want anything to complicate it . . . do you understand?"

After a short pause Ochee said "okay, that's fair at the moment, so go on."

"So last night we staked it out, the boathouse, the beach the entire place, but we didn't find anything, we're going back tonight."

"Do you want some help?" Robert asked and Jimmy felt for the first time that he really could trust Robert.

"No, not right now. Lester's pretty good at this, but we might later, I just don't know . . . I could use your phone number, that'd help us," he said as an afterthought.

"Listen, Jimmy, write down our cell phone numbers. Don't bother calling us at the station. It will just get back to Desmond and that's not going to be good for anybody. So write these numbers down, you ready?"

"Just a minute," Jimmy stood up walked to the kitchen table grabbed a pencil.

"Ready."

He wrote down both of their cell phone numbers on the side of the Virgin Islands Chart.

"Remember, Jimmy, call us any time if we can help, Frederick and I mean it. Okay?"

"Alright . . . and thanks, Robert."

"Your welcome kid, keep us posted, and good luck," then he hung up.

Jimmy walked back to the couch and sat down. Lester was sitting up and they looked at each other, finally Lester asked "Was it good or was it bad?"

"It was mostly good, but it was also bad."

"How's that?"

Jimmy glanced at Lester and shook his head, "the cops told me they believe me, they think I'm innocent."

"That must be the good news," Lester said, "so what's the bad?"

"Well," Jimmy said casting his gaze to the floor feeling dejected just thinking about it.

"They asked me for information, Lester. They asked me what I know, you know what that means, don't you?"

"I think so."

"It means, they don't know shit, Lester. The cops don't have a clue."

Chapter 41

Lester, Jimmy, and Flip were hanging out in Jimmy's small cottage, watching the minutes slowly ticking by, driving each other crazy. The frustration that they felt was palpable. Each of them was so eager to get back to Cantelle Bay Resort but they knew they couldn't, not yet, not until nightfall, and that was hours away.

Early in the afternoon Jimmy and Flip walked down to the dock and fueled the powerboat that they would take out to Three Cove Island while Lester stayed behind and made some calls trying to find out who owned the resort. Jimmy checked the weather and it didn't sound bad. Fifteen knot winds and three foot seas, at least it was going to be better than last night.

Back at Jimmy's the sitting around became too much to handle so the three of them went to the Hook for an early dinner and were back home just as the sun was setting.

"What time do you want to go, Lester?" Flip asked impatiently, walking around Jimmy's living room, acting like a zombie.

"Well . . . we need to make sure everyone is asleep before we start walking around that island. So I figure we should try to get there around eleven, take it slow and give ourselves some time to get situated."

"Lester, what about guns? I mean suppose we find them and then what?" Jimmy asked and he knew Flip was wondering the same thing because they talked about it when they were refueling the boat.

Lester let out a deep sigh and slumped back on the couch. He looked at them and slightly raised his hands up before dropping them on his lap.

"I don't know. I have my Glock 9 millimeter but that's all I brought with me. Do you know anybody that's got a weapon they'd loan you?"

Flip and Jimmy both shook their heads, "Lester, around here guns are a real issue and most people who have them wouldn't let anybody know. I can't think of a single person that I could borrow anything from that was bigger than a slingshot," Jimmy said feeling for the first time in years that he wished he owned a pistol, a shot-gun, maybe an AK-47, something.

"You could call the detectives and ask them but I doubt they will have any firearms to hand over to you two. Guns screw a lot of things up . . . but they also can save your ass," Lester replied.

"You're right, and tonight I sure wish I had one," Flip said.

"Me too," Jimmy agreed.

Lester shook his head, "Well, tonight I'll be with you Flip. I didn't accomplish much last night bobbing around out there, so if something comes up at least we will have the Glock."

"Yeah, at least we have that. Listen Lester, I've got to do more tonight, I didn't accomplish anything last night either," Jimmy said and again he knew Flip felt the same way, because they had talked about that as well.

"Okay, you're right, but our bottom line is always the same, we can't get caught and we can't spook whoever is on the island."

'Right. Don't get caught," Flip echoed.

Time dragged by so slowly Jimmy thought it would have gone by faster if he was having a root canal. It was after nine and they were still just sitting around, Jimmy trying to read a book about the around the world Vendee Globe single hand sailboat race, when suddenly Lester's cell phone rang. It was so unexpected that all three of them jumped. Lester flipped his phone open and listened for a minute without saying anything.

Finally he thanked whoever called and put the phone in his pocket. Jimmy and Flip's eyes were glued to him.

"What?" Flip finally asked as Lester seemed to be lost in thought.

"That was my contact at Cantelle Bay. A very large yacht just anchored off the resort fifteen minutes ago."

Jimmy and Flip wondered what that meant, if anything.

"So what?" Jimmy said a few moments later still staring at Lester.

"Maybe its nothing," Lester said looking at them" but I think it changes everything."

"How's that?" Flip asked.

"Well for one thing that yacht has radar so it will be able to see us coming for at least ten miles. So forget sneaking up to the island in the dark," Jimmy said wondering what else might have just changed because of the yacht.

"That's just for starters," Lester said as he stood up, followed by Jimmy and Flip and they walked to the dining table and looked at the chart.

Lester pointed out Cantelle Bay resort and Honeymoon Beach.

"The yacht has to be anchored here," Lester said as he took a pencil and made a small x just outside the reef, "so that means we can't approach from any of these directions," Lester ran his hands over the chart on any area that the yacht's radar could scan.

"Right Lester," Jimmy jumped in, "anywhere in that space his radar will see us."

"Jesus, that cuts off half the damn Caribbean. We'd have to swing all the way around here, to the back of the island" Flip said as he started drawing lines on the chart.

"Right, it does that indeed," Lester replied looking at Flip's pencil lines.

"It also does a lot more than that. We can't use the cove we used last night to pull the dinghy up and I don't know what you're going to do with the boat if you go ashore with Flip tonight," Jimmy said looking up at Lester then staring back at the chart.

"I was going to anchor the boat here," again another mark on the chart at a small cove half a mile from the resort.

"Well that's out," Flip said as Lester's mark was now inside the radars view.

"Right Flip. This changes a lot of things for us and it makes tonight a lot more dangerous."

Jimmy and Flip both raised their eyes from the chart and looked at Lester.

"Dangerous?" Flip asked.

"Yeah. Dangerous, because I'm going on the assumption that the yacht is there because the girls are there."

"What!" Jimmy exclaimed.

"I've thought from the very beginning that whoever had the girls wouldn't murder them, it would be to much of a waste, it wouldn't make sense," Lester paused and looked at Jimmy and Flip, giving them a chance to really hear what he was about to say, "I've thought all along that whoever had them would sell them."

"Shit," Flip said, "Sell them like . . . merchandise?"

"More like slavery, white slavery," Jimmy said as the horror of Lester's statement settled in his mind.

"Yes, Jimmy, white slavery. Think about it this way. Human trafficking is a huge business. We've all heard about refugees trying to get into the states, but that's nothing compared to other parts of the world. Believe me. Slavery still exists all around our planet. So . . . if somebody needed for the girls to disappear because of what happened that night on Sea Horse why would they kill them? I don't think they would, not if they thought it through. Not if they had the right connections. Three young white women would bring a fortune in the right situation. Plus the beauty of it is they would disappear anyway, which is what somebody wants, right? I mean they could easily be swallowed up somewhere, disappear into some middle east kingdom never to be seen again, held by some rich sheik or some other asshole. Think about it and you'll see I could easily be right. Actually I hope to hell I'm right."

"Jesus, Lester," Jimmy and Flip said at the same time.

"That's why I haven't lost hope in any of this. I've always believed the girls are alive. Now I think they are at Cantelle Bay resort, or if they're not there then I think it is the rendezvous place. That yacht is the last piece in the puzzle for me."

"Why is it the last piece of the puzzle?" Flip asked although he thought he knew the answer.

Lester again looked at both of them, stared into their eyes trying to get the seriousness of this across to them.

"Because, like I said, I think that yacht is there because the girls are there, but . . ." he paused almost afraid to continue, "believe me when I tell you this, if I'm right and the girls get on that yacht and it sails away, we will never find them."

Chapter 42

Jimmy was stunned as he listened to Lester. At first he thought he must be crazy but as he sat there thinking he started to hope that Lester was right. If he was then the girls were still alive and that was all that mattered at the moment.

"Do we call the police?" Jimmy asked looking at Lester.

"I don't know. It depends if you trust them or not, they could screw things up as much as they could help us."

"I think I should call them, Lester," Jimmy said quickly weighing it all in his mind.

"What are you going to tell them? I mean right now it's just circumstance." Lester spoke softly as if his thoughts were far away.

"That boat house is not circumstance," Jimmy replied.

"You're right about that," Flip said, then paused as if thinking about something else before discarding it and saying, "what about the coast guard?"

"I think we call them for sure. But this is very important, what we need from the Coast Guard is back up if necessary. The last thing we want is a helicopter buzzing around out there. That will just send everybody running with their tail between their legs and we will never find the girls," Lester said looking up at Jimmy and then over at Flip.

"What we want, Lester, is to make sure that yacht doesn't sail away if they have the girls onboard," Flip said after a moment of uncomfortable silence.

"Right, that can't happen."

"Suppose you're wrong, suppose we stake out Cantelle Bay and nothing . . . then I'd feel like an idiot calling the cops and the coast guard," Jimmy said.

"That's the chance we take. It's up to all of us to decide, not just me," Lester said letting the importance of this next decision settle in.

They sat in silence for a few minutes trying to think it through. Jimmy was looking at the chart of honeymoon beach trying to digest all that Lester had just said. He didn't know what to think, and trying to figure out if they should call the cops and the coast guard was getting more confusing by the second. He knew they only had one chance and if they called in the reinforcements and nothing happened it would be pretty tough to call them again. After a few minutes it was Lester who broke the silence.

"My thoughts, guys, are . . . we call the coast guard and ask them to be available if we need them, that's all we want from them right now. As far as the cops, I say call them also, at least they have guns."

"Alright," Jimmy said then turned and walked into his bedroom where his phone was.

Flip exhaled deeply, slid back in his chair and looked at Lester,

"I'm with you no matter what Lester, you know that. If we have to put these people down then I'm able."

Lester reached his hand across the table and grabbed Flip's huge hand.

"I know, Flip, I know . . . and thanks."

*

Bella Bella sat in forty feet of water, her anchor set and connected to three hundred feet of chain. The captain had just turned the twin diesels off and only the hum of the generators purred through the yacht. Laurie was standing next to him looking at the resort in the dim light. She had been trying to stay away from Tigran and especially Louis all day. She still figured she was as good as fired, but no use getting in their way. Lunch and dinner had come off pretty well she thought and neither of them wanted any drinks after dinner so once she cleaned up she had spent most of the evening hanging out in the pilothouse with the captain. The two crewmen she hadn't seen except at dinner and that was alright with her. Besides the captain she didn't like anybody on board.

"Now what?" she asked the captain once the rumble of the engines died.

"Well, not much. We're secure for the night. I have the depth sounder alarm on as well as the radar alarm. That's about it, time to kick back."

Laurie laughed, "Maybe its time to lock myself in my room, barricade the door."

The captain laughed as well." I don't think it's that bad."

"Yeah, you're probably right . . . maybe."

Laurie stayed in the pilothouse watching the captain as he turned switches off and others on. He played with dials, checked gauges, and then wrote in a book that she figured was his log book. Basically she knew he was getting Bella Bella ready for the night.

"Well, I'm about finished up here, want to go downstairs for a night cap?" he asked her as he closed his log book and set it on the chart table.

"Am I off duty?"

"Yeah," he laughed again, "you're off the clock, darling."

"Then a nightcap sounds good, skipper."

She followed him out of the pilothouse, down the steps into a small hallway that led either into the galley or to the main salon and the rest of the boat. As the Captain reached the bottom step she thought he would walk into the galley but he stopped and she wasn't expecting it, and she bumped into him before she heard,

"Good evening, captain," and she knew it was Tigran.

Shit, she thought, she'd hoped she wasn't going to see him tonight.

"Please join us," she heard the Russian say with a laugh that sent chills up her spine. Following the Captain she walked out into the salon. Tigran and Louis along with the two crew were sitting on two large sofas surrounding a large glass coffee table, a few bottles of alcohol, some empty beer cans, and some shot glasses spread out before them.

"Good job, Captain, won't you please sit and join us for a drink,"

Tigran asked although it sounded less like an invitation and more like an order and Laurie knew he wasn't going to take no for an answer.

"I'm kind'a pooped Tigran, it's been a long day," the Captain replied and Laurie could hear the tension in his voice.

"Yes, yes, but I insist, please. Besides it's the end of a successful voyage and that calls for at least one drink . . ." then he looked at Laurie, smiled and said, "please, my dear, join us as well."

There wasn't much either of them could do so she sat down, tried to smile, but she knew it didn't fool anybody. Tigran seemed in a very good mood but somehow Laurie sensed that not everything was as it seemed, maybe it was the crew or Louis, maybe the expressions on their faces she wasn't sure but something wasn't right and that made her even more nervous.

"What would you like? I have some excellent single malt?" Tigran said as he sat up, reached for two empty shot glasses on the table, without giving either of them a moment to reply.

"That sounds good Tigran, I'll take a shot," the Captain said.

"And you?" he asked looking at Laurie although he was already pouring her a shot glass as well.

"I guess I'll try one too . . . thanks."

Tigran finished pouring the two shot glasses and slid them across the table where they stopped in front of Laurie and the Captain, just like in the movies, Laurie thought.

"Alright now, to a great voyage and a great tomorrow, to our health," Tigran toasted and Laurie noticed everybody but her and the Captain were drinking beer.

The scotch burned Laurie's throat as it went down and she thought it tasted terrible. She finished with a slight gasp which brought a laugh from everybody but the Captain who finished his in silence.

"Wonderful," Tigran said then stood up and suddenly the party was over. Laurie and the Captain each made it back to their own small cabin before the drug set in. Neither would hear a thing tonight no matter what. They were about to slip into a drug induced coma that a bomb going off in the next room wouldn't wake them from. It was goodnight sweet Irene for both of them.

Chapter 43

The powerboat with Lester, Flip, and Jimmy on board raced through the night, there was no moon and the boat's running lights were turned off. It was impossible to see as they crashed through the waves with Jimmy wedged tight at the helm. The GPS plotter on the dash board showed the next way-point to be three miles away. They were exhausted from the bashing the boat had taken and they still had a few more miles to go. Having to come around the back side of Three Cove Island added another hour to the trip. Because of the yacht's radar the nearest beach they could pull the boat onto undetected was two miles from Cantelle Bay Resort. It was going to be a long night and they all knew it.

As Jimmy hung on to the steering wheel he worried about the fact that he hadn't been able to get hold of the cops. Neither of them had answered their cell phone. Jimmy had tried each of them three different times, but the detectives must have turned their phones off. Looking at the bright side as the powerboat smashed through the darkness at least he had been able to get hold of Commander Leboske, although he had to call him at home, finding his number in the phone book. The conversation had been short but effective. Leboske told him that whatever the Coast Guard could do they would and to keep him posted. At least that was something Jimmy thought as suddenly the GPS flashed and he reached over and scrolled down to the next waypoint he had pre-programmed and then hit enter. They were now only a mile away and still he couldn't see the island. Just stars and a dark sky. None of them had said much the entire trip, there really wasn't much to talk about that they hadn't already worked out. But Jimmy kept thinking about a gun and wondering if he could use it.

Jimmy slowed the boat down as the depth sounder started showing the depth gradually decreasing and then Three Cove Island appeared in the darkness about the same time that the last way-point flashed on the GPS. They were now a hundred feet off of the beach. Jimmy continued watching the depth sounder as the water suddenly started becoming shallow. At eight feet with the boat barely moving Jimmy killed the engine then hit the tilt switch and lifted the engines and propellers out of the water and moments later the bow slid into the sand. The instant the boat stopped they all scurried over the bow, Jimmy carrying a long rope with an anchor attached to it. He walked thirty feet up the beach, knelt down and buried the anchor. The boat wasn't going anywhere.

They walked up the beach until they were just inside a row of tall palm trees then stopped and gathered around Lester.

"Okay, Jimmy, like we planned, you go around to the far side between the resort and the boathouse. Flip you get up on the hill overlooking Honeymoon Beach and you call us if you see anything. Jimmy, your phone is on vibrate, right?"

"Right, Lester."

"Make sure, because that could be a big screw up otherwise. Mine's on vibrate as well," Lester said looking at Flip and then back at Jimmy, "so again, either of you see anything, you call me."

"Where are you going, Lester?" Flip whispered.

"I'm going to work my way in close to the resort along the beach, from there I don't know."

There was a long silence before Lester reached his hand out and both Flip and Jimmy grabbed it and they gave each other a strong shake then Jimmy turned walked into the palm trees and disappeared. Lester started walking down the beach toward Honeymoon

Beach and Flip headed up the rocky path and the long hike he would have to make to get where he was last night and moments later all three were gone.

*

The inflatable bumped hard into the dock as Tigran pulled into the boathouse then killed the engine. It was so dark that when Louis finally climbed out of the boat he couldn't even find a cleat to tie the boat off too. Tigran's lover stood there for a minute, not sure what to do before the Russian climbed out and gently kicked around with his foot until he hit a cleat. He grabbed the dinghy line from Louis and wrapped it tight.

"Just be patient, my love, Frankie will be here soon," Tigran whispered in the darkness.

"Patience, I can hardly wait, we have come a long way for this."

"Yes we have."

A few minutes later the boathouse door swung open and Frankie walked in then closed the door behind him, the glow of his small flashlight shining on Tigran and Louis. Frankie smiled when he saw Tigran, walked up and gave him a big hug. He turned and looked at Louis who he had never met.

"Who is this?" Frankie said as he rudely shined his light into Louis's face

"Frankie, this is Louis, he is my . . . business partner."

Frankie couldn't imagine what kind of business dealing these two could have, but then he figured what the hell who was he to say anything.

"Louis, okay, nice to meet you," he said without meaning it, then turning his attention back to Tigran, "it's good to see you again."

"I think the pleasure will be all mine on this trip Frankie."

Frankie laughed, "you know what my friend, I think you're right."

"We have come a long way, obviously I think so as well, but we shall see soon enough."

"I know its been a long trip for you so I suggest you view what you have traveled so far to see, then let's have a drink . . . friendship before business?"

"Frankie, I think that is an excellent idea," Tigran replied, as Louis stood in the shadows feeling left out and disliking Frankie more by the second.

"This way," Frankie said as he pointed the beam of the flashlight toward the door and slowly led them out of the boathouse. Once outside Frankie turned the flashlight off, closed the boathouse door behind them, then started walking in the darkness, following a small foot path toward his house.

They walked in silence until Frankie reached the small door that led into his cistern room. Stopping, he waited until Tigran and Louis were standing next to him, "Shhh," he whispered as he held his right index finger to his lips. Then he turned, swung the heavy door open and they went inside. The room was almost completely dark, a small glow of light coming from another room through a little window in a door. The three men stood in the darkness of the cistern room and Frankie pointed to the little glass window and whispered into Tigran's ear, "they won't know you are here if you're quiet."

Chapter 44

It was so dark that Jimmy almost missed them. He was fifty feet from the resort, sitting in some tall weeds watching the yacht float up and down on the swell. A few lights on board made her outline barely discernable in the distance. Jimmy had been sitting for almost an hour, his legs were cramped and he kept thinking it was time to move, but something held him back and it was a good thing he listened to that inner voice of his.

He saw them first out of the corner of his eye, just shadows, his mind not really seeing shapes as much as movement in the darkness. Focusing his attention toward the boathouse and the walkway that led from it he stared into the black of night wondering if his mind was playing tricks on him. But it didn't take long before he definitely saw three men walking, visible for a second or two then the next moment disappearing again, and they were coming toward him. Following them in the shadows was almost impossible. It became a guessing game where they would appear next. He lost them when they reached a large building as they simply blended into the darkness and disappeared as quickly as he had first seen them.

Turning to his left he watched the back of the building, hoping to see them reappear, the dim reflection of an overhead light near the resort entrance giving him just enough light to see. After a few minutes they didn't appear and he realized they must have stopped. His heart raced, now what he thought? Slowly doing everything he possibly could to not make a sound he started crawling closer to the building, stopping often, trying to hear anything in the silence of the night. It took five minutes before he could tell the building was a house, his eyes continuing to play tricks, the shadows of swaying palms causing him to see things that weren't really there. It took another few minutes before he thought he could vaguely see the outline of a low door in the side of the building. He crawled closer, now he was only fifteen feet away, and there definitely was a door and somehow in his heart he knew the girls were there. He wanted to jump up, run to it, swing it open, and rush inside. If anybody stood in his way he would take them out, simple as that. His body was full of adrenaline and he knew the warrior that he spent years developing was just below the surface, ready. But he didn't move, instead he just laid there and watched, understanding that there was only one chance tonight. No Rambo shit he remembered Lester telling him.

Still it took all of his self control to keep himself in check. His mind was racing with the hope of finding the girls safe, his emotions overflowing, and he suddenly realized with a surprise, another emotion raced through his mind as well, it was hatred. Whoever took the girls was going to pay.

Turning around so he was facing away from the house he reached into his pocket and pulled out his cell phone. Keeping it directly in front of him so what little light it would cast when he opened it could not be seen by anyone he flipped his phone open. He scrolled down and found Lester's number and hit send. It took a few seconds before he realized that his phone wasn't doing anything. He looked at the screen, then looked at the coverage bars, there weren't any.

"Shit," he uttered softly to himself when he realized there was no phone service. That was something none of them had even thought about. He closed his phone, put it in his pocket, turned back to the house and felt very vulnerable, now what? What else had they overlooked? What other un-foreseen miscalculations could come back to haunt them tonight? Any small detail could make the difference between success and failure, he knew. It only took one screw up and everything could go to shit so fast he wouldn't believe it.

*

Frankie turned and looked at Tigran and Louis as they stood in the small room looking through the little glass window. The three were quiet but Frankie could feel the excitement in the air. The girls were asleep, one of the blondes facing toward them, the other two with their backs to them. Louis gently nudged Tigran in the ribs and then bent over and gave him a kiss. Frankie ignored it. The girls looked so peaceful Frankie thought. They almost looked angelic laying there in the dim light, and a sense of guilt that surprised him ran through his mind, but it didn't last. He'd learned years ago to get rid of guilt. In his business there was no room for it.

Frankie reached into his pocket and pulled out a ring of keys and held them up for Tigran to see. The Russian smiled and nodded his head as Frankie sorted out one key and inserted it in the lock.

The girls bolted awake, fear driving sleep instantly from their minds as the door to their cell swung open on noisy hinges. Frankie walked in followed by Tigran and Louis.

The girls moved fast scrunching up tight against the headboard as far away from their captors as possible.

"Good evening, ladies," Frankie said his voice almost friendly.

The girls were terrified.

After a very long moment which Frankie thoroughly enjoyed he continued, "this is Tigran and his friend Louis," he said pointing to each man as he spoke.

The girls stared at them and Tigran and Louis could see the fear in their faces, they could smell their fear like a lovely scent, enticing, erotic, sexual.

Louis walked to the edge of the bed and sat down never taking his eyes from them. He smiled as he reached out his hand and the girls moved even further away from him.

"My loves," he whispered his voice full of tenderness, "I have waited long to see you. I have thought much about how delicious you will be. I have built dreams and together we will discover what those dreams are. Yes together we will make many discoveries that I promise you."

Then he sat there looking at the girls hoping one of them would say something, hoping for some defiance, some fight, but nothing, they just stared through hopeless eyes and for a moment he was disappointed, then he started to think of what pleasure he could take from them, force from them, and that made his disappointment vanish.

Tigran kept his eyes on the girls and didn't express any emotion, didn't say a word just looked at them, a slight smile on his face. He stood like the judge, jury and executioner and the girls quickly realized that their fate rested in his hands.

Chapter 45

Jimmy didn't know what to do, his mind was racing with so many different possibilities. Should he stay where he was and guard the door in case they decided to move the girls to the yacht? What if they had guns, then what could he do? He didn't want to leave, but he knew he needed to find Lester and Flip fast. Together the three of them could come up with a plan, besides he thought, Lester had a gun. After a few minutes of indecisiveness he knew he needed their help. Slowly he moved back away from the house then turned toward the beach. He kept himself in the darkness, crawling a few steps, stopping, listening then moving forward only to repeat the process all over again. He knew that Lester was hiding somewhere near the beach, but how could he possibly find him. Suppose Lester had tried to call him, and the fears just started growing until he could hardly move. Maybe Lester would find him, but then maybe somebody else could find him just as easy. There was nothing else he could do, he needed Lester and Flips help, he had to keep going. Slowly through the darkness he continued, and soon he was at the side of the resort, the beach thirty feet in front of him. He crawled until he reached a large pillar at the entrance to the bar, then he slowly stood up, and didn't move. For five minutes he stood there frozen, like a statue in the darkness, he didn't even turn his head at the slight sound when he first heard it. Something had caught his attention as he listened, his senses becoming riveted trying to decide if his mind was playing tricks with him. A minute later there was no doubt, somebody was here, the sound coming from inside the bar. Was it Lester? Was it security? Any sound, any alarm would destroy all hope they had of surprising whoever had the girls. The sound now became a shuffle, feet against sand on a hard surface, a slight scrapping sound that in the light of day he would never have heard. Closer the steps came. He froze, keeping his breath controlled. Now coming closer, heavy footsteps and he knew it couldn't be Lester. His back was against the pillar so it blocked his body from whoever was coming. Suddenly a foot stepped out past the pillar then one arm carrying a large nightstick then a big man stepped past him. For some unknown reason, some animal self-preservation instinct from mankind's ancient past somehow Charlie Markenson sensed Jimmy's presence as soon as he stepped past him. He spun to his left his nightstick swung toward the pillar. Jimmy ducked as the nightstick slammed where his head had been moments earlier. Jimmy wasted no time. If this guard was smart he would just yell and their entire plan would evaporate in a heartbeat. Instead the guard pulled the stick back attempting to hit him again. Jimmy charged, his right forearm slamming into the fist that held the nightstick jamming it high in the air. Then almost gracefully he ducked deep and came under the huge man and stepped behind him. Jimmy's motion was effortless, fluid, no hesitation as he reached his left arm up and hooked the man's neck from behind in his elbow, then his right hand came up behind Charlie's neck and Jimmy grabbed his own left bicep, and squeezed inward, instantly constricting the carotid arteries to Charlie's brain. The big man struggled but only for a few seconds then his knees gave out and he started to collapse. Jimmy kept the choke hold tight holding him up until the man was motionless, dead weight in his arms. Still Jimmy was afraid to let go but he knew the man would die if he didn't release his grasp. Jimmy finally eased his left elbow out from Charlie's throat and dropped him to the floor.

Jimmy didn't know what to do now. If he left to find Lester the man would soon regain consciousness, sound the alarm, and that couldn't happen. But he couldn't just stay here. This was now a new nightmare, another unforeseen event that could decide the outcome of this evening. Suddenly another sound caught his attention and he spun to his left ready for more combat. But it was Lester who stepped out from the shadows of the beach.

"Glad to see you," Jimmy whispered his adrenalin rushing, his body tense as a bow string.

"That was pretty good, Jimmy, damn good."

"Did you see the three guys walk up from the boathouse?"

"I didn't but Flip saw them through the night vision glasses," Lester said as Flip stepped out of the darkness next to Lester.

"Good. Okay, I know where the girls are, I think anyway. But what do we do with this guy?" Jimmy asked.

Lester smiled then reached into his pocket and pulled out a roll of duct tape and some plastic ties.

"The duct tape's not FBI issue but it will work, never leave home without it," Lester said still grinning, which Jimmy thought was weird at the moment because he was still about to explode.

They rolled the big man over securing his hands and feet behind his back with the F.B.I issued plastic ties, then Lester taped his mouth shut as well.

"Flip, can you drag him somewhere? Maybe down to the boathouse or something. He's not going to get free from this until somebody cuts him free," Lester said looking at Flip.

"No problem."

"Okay listen you guys," Jimmy said his voice a soft whisper, "from the boathouse there is a small path that leads to what I think is the main house. There is a cellar door, like a basement or something on the right side of the house. I think that is where the three guys went. If they went there then that's where we'll find the girls."

"Fine, Flip, meet us near the house after you drag this guy to the boathouse, we'll go there now and keep a look out. Be careful, be quiet and be safe," Lester said.

"Alright, Lester," Flip said before he reached under Charlie's arms, lifted his shoulders up and started dragging him away into the darkness.

Jimmy turned and slowly started making his way back toward the side of the house. Lester was right behind him, holding his glock in his right hand. Jimmy parted low bushes and palm fronds as they continued, making it easier for Lester to follow. Onward through the darkness they walked, stopping often, listening then moving again. This time Jimmy stopped near the footpath, about five feet away from it, standing in the brush and small trees that made good cover.

He knelt down and Lester did the same.

"There is a door right about there," he pointed it out to Lester who couldn't see it, "that's where the three guys went. So I figure that's where the girls are."

"Good, Jimmy, really good."

"Now what, Lester?"

"Hell if I know."

Ten minutes later the cistern door opened and three men following the beam of a small flashlight appeared. Jimmy and Lester froze, their eyes trying to focus on shadows as the men moved away from the door and moments later disappeared into the darkness, before a light flicked on in the house a minute later. Somebody put some Bob Marley on the stereo and soon it sounded like a party was beginning.

Jimmy and Lester sat for a long time, neither speaking, each knowing that soon they would have to move, but neither knowing when. It was Lester that finally reached over and nudged Jimmy with his elbow, then stood up and started walking toward the cistern door.

Chapter 46

When Lester and Jimmy finally reached the side of the house and the small doorway they saw the door was securely locked by a large padlock just above the door handle. Jimmy turned the handle and pulled the door open an inch but the padlock stopped the door from opening anymore. Stepping to his right Jimmy looked at the door hinges hoping they were the kind that the pins could be popped out but this door was heavily built and the hinges were sticking out of solid concrete, and the pins were solid half inch steel.

Lester put his hand on Jimmy's shoulder and shook his head then they stepped back away from the door and walked into the brush and trees. Twenty feet from the house they knelt down and Lester whispered, "we need to get that door open."

"We need bolt cutters or a hack saw."

"Right. That's a good idea . . . where do we get one?"

Jimmy was silent for a moment wondering if there was any other way to get that door open besides cutting the lock.

"Maybe the boat house would have some tools," Jimmy whispered once he realized the only way they were going to get through the door was to cut the lock.

Lester nodded, stood up and said, "I'll go, and I'll keep an eye out for Flip. He should be heading this way."

"Alright, Lester, find something to cut that lock, I'll stay here and watch."

Lester nodded then turned, took five steps and disappeared toward the beach.

The party was getting louder upstairs as Jimmy sat in the brush and palm trees hoping that Lester could find a hack saw and make it back in time to cut the lock.

*

Flip reached the dock and pulled Charlie out of the surf, his arms and back were aching from having to drag the big man through the water. Flip knew he couldn't risk leaving a trail on the beach for somebody to follow. Charlie was awake but he didn't put up any fight, which would have been a mistake because Flip felt like beating the hell out of him.

Once at the boathouse door Flip stopped and looked around. He didn't hear a thing and he couldn't see anything either because the night was pitch black. With one hand he slowly opened the door then pulled Charlie through and closed it behind him. Flip turned on his small flashlight and shined it to his left seeing a long workbench and some boxes piled on the floor around it. Looking out through the wide entrance of the boathouse he saw a few lights from the large yacht shining in the darkness on the other side of the reef.

Putting the flashlight in his mouth he dragged Charlie to the far corner of the boathouse then dropped him next to the wall. Looking around he found an old sail and unwrapping it he threw it over him, then he knelt down next to Charlie and pulled the sail back, shining his light right in his face, blinding him. Flip brought his lips down to Charlie's ear and whispered," You move you son of a bitch, you make one sound, and you're dead."

Then Flip stood up and threw the sail back over Charlie's head. He felt like giving him a good hard kick but he didn't. Turning to his left he walked to the door and turned his flashlight off then he just stood there for a few minutes, listening, thinking, re-focusing his thoughts. Now it was time to head for the house and find Lester and Jimmy. He opened the door, stepped outside and closed the door behind him, and started following the pathway toward the resort. Flip never saw the small inflatable dinghy pulled up on the beach just south of the boathouse or the two armed crewmen from Bela Bela as they made their way into the palm tress that lined the beach.

*

Lester followed the little walkway from the house, stumbling a few times feeling like a blind man as he groped his way toward the beach, the sound of the surf and croaking frogs all that he could hear. Crouching low trying to keep his silhouette small he walked with short steps, careful not to trip or kick anything in the darkness. His flashlight was turned off, there was no way he could risk using it. He was just starting to think he should be near the beach when he heard something. He stopped and listened, was his mind playing tricks with him, he couldn't tell, all he heard was the surf, then he realized the frogs had stopped croaking, and a chill went up his spine. The shadows danced around him, and a slight gust of wind rattled branches and leaves, making strange noises in the night. He took three more careful steps before he heard footsteps and they were coming his way. His first thought was it must be Flip and he almost continued walking but something made him hesitate so he stepped a few feet off of the path and knelt down, motionless. In what seemed like the next second he vaguely saw two men appear out of the darkness coming his way on the little footpath and he froze. Both men were short and he could now see each of them carrying some sort of rifle probably a shotgun.

Shit! Now what he thought? Moving was impossible, so he didn't move, didn't even breath as they came closer. Huddled in the darkness he realized with a sickening feeling that he had to do something, he had to act now, he couldn't let them surprise Jimmy, even if that meant blowing their cover. The silent figures were now two steps past him walking side by side when he stood, swung his right arm around and jammed the barrel of the Glock against one of their heads.

"Freeze asshole," he whispered.

Both men stopped in their tracks.

"Drop the guns," he said as he pushed the barrel harder into the back of the man's head, forcing him to take a step forward to keep his balance.

Then faintly Lester heard another sound behind him and in that moment, less than one second, his reaction overcame his training and ever so slightly he turned to look behind him. The man with the Glock to his head felt the barrel waver and he dropped to his knees as he swung the shotgun butt up behind him and it slammed into Lester catching him directly in the groin. Lester gasped, started to collapse but as he fell forward he slammed the butt of his Glock against the man's head dropping him instantly.

The other man was already turning raising the barrel of his gun toward Lester who now was on his knees hunched over, paralyzed with pain and he couldn't do anything to protect himself. Seeing the barrel swinging up toward his head Lester knew he was dead. The shotgun arched high, coming up fast and it slammed under his chin, snapping his head backward, knocking him off of his knees and he landed with a painful crash on his side. Then the cold steel lodged against Lester's forehead and a foot slammed into his stomach, the Glock was kicked out of his hand and then the barrel of the shotgun slammed into his forehead again and that was the last thing he remembered as he drifted from the pain and terror into darkness.

*

Flip was slowly following the walkway up from the boathouse. He was thinking about Jimmy and Lester and how the hell he was going to find them when out of nowhere a figure suddenly emerged and before he could even think the butt of a shotgun slammed into his rib cage, breaking ribs, knocking the air from his lungs. The cold blue steel then arched upwards and hit him under his chin, snapping his head back and he was unconscious before he slammed on the ground.

*

Jimmy sat in the shadows, looking at his watch wondering what could be taking Lester and Flip so long. How hard could it be to find a damn hack saw, he thought?

Chapter 47

When the lights above him flipped off Jimmy jerked and almost fell over. He wasn't sure if he had fallen asleep or not but he must have been close to drifting off. Now wide awake, adrenalin surging through his body, he looked up at the dark house and had a sudden fear about Lester and Flip. Glancing at his watch he realized Lester had been gone for over fifteen minutes. Something wasn't right, but he didn't have time to think about it because he suddenly saw the beam of a flashlight appear from the back of the house. Then three men walked around the corner following the light and they traveled part way down the foundation wall and stopped at the door. Jimmy watched as the man holding the flashlight reached into his pocket and took out a key and unlocked the padlock. Putting the lock in his pocket he turned the door handle and the three went inside and moments later the door closed behind them.

Jimmy was up the moment the door closed. He walked toward the house, not sure what to do next, stopping only when he reached an area ten feet from the foundation wall that had all the trees and shrubs cut back and he had no cover to hide in.

He turned to his left and walked fifteen feet down the pathway away from the house, then knelt down a few feet off the path in the last of the brush that he could use for hiding.

Shit, shit, shit, he thought, where the hell were Lester and Flip? He kept hoping that at any moment they would come out of the darkness, he kept looking around him, trying to see them, trying to hear them, trying to sense their presence but nobody was there.

Suddenly his attention was brought back to the door as it opened and out walked a man followed by the twins, Megan and then two more men, one of them holding the flashlight and in its dim glow Jimmy thought he saw the other man holding a pistol pointed toward the girls. The light bounced back to the walkway and Jimmy lost sight of the gun. Adrenaline, hatred, fear, all flowed through Jimmy at that moment and he felt a sudden urge to jump up and attack right then, kill them all if he had to but instead he waited, fearing a gun and knowing that timing was everything.

The man with the pistol had his right hand on one of the twins shoulders, holding her close. Everybody stood in silence waiting until the cellar door was closed then the man with his hand on one of the twins pushed her forward and they all started down the path. Jimmy was crouched low, his legs coiled springs, tight, ready. His eyes were focused on the man with the pistol, nothing else mattered but that gun. The first man walked right past Jimmy and didn't notice him, then the twins, then Megan and suddenly the man holding the pistol was three feet away and Jimmy leaped.

The Russian never had time to even react as Jimmy sprang from his hiding place and kicked Tigran's left hand high into the air. The barrel flew skyward as it jerked his trigger finger and the silence was shattered by the explosive sound of a round being fired harmlessly into the night sky before the gun flew from his hand and disappeared into the darkness. Jimmy grabbed Tigran and slammed his right fist into his rib cage. The Russian gasped, instinctively he tried to swing his left elbow at Jimmy but Jimmy stepped back out of the way, grabbed his elbow, jammed it up then crashed his knee into Tigran's groin. As Jimmy's foot hit the ground he slammed his right fist into the side of Tigran's head and he fell on his face in the dirt. The girls screamed, scrambled to get out of the way as Jimmy stepped past the Russian and kicked his right foot out hitting the man carrying the flashlight in the stomach. Then following his momentum he spun, his left arm extended, his body a whipping arc of power and he slammed the back of his knuckles into the side of Frankie's head, dropping him to his knees. Another well placed kick sent him tumbling backwards into the night. Jimmy turned and charged Louis who gave a scream like a wounded animal but was to terrified to move. Louis screamed again as the heel of Jimmy's right foot slammed into his mid section causing his lungs to explode with pain and he went flying backward. Jimmy followed the falling Louis and kicked him again with a front kick under his chin that lifted Louis off of his feet and he hit the ground with a gurgling scream of agony as his right forearm shattered on impact.

Tigran was on his knees trying to get up, confusion on his face when Jimmy spun and with a running leap slammed his right foot into his chest which flipped him over and he smashed into the ground with a terrible gasp.

Jimmy was beyond self-control as he dragged Tigran to his feet and hit him in the face with a right hand that knocked teeth loose. Another punch almost fractured his jaw. The Russian was limp in his grasp, not even able to scream, wavering between unconsciousness and death. Jimmy dropped him as he saw Frankie charging at him out of the darkness. In that second all Jimmy knew was fear and hatred and they both propelled him. He kicked high hitting the rushing Frankie once again in the face, lifting him off of his feet, breaking his nose, sending him somersaulting into the darkness. Spinning Jimmy looked at Louis but he hadn't moved, he just lay there whimpering holding his right arm, and in that moment Jimmy knew he was victorious. None of the men moved, yet, still the fear pushed him to fight more. Frustration overcame him as he turned back to Tigran and Frankie to find them motionless. Then he saw the girls huddled close to each other and he stopped for a second and reality came crashing back to him before he rushed into their arms, tears flowing. The girls threw themselves at him, hugging him in between their sobs of joy and sorrow and fear. Their hearts were exploding, their minds seeing but somehow not really believing. Jimmy was alive and he had saved them.

*

The crewman from Bela Bela had been slapping his unconscious friend, trying to get him to respond when Tigran's shot echoed through the night. He stood and looked at the pile of bodies around him. He didn't know what to do. He had done a quick search of Lester and Flip and didn't find anymore weapons. Tucking the Glock in his belt he grabbed the other shotgun and started walking toward the house. His pace was brisk but not foolish, a shotgun in each hand held waist level, safety's off, and a round in each chamber. He walked a hundred feet and he could now hear voices crying hysterically in English gibberish that he couldn't understand. He slowed his pace and came around a corner and stopped, there were people on the ground, and he knew it was Tigran and Louis. Still crying and holding each other tight were three women and a man. They were so focused on each other that they didn't see him even though he was only fifteen feet away.

Taking three more steps they finally heard him as his feet intentionally kicked a rock in the path sending it spinning toward them. Silenced slammed into the night as they all turned and looked at him. Then just for effect he slid the pump action of the shotgun in his right hand ejecting one round and replacing it with another. It may have been a waste of a round but it was worth it. It doesn't matter what language you speak, everybody understands the sound of a loaded shotgun.

Chapter 48

Tigran and Frankie both staggered to their feet helping each other stand. It would have been impossible for either man to do it alone. Louis hadn't moved. He just lay moaning curled in a little ball. The crewman with the shotgun stood five feet from Jimmy and the girls, who were still in each others arms but none of them dared to move. Frankie could hardly breathe and Tigran was in such pain he stumbled and fell twice just walking the few steps that it took to reach his crewman before he pulled the shotgun from his hand. Then he spun, staggered, almost fell, caught himself and took one step toward Jimmy and pointed the barrel right at Jimmy's face.

"You bastard," he tried to scream, but his words came out garbled, almost incoherent. He took another faulty step toward Jimmy, about to pull the trigger but he suddenly realized that the girls were in the way. Confused, Tigran stood there looking at them, unsure what to do next.

Frankie came staggering out of the darkness, "no!" he shouted, not knowing if he could reach the crazy Russian before he pulled the trigger.

Tigran turned and looked at Frankie.

"No, Tigran, not here, not now, too noisy, I've got guests!" Frankie managed to say his head exploding with every word.

The Russian was suddenly beyond reason, his rage crashing back, and all he wanted to do was kill the man standing in front of him. The man who had dared to attack him, who had caused this anguish and pain that he now felt, this humiliation that he would find hard to live with the rest of his life. Tigran turned away from Frankie and back to Jimmy who knew he couldn't move because the girls were too close around him.

Frankie took two quick steps then brought his weight forward and hit Tigran with his right fist crashing into his injured jaw as he pushed the barrel upward with his left hand. Tigran's head snapped sideways, he fell to his left knee and Frankie pulled the gun from him as he collapsed on the ground. Frankie spun to his left and pointed the weapon at Tigran's crewman who still held the other shotgun. Frankie stared at him for a few seconds that seemed like hours, the man's face almost lost in the darkness.

"No trouble," Frankie whispered hoping the Russian understood.

Tigran was now up on his knees bent over at the waist his head inches from the ground, a string of Russian curses escaping from his lips.

"Alright, you son of a bitch," Frankie said spinning back to Jimmy as he leveled the shotgun at him and he motioned toward the cellar door.

Jimmy and the girls didn't move. Frankie waited only a second before he took a step closer to them and shoved the barrel under Megan's chin.

"I said move, asshole!"

Jimmy had no choice and a minute later he was thrown into the small hurricane safe room that had held the girls for so long. When the door slammed behind him he dropped on the bed, defeated, knowing that he had just failed and once again the girls were lost. What happened to Lester and Flip he had no idea and Jimmy flung himself back on the bed, stared at the ceiling and felt such anguish that death would have been better. He had freed the girls, for a very short moment they were safe again but then he became foolish, dropped his guard and now he was as good as dead, the girls were going to disappear forever and he couldn't do a damn thing about it.

*

By the time Tigran, Louis, the girls and the crewman who was dragging his still unconscious friend reached the boathouse, Lester was just stirring, he was laying off the walkway in some bushes, blood covering his face and his head throbbed. He stared into the darkness trying to remember what happened, how did he end up here? His mind tried to block out the pain by blocking out the memory. Then slowly his eyes adjusted, and his head stopped spinning just enough for him to recognize Flip lying a few feet away from him. Lester painfully rolled to his right and pulled himself over to his friend. He brought his face down close to Flip who at least was breathing in short gasps sandwiched between moans.

"Flip, Flip," Lester said softly, each word wracking him with pain as he pushed Flip trying to get a response.

"Flip, Jesus, Flip," he managed to say. Then he almost fainted, almost hoping for the sweet release from his agony that unconsciousness would bring but he fought it off, he had to.

He shoved Flip again then slapped his face as best as he could from his awkward angle and slowly Flip started to stir. With every deep breath Flip took his moans became louder until he sat up dazed, confused and suddenly very scared as his mind raced back to the events of the last few minutes.

"Fuck, Lester, what happened?"

"We screwed up."

"Where's Jimmy?"

"I don't know."

"Did you hear any gun shots?"

"No, thank God."

"That's good."

All that they could do for the next few minutes was to sit there, listening to nothing but the croaking frogs and the distant waves crashing on the beach. The night was eerie, almost haunting and they both knew they had lost.

"Can you get up?" Lester finally asked him.

"I don't know, but I'll try."

They struggled and together leaning on each other they finally stood. Each man was racked with pain, neither certain what to do next.

"Lester, we need to get to the boathouse, that's where they will take the girls."

"Right."

They started down the little pathway arms around each other, neither of them being able to walk alone without the help of the other. Each step caused their bodies to scream with pain, each foot in front of the other a struggle of their collective wills, but they didn't stop. They came out of the palm trees onto the beach and they could see the outline of the boathouse reflected in the dim light of the moon. Looking out toward the yacht they could see lights and the phosphorescence of the small waves as they crashed upon the reef. The waves and light played tricks with their eyes, shadows racing across the waters, each of them seeing things that were not there. Then in the dim light for a fleeting moment they both saw the inflatable dinghy heading out through the reef. Lester collapsed in the sand, all of his strength evaporating as he watched the boat disappear into the darkness as quickly as he had seen it. In that moment before his knees buckled he had seen the flash of long golden hair reflecting in the moonlight and he knew that his daughters were out of his reach and were gone forever.

Flip collapsed next to him and put his right arm around Lester. They both watched as the moonlight continued to play tricks allowing quick glimpses of the inflatable as it headed out to the yacht.

Time stopped for both men as they sat there, and it seemed liked hours but it was only a few minutes before they heard something behind them and slowly they turned and looked up into the barrel of a shotgun. A tall figure stood before them, his face lost in the darkness but the barrel was inches from their face's and they knew it wasn't Jimmy coming to their rescue.

*

Bela Bela floated on the sea like a darkened city as the inflatable pulled up next to her. Once the small boat was secured strong hands pulled the girls up a short set of steps and onto the lower deck.

Tigran and Louis were next, the crewman who had been knocked out by Lester was now conscious but moving slow as he followed.

"Take them forward, into the starboard anchor well. I'll deal with them shortly," Tigran mumbled as he looked at his crewman. The man nudged the barrel of his shotgun into Megan's back and the three girls started walking down the dimly lit deck toward the front of the boat.

"Tigran I need a doctor," Louis whimpered holding his arm feeling like he was going to vomit at any moment.

"Yes. We both do. I will get us a doctor soon, but first we must deal with our cargo."

*

The girls had struggled but there was nothing they could do as one of the crewman held their arms and each one felt the small prick of a hypodermic needle as Tigran jabbed it into their vein. It took only seconds before the drug was flowing to their brain and shutting it down. Once they became unconscious each girl was strapped to a small bunk lying on their side held tight by three pieces of webbing that didn't allow for them to even turn over.

The crewman was the last to leave the small room of the starboard anchor locker. He flipped the small light off, climbed the three steps out of the narrow hatch then leaning over feeling in the darkness he twisted the recessed hatch tight sealing the room off. Only the faint purr of a small fan, that brought outside air into the girls dungeon could he hear, and that was only because Tigran had told him to make sure the fan was on or he would have never been aware of it. Standing up he started piling four hundred feet of ½ inch chain back over the hatch. It took fifteen minutes before he finished, his arms and back aching from moving all that chain. Breathing heavily, sweat dripping from him, he stood in the near darkness of the tiny space thinking that nobody would ever find them, even if an army tore Bela Bela apart, nobody would look under all this chain.

Chapter 49

Jaskee held the shotgun on Lester and Flip as they walked toward the house. He was nervous. He had never held a gun on anybody before. The two men walked five feet in front of him, side by side, hands in the air and he hoped they were smart enough to not try anything stupid. He didn't want to shoot them, but he wasn't going to screw up and let them get away. That was for damn sure. Not after Frankie had woken him up with a sharp kick fifteen minutes ago, handed him a shotgun and told him to start looking for two men on the path to the boathouse. Frankie hadn't told him much more than be careful, try not to shoot anybody unless you have to and if you find em' lock them in the hurricane room.

"Are you alright?" Jaskee had asked Frankie as he had climbed out of bed, confused and scared.

"I'm fine, just find them. I'll be in my office with a bag of ice on my ribs. Let me know when you have them locked up, and don't screw up," Frankie had said before he turned and headed out the door slamming it behind him.

It didn't take Jaskee long to find the two men standing on the shore near the boathouse. He spent five minutes carefully walking in their direction before they unexpectedly dropped to the sand and just sat. Catching them was easier than he had thought it would be, and he wondered what his reaction would be to somebody shoving a shotgun in his face on a deserted beach at three o'clock in the morning?

At the cistern room door Jaskee stood back a safe distance and had the large black man un-lock the door. Once they were inside he made them get on their bellies before he unlocked the hurricane room door and told them to crawl in on their hands and knees. He had seen that somewhere in a movie once and it seemed like a good idea at the moment. Jaskee was surprised to see another man in the room but he kept his wits about him and soon all three were locked up tight.

Jaskee stayed in the cistern room for a few minutes looking through the little window into the hurricane cell watching the men. The two that he had found on the beach sat on the floor their backs slumped against the wall. The third man sat on the edge of the bed looking at the others but nobody said a word. Jaskee had seen defeated men before but he had never seen it like this. These three had lost, and he knew it was something to do with the girls. What Frankie was going to do with them he didn't want to know, and he hoped to god that he wasn't going to have to be part of it.

*

Frankie lay in the darkness on his couch, with a bag of ice on his head, another one on his ribs thinking about the damn Russian and the girls. Bobby sat in a chair across the room. The shot from Tigran's pistol had woken Bobby with a start and it had taken him fifteen minutes of frantically searching the resort before he finally found Frankie, beat up but at least alive in his office.

"That fuckin Russian got off the island, took the girls, and didn't pay me a damn penny," Frankie said not looking at Bobby.

"Lousy deal."

"Right. Maybe that asshole will wire me some money, but just as easy he could tell me to go to hell. What can I do, that jerk could be anywhere in the world by tomorrow."

"Really shitty Frankie . . . sorry . . . I wonder where Charlie is?"

"That idiot, probably asleep somewhere, so much for security."

"I doubt it."

"Well, then where the hell is he?"

"I don't know."

"Well I know one thing. I've got more shit to deal with . . . in my hurricane room that is. I traded three young babes, worth a fortune they were, for three guys and all I can do with them is use em' as fish food."

Frankie exhaled a deep sigh, stared at the ceiling for a few minutes before he continued.

"Bobby, what a really shitty day."

*

Bela Bela departed Three Cove Island with Tigran at the helm. He stood in front of the small joy stick that he used to steer his yacht and looked at the Garmin GPS 800 screen before him. His entire body hurt as he pushed in way points charting the fastest course to downtown Charlotte Amelia on St. Thomas.

Louis was down below laying on the dining room sofa bags of ice taped tightly around his arm. He hadn't been able to do a thing to help get Bela Bela going. Fortunately for Tigran both of his crewmen were well and able to help get the yacht under way.

Tigran had driven Bela Bela often when he first bought her but once he started hiring captains he left most of the work to them. Now in spite of his pain he was almost enjoying pushing his yacht through the darkened seas. Carefully he leaned back into the helm seat and looked at the radar screen. Three Cove Island was disappearing behind him, and so was Frankie Balero and even better was the fact that he had what he came for and he still had all of his money. Not a bad night all in all, he thought, praying for the pain medication that he took out of the first aid kit to start working.

Tigran wondered what Frankie was thinking about at the moment. He certainly had to be pissed that he hadn't gotten paid but that was just how business goes sometimes Tigran thought as he punched in the last way point. He also wondered what would happen to the men who had attacked him this evening, but instinctively he knew that Frankie only had one choice. Those three men were going to die very soon, there was no other option. He thought about the one who had beat him and Louis up so badly, tried to see the man's face in his memory. That bastard the Russian thought, he should have blown him into a thousand pieces when he had the chance. But he had been weak, hesitated when Frankie had yelled at him in the darkness, and Tigran hated himself for that weakness. But now that he had time to think, the medication starting to free his body from the pain that had overwhelmed him earlier, he started thinking of how he would kill that guy if he had the chance. Maybe he would chain him down, cut him a hundred times and dump salt water, bleach or better yet battery acid on his wounds, yeah, he thought with a sense of almost regret, it's a good thing that Frankie has to deal with that guy, because if it was up to him he could come up a with a thousand painful ways to kill that bastard.

Tigran then started thinking about the Captain and the new stewardess and what they would think when they finally woke up from their drug induced slumber and found they were in St. Thomas. After a few minutes he decided that if they asked too many questions he would just fire them on the spot.

Now that Bela Bela was in deep water it was clear motoring all the way to St. Thomas. He turned on the auto pilot, interfaced it with the GPS and the radar, and shoved the throttles forward. He was pushing his yacht hard, cruising at nineteen knots, burning over ninety gallons of fuel an hour. It didn't matter. He had to get Louis and himself to a hospital as fast as he could.

Sitting back in the darkness of the bridge, the only light coming from the instruments before him he peered out into the darkness. Racing Bela Bela through the night was like how he lived his life, he suddenly realized. He knew that in life, you must first understand what you truly want, and only then can you make decisions that lead to those goals. He had traveled half way around the world for these three and he now owned them . . . simple as that, he owned them, and they were his. Maybe sometime in the future on a little Greek island that he knew and loved so well he would have a wedding ceremony, a very simple one, three brides and himself. He loved weddings, especially the vows, and his favorite verse was . . . until death do us part.

Chapter 50

At the first light of dawn Bela Bela was only two miles out of St. Thomas on a course for the Royal Bay Marina. The thrill of racing his yacht through the night had disappeared long ago only to be replaced by the growing pain that raced throughout his body. He was glad they had finally arrived. His ribs ached, his balls felt shattered, his mouth felt frozen in place and the three pain pills plus whiskey he had somehow managed to swallow did little to stop the pain anymore.

He backed the throttles off and grabbed the radio, scrolling to channel 16, the United States Coast Guard channel.

"United States Coast Guard this is the Motor Yacht Bela Bela, we have an emergency and request immediate permission to dock, over," his words sounding like mush.

A woman's voice came back immediately, her concern easy to hear.

"Bela Bela what is your emergency, over"?

"We took a freak wave last night, one of my crew has a broken arm and I have injuries as well."

"Roger that, where is your vessel registered?"

Tigran wanted to ask her what the hell it mattered but he didn't.

"We are flagged in Georgetown, Cayman Island. I request to have an ambulance meet us."

"Roger that, what is your location?"

"We will be arriving shortly at Royal Bay Marina. I have been here before. I will tie up to the outside breakwater, repeat I request immediate medical assistance, over."

"Roger Bela Bela please proceed. I will contact the hospital and have an ambulance meet you. We will also try to have Coast Guard Officers there as soon as possible. Due to your injuries we will take care of clearing you in at a later time. If the ambulance arrives before our officers do please depart immediately for the hospital."

"Roger that, thank you," and he turned the radio off.

He grabbed a small hand held radio used only for communication onboard his yacht, clicked it on and said, "Vonderick, we will tie on the port side, have everything ready. Once we are secure help Louis to the dock. An ambulance should be waiting."

"Yes sir," he replied back.

"Also I don't think the captain or our new stewardess will awake in my absence but if they do just tell them to wait. I will explain everything to them when I return."

"Yes Tigran."

With expert skill Tigran docked Bela Bela on the outside breakwater. By the time he turned the engines off he could see the flashing lights of an ambulance as it raced through the morning light heading toward the marina.

*

Frankie was almost asleep trying hard to use his mind and three shots of bourbon to turn off the pain. Bobby had fallen asleep in the chair and was softly snoring which made it even harder for Frankie to fall asleep. That damn Tigran he was thinking when suddenly the door to his office exploded with a crash, flying off of its shattered hinges and crashing into the room. Before Frankie and Bobby could even react a man neither of them had ever seen before was standing in the ripped out doorway pointing a pistol at them.

"Son of a bitch," Frankie shouted, as he jumped to his feet without even thinking.

Bobby spun to his left diving off of the chair. He acted more from instinct than reason and the pistol barked once, its sound muffled by the four inch grooved silencer. Bobby screamed and landed on the floor grabbing his left leg a puddle of blood already oozing out onto the carpet.

"Move again and you're dead."

Frankie couldn't believe it and he crashed down onto the sofa, bouncing softly once, absorbing his impact before kneeling down next to Bobbie, who lay sprawled on the floor.

"Where are they?" the dark skinned man asked.

"Fuck you," Frankie yelled.

Another round blew a hole in the floor inches from Bobby's head.

"Alright, goddamn it, who are you?" Frankie stammered too confused to even speak right.

"I want you to take me to them."

"To who?' Frankie bluffed but he knew it was pointless as he stared at the pistol then up to the dark eyes of the man.

"To Lester and his two friends, my patience has ended the next shot will go through your friends ass and out his balls, understand?'

"Fuckin shit . . . asshole, yeah I understand," Frankie said as he stood up and started for the door.

"Bring him," the black man nodded at Bobby.

"Christ he can't even stand, he's bleeding all over the place."

"Help him up."

Frankie swore under his breath as he reached down and pulled Bobby to his feet.

"Tie it off, it's just a flesh wound," the man holding the pistol said keeping the gun pointed right at Frankie.

Frankie pulled his tee shirt off then tied it around Bobby's leg.

"Now show me my friends."

Frankie knew this was no time for any stupid heroics.

The man stepped back away from them and waved the pistol toward the broken out doorway. Frankie lifted Bobby's right arm over his shoulder and they stepped out of the office and toward the back door. There was just enough light to see as they walked outside, stepping carefully, the pistol never far from the back of Frankie's head. They turned the corner at the back of the house then walked until they reached the cellar door.

Frankie turned and looked at the gunman, a moment of indecision about whether to attack or not, but the look in the man's eyes made Frankie cringe. Also looking at the silencer he suddenly realized that this was no small time punk. Punks don't use silencers.

Opening the outer door Frankie and Bobbie walked into the dimly lit cistern room. The man with the gun looked around saw the doorway to the hurricane room and its small window.

"Close the door behind you," he whispered and Frankie did as he was told.

"Lay down both of you, now," the man barked the order as he walked to the hurricane room door and pulled the large deadbolt back sliding the door open a few inches.

"Lester, it's Hobbs," he didn't have to finish as Flip, Jimmy and Lester had already jumped at the sound of the door opening.

"Hobbs, son of a bitch!" Lester said as he walked out of the cell and gave the man a hug.

The man named Hobbs just gave a short laugh, then turned his attention back to Frankie and Bobby laying on the floor.

"Do I kill these two?" Hobbs asked.

Lester couldn't see the men's faces as they lay on the floor. But he was filled with rage at what these two men had put his girls and him through. He reached down, grabbed the man closest to him by the hair and jerked his head up, and looked at his face. Lester couldn't believe what he saw, he blinked as if trying to change the image before him, as if something in his mind would refocus and give him a new face to see, but in that millisecond he knew it was real, and his mind wasn't playing tricks.

Lester gasped then kicked out with all of his strength connecting with the man on the floor causing him to shriek in pain. Jimmy and Flip both looked at Lester surprised by his violence then even more surprised as Lester reached down grabbed the man by his hair once again and dragged him to his feet. Jimmy and Flip could see recognition in both men's faces and Lester slammed his fist into Frankie's stomach doubling him over.

"I don't believe it, son of a bitch!" Lester screamed as he smashed his right foot into Frankie's balls dropping him to his knees. Lester went to kick again but Jimmy grabbed him and held him back.

"Lester what is it?" Jimmy said shocked to see his friend act this way.

Lester shook Jimmy loose then took two steps back moving like a drunkard before he leaned against the hurricane room wall.

"Fucking Frankie Balero, that's what. I don't believe it."

Frankie tried to stand but couldn't and he collapsed on the floor, his ball's killing him, his breath coming in short gasps, making it almost impossible to talk.

"Those are your daughters," he managed to spit out, "oh my god."

Chapter 51

"What do you want to do with them, Lester," Hobbs said breaking the awkward silence.

Lester's legs' had given out and he had slid down the wall and now sat slumped against the hurricane room with his hands to his face as if trying to protect himself from the insanity of seeing Frankie Balero on the floor. Lester finally looked up at Hobbs then back at Frankie.

"I want the girls, Frankie. I want the name of the yacht."

"Go to hell," Frankie spit out still doubled over on the floor.

Lester slowly forced himself up, everybody watching him as he took two steps then knelt down in front of Frankie.

"Listen to me Frankie, what happens to you means nothing to me at this moment. I want my girls, and you will tell me what I need to know. Do you understand me?"

Frankie could see the confusion and fear in Lester's face, he could see the suffering in the eyes of a man who had just lost the most important thing in his life and now suddenly maybe had a chance to get it back. Frankie could see vulnerability and he knew that he had to play Lester for all that he could.

"Fuck you Lester," he spat out gambling that Lester would feel the hopelessness of the moment, and he would be able to bargain his way out of this mess.

"That's the wrong answer, Frankie, one more time. What is the name of the yacht?"

"Kiss my ass, how's that," he said bringing his eyes up to Lester's.

But in that moment Frankie realized that he played him wrong, dead wrong. Lester smiled as he stared at Frankie and slightly shook his head before standing and walking over to Hobbs. He didn't say a word as he grabbed the pistol and forcefully pulled it out of Hobb's hand. Lester turned back toward Frankie, his motion slow, as if he was about to collapse once again, as if all that had happened in the last few days was too much for him to bear. He knelt in front of Frankie and put the barrel against his forehead, pushing it hard into Frankie's skin.

"You have any last thoughts, asshole?"

Frankie started to say something but his words suddenly became a jumble as his mind froze with sudden fear, and in the next second before he could utter a sound Lester pulled the trigger blowing the back of Frankie's head off, sending his body careening, blood and brains splattering across the floor and the cellar door. Before anyone could move Lester swung the pistol and pushed the barrel against the side of Bobby's head.

"Don't shoot, Lester, shit, don't shoot," Bobby screamed, his eyes bulging, his face white as a ghost, the smell of crap suddenly filling the small room as Bobby shit his pants.

"The guys a fuckin Russian, name Tigran. I don't know the name of the boat, I swear. I don't . . . but he's Russian, Tigran, his names Tigran, a drug dealer, keeps his boat in Antigua, god Lester don't shoot . . ." Bobby saying anything he could think of to stop Lester from pulling the trigger.

Jimmy and Flip didn't move they were caught up in the drama of the moment, shocked at Frankie's murder, neither could believe that Lester could kill in cold blood. Only Hobbs wasn't surprised at Lester's violence, but that was because he knew Lester better than any man in the room, knew Lester's past, before marriage and kids, and farms in Virginia, he knew this Lester and he had no idea if Bobby was a dead man or not.

Lester pushed the barrel harder into Bobby's head.

"I swear Lester, I'll tell you everything, god just don't kill me, please god."

"Alright," Lester said casually as if he had just asked a waiter for a menu, "alright, what's your name?"

"Bobby, Bobby from Chicago I work . . . I used to work with Frankie."

"Well you don't any more. Now once again tell me everything. I have more reasons to kill you than leave you alive right now . . . so don't miss a thing."

Bobby sat up looked at the men standing around the room, looked at Lester who took a few steps back then sat down once again leaning against the hurricane room wall, keeping the pistol pointed.

"I know Frankie wanted to sell the girls to the Russian, he didn't want to kill them. This really wasn't even his mess it all started with his damn nephew Tommy, who I think your friend there," he looked at Jimmy, then back to Lester before he continued, "fed to the sharks. Frankie didn't want any of this."

"That don't make much difference now," Lester said his voice as cold as ice.

"Yeah, so the Russian keeps his yacht in Antigua, probably has a plane there, I think that's where he will go. He has to get the girls out of here. Once he gets on that plane they're gone, Lester, you know that."

"Right. I realize that, so what do I do with you?"

Bobby didn't know what to say, he was thinking so fast about the Russian and the girls that Lester's question caught him by surprise.

"With me . . . God Lester . . . I want nothing to do with this, shit."

"Isn't it a little late for that?"

Bobby switched his thinking about the Russian to his survival, weighing his options, his mind racing, trying to figure out what to say next, staring at a man who was capable of cold blooded murder.

"Listen Lester," Bobby said softly, trying to keep his voice from breaking, trying to keep the fear locked deep so it wouldn't show.

"I have no idea who or what you are . . . but I know you are somebody not to fuck with. I don't know how you knew Frankie, what your connection was, but, lets say I'm in the same business as Frankie . . . I know a lot of people, and that is worth something. I know a lot . . . and I'm willing to trade what I know for the chance to live . . . understand me?"

Lester didn't say anything for a minute, just left Bobby's statement hang out there.

"Does the name Joseph Flynn mean anything to you?"

"Shit!" Bobbie muttered.

"How about Washport Bay, Washington, how about Joey "bright eyes" DeSilva?"

"Oh god . . ."

"Prayin' won't help you much Bobby, but answering some questions just might save your life," Lester said softly, like he was talking to the waiter once again.

Chapter 52

The emergency room at the hospital was a disaster. The small waiting room even at this time of night was filled with sick people, injured patients and frantic relatives. Tigran and Louis had been impatiently waiting for twenty minutes after arriving by ambulance. One gunshot victim had already been wheeled in after they arrived, a paramedic beating on his chest, another holding an IV bag as they rushed through the door and disappeared down the hallway.

Tigran was furious, he wasn't used to waiting on others, and he had to get out of St. Thomas as fast as he could, and every minute spent in this hospital was a minute he could not afford to spend.

After a fat woman was brought in, who seemed to know one of the nurses behind the counter and was immediately whisked away down the hallway Tigran had enough. He stood up and walked up to the front desk. There were two nurses standing talking, a third had her back to him looking up something in a large file cabinet against the far wall. Neither of the nurse's seemed the least bit concerned that Tigran and Louis had been waiting for a long time and they ignored him as he stood at the counter.

"Hello ladies," he finally said not believing that they could be so rude.

"Yes, can I help you?" the fat nurse said turning away from her friend and giving him a look like he just interrupted a very important conversation. The Russian felt like hitting her with the phone on the desk but he knew it would be counterproductive.

"How long before we see a doctor?"

"Sorry, it could be a while," the fat nurse said with a look on her face that was meant to put Tigran in his place.

"I don't want to wait, neither does my friend," his tone suddenly harsh, menacing.

"Well, that's just too bad. There's not much we can do," the other nurse said enjoying her moment of authority and power.

"Yes there is, bitch," he said as he pulled his wallet out and started putting hundred dollar bills on the counter.

"I want a doctor now," he demanded his face full of rage, which instantly stopped both nurses in their tracks.

The fat nurse looked at her friend whose eyes bulged at seeing ten one hundred dollar bills sitting on the counter. Both nurses glanced over their shoulders at the third nurse who was still looking through files oblivious to the entire transaction. In one fast motion the fat nurse reached over grabbed the money, put it in her pocket, turned again to see her co-worker still at the files then turned back and smiled at Tigran.

"I think the doctor will be with you very shortly sir, very shortly," then she gave her friend a wink, turned and started running down the hallway.

*

Bobby and Charlie sat locked in the hurricane room prison. Charlie was trying to get over the shock of seeing Frankie dead on the floor and he had started making dumb shit excuses about how he got caught, and it wasn't his fault. Bobby finally told him to shut his mouth. All Bobby could do was think about how close he had come to dying, and that Frankie Balero was now just a memory. He couldn't believe he had shit his pants but what the hell, seeing Frankie blown away like that was just too much. Before they locked Charlie in the room with him Bobby had spilled his guts to Lester, telling him everything he knew about Joey "bright-eyes" and the contract hit at Washport Bay, and he knew a lot. He knew how much was paid for the killing, who the money was given to and lastly he new that Frankie was a big player in the hit. Other people may have wanted Joey dead for one reason or another but Frankie had paid for it.

Damn Frankie, he thought, looking at his body, what a waste. He didn't deserve any of this. All he wanted was to retire and hang out in the islands, running his little paradise, getting tan and enjoying life. Now Frankie lay right where he fell, sprawled out on cold concrete the back of his head blown off. Jesus. Bobby had no idea how this was all going to end but he knew if he was in Lester's shoes the less witnesses the better. That was for damn sure. All Bobby could do was sit and pray, and hope to god that Lester had enough blood on his hands for one day.

*

"Call him" Lester said as he handed Jimmy the phone. They were sitting in Frankie's office, lights on and Jimmy had his wallet out and a piece of paper laying on the desk in front of him.

"Alright," Jimmy dialed Commander Leboske's number. He glanced at the small clock on the desk, it was 4:14 in the morning. Jesus he didn't want to wake Leboske but right now every minute counted, they all knew that.

The phone rang and rang and Jimmy kept looking at the clock, then Lester, then back to the clock. It seemed like it took a very long time before Leboske picked up the phone.

"Commander this is Jimmy McBain," he didn't give Leboske a chance to even speak, "this is an emergency, sir, sorry for calling you so early, but we can't afford to waste time."

"Alright" Leboske managed to say as he sat down on a chair at his desk in his underwear.

"We found the girls, sir, but . . . they were taken away on a large yacht. Some of the yacht's crew are hurt and we think they will need medical attention."

Leboske interrupted" Where, Jimmy, where were the girls?"

"Three cove island sir, at a small resort called Cantelle Bay. The kidnappers were able to escape with the girls and we fear they will be long gone if we don't find them right away."

"What's the yachts name?"

"We don't know, all I do know is that it is based in Antigua and the owner is a Russian drug dealer, named Tigran."

"Russian drug dealer, from Antigua?"

"Right sir."

"That's not much Jimmy."

"I know sir, but it's all I have. The girls are alive, we found them, we had them . . ." his voice dropped as he thought about how close he had been to saving them tonight, "but not anymore. Can you help us?"

"Sure I can help, just not sure what I can do with a yacht from Antigua owned by a Russian drug dealer. If they're in American waters, and we can identify them, then maybe I can do something, but once they're in international waters, Jimmy, I'll need a damn good reason to stop and board them."

"I understand, sir, and thank you, we'll be back in St. Thomas as soon as possible and we'll call you then."

"Alright, Jimmy."

Jimmy hung the phone up and looked around the room at Lester, Flip, and Hobbs.

"He didn't sound too promising."

"Call the cops." Flip said.

"Good idea," Jimmy replied as he looked at the piece of paper before him and dialed Detective Klein's number.

A minute later an upset detective answered the phone, his voice mumbled, his mind numb with sleep.

"What?"

"Detective Klein, Jimmy McBain here, sir, sorry to call you at this hour but we found the girls and we need your help."

"Why do you need my help if you found them?"

"Because we fucked up . . . but that's not the point."

"McBain, this had better not be bullshit."

"It's not. We had the girls but we were taken by surprise and just now escaped from a prison cell. The girls are on a yacht and they are heading somewhere, we just don't know where," Jimmy said suddenly realizing that he wasn't making that much sense.

"What's the . . ."

"We don't know the yachts name, but it is based in Antigua, owned by a Russian drug dealer named Tigran."

"That's all you have?"

"Sorry sir, but it is. But please understand we had the girls, we held them, they are alive and now they are on that yacht."

"Jesus, McBain!"

"I know, detective we need your help. You told me that you and Ochee believed me, well believe this. Lester is right here if you want to talk to him."

"Christ Jimmy, I need coffee before I can even think."

"There's no time for coffee. We need to find that yacht before it gets in international waters!"

Klein was surprised by Jimmy's statement.

"So you understand that, Jimmy?" he asked.

"Yes I do, once that yacht is in international waters there's not much we can do . . . right?" Jimmy hung his question out there.

Detective Klein was silent for a moment that felt like hours with Jimmy about to explode, finally Klein said, "lets just hope they're close, McBain. I'll call Ochee, we're on it."

The phone went dead and Jimmy hung up, then he looked around the room and said, "we'd better find that yacht soon. If it gets in international waters we are screwed."

Chapter 53

Laurie woke slowly her mind reluctant to leave her drug induced coma behind. She rolled over, looked around her small cabin, then sat up on her bunk. Something didn't feel right but her foggy mind couldn't quite figure out what was wrong. Dragging her feet off the bed, she stood up then had to sit back down on her bunk before she fell down.

What was going on, she thought as she looked around her room. Something was wrong, then she realized Bela Bela wasn't moving, and that could mean only one thing, the yacht had to be tied up to a dock. If they were still at anchor no matter how calm the seas, there would be some motion to the boat. Still too confused to do much more than sit up she forced her mind back to last night and with a sickening feeling thought about the drink Tigran forced on her and the Captain. Then it suddenly dawned on her that she was still wearing her uniform, she had slept in it and that was something she would never do. With a sickening feeling she realized that there was only one answer that made any sense, Tigran had drugged her last night.

She forced herself up and walked to her small bathroom, ran the sink for thirty seconds then cupped her hands and brought cold water to her face. It did little to help her racing mind. She reached down and cupped her hands and rinsed her face again then looked at herself in the mirror. What about the Captain, she thought, was he part of this? She hoped not, he was the only person on Bela Bela she liked.

If she had been drugged last night, why, she asked herself? She hadn't been sexually abused, that was obvious so what could have happened?

She ran a brush through her hair a few times, quickly brushed her teeth and walked out of her little cabin, up three steps and down a short hallway before entering the main salon. She stood there looking out a big window, staring at a dock and it took her only a moment to realize they were at Royal Bay Marina, in St Thomas. How the hell could they be here, she wondered?

Standing there she suddenly noticed that Bela Bela was empty, nobody was around, a haunting silence filled the huge yacht and she shuddered, a feeling of doom and then panic filled her heart. She wanted to turn and race off the yacht but she didn't. Fighting her panic she walked up the stairs to the pilothouse hoping to see the Captain but he wasn't there. Nobody was onboard. With that sense of foreboding still racing through her mind and getting stronger each second that she stood there she became almost frozen in place, her body incapable of moving, her mind still numb, trying to finds answers that made sense. Fear finally forced her to move, she had to get off Bela Bela as fast as she could that was all she knew at the moment. Forget trying to find anybody she told herself, forget that there might be some logical explanation, forget everything but self preservation and get off this yacht, her mind screamed at her.

Quickly she retraced her steps back to her cabin and opened her small suitcase which had some clothes, her passport and not much else in it. She threw in some makeup, a few books and a few pictures and was walking out her cabin door a minute later. Once again in the salon she stopped long enough to look around. It was the silence she realized that scared her, that made everything so out of place, the silence turned Bela Bela into a grave, it was time to leave and never look back. She walked twenty more feet, slid the large glass door opened that led to the stern of the boat, walked down two steps past the hot tub and the large inflatable dinghy, then threw her bag onto the dock. She was glad she was wearing tennis shoes as she took a small leap and landed on the dock next to her bag.

She thought maybe one of the crew or Tigran or somebody would suddenly yell at her as she started up the dock but nobody appeared, only silence which made her walk even faster. The outside breakwater that Bela Bela was tied up to was a long finger of concrete forty feet wide and a hundred and ninety feet long. At the end of the breakwater was a small parking area and off to the right was a restaurant and bar. Laurie walked slowly forcing herself not to run, she was off the yacht, but somehow she knew she was still far from being safe.

As she reached the asphalt she was surprised to see a man walking around a row of tall shrubs from the parking lot and with a surge of fear she realized that he was looking right at her and heading her way. Laurie took a step to her right and started to pass him when he gently put his hand on her left shoulder, "excuse me," he said as he stopped and looked at her.

Laurie took two more steps fighting the urge to run, to flee from this stranger who must have something to do with Bela Bela and the nightmare that she was trying to escape.

"I'm Detective Klein, Virgin Islands Police Department, can you give me a minute?"

Laurie was too fearful to say anything. She just stood there like a deer in headlights and she didn't know what to do.

"Laurie, sorry but I watched you climb off of Bela Bela and that is the reason I'm here. I need five minutes of your time, that's all, just five minutes."

"Why?" she whispered, shocked at hearing her name.

"Let me buy you breakfast and I'll tell you why. You need to trust me, because I need your help."

Then he walked up to her, put his arm back on her shoulder and gently turned her towards Tickles Bar and Grill and she felt to numb, too helpless, to afraid not to follow and they started walking in an awkward silence. Laurie just felt more confused and more fearful with each step she took.

The restaurant was empty and soon Laurie was holding a cup of coffee sitting there looking at Detective Klein knowing that she was caught up in something that she definitely didn't want a damn thing to do with.

Klein smiled as he looked up from the menu.

"Might as well order breakfast, Laurie."

"You know my name," it wasn't a question just a surprised statement.

"Yes, we also know the boat you're on is owned by a Russian named Tigran and you left Antigua two days ago."

"What's going on?"

"That's what I want you to tell me."

"Tell you what? All I know is that last night we anchored off of an island at some little resort and this morning I wake up here in St Thomas with nobody aboard, nobody and that's way too weird for me."

"You didn't know you arrived in St. Thomas, how can that be?"

Laurie looked at him, not sure if she wanted to get anymore involved in this entire crazy situation. She knew she hadn't done anything wrong, and whatever was going on she didn't want a damn thing to do with it. Just keep quiet, let this cop buy you breakfast, find another boat, another job, and just get on with it, she thought, but she didn't.

"Last night something happened to me," she said, then paused trying to think of the best way to word her suspicions.

"What happened?"

"I think I was drugged."

"Why do you think that?"

"Well . . . because once we arrived at the resort and the Captain shut the boat down Tigran and his friend made us have a drink with them."

"Made you?"

"Well they didn't pour it down our throat, but Tigran insisted that the Captain and I sit down and have a drink. He poured us a glass of scotch and as soon as the Captain and I finished it . . . well the party was over and everybody got up and I headed to my cabin. I never even changed out of my uniform. I'd never do that, never. I passed out and didn't hear a thing until I woke up this morning in St. Thomas."

"Maybe you're just a heavy sleeper, or you can't handle your booze," Klein said but he knew that wasn't the case. It made perfect sense to him that Tigran drugged her if he was going to transfer the girls aboard last night.

Laurie laughed, "In my line of work being able to handle a drink or two is more important than being able to cook. Women who can't handle alcohol get taken advantage of real fast."

"You speak from experience?"

"Listen . . . I'm telling you what I think. Something happened last night and I don't really want to know what is going on. I'm off the boat and out of here. Alright? That's all that matters to me at this moment. I'm gone and Bela Bela is just a memory."

Detective Klein sat back in his seat, paused for a moment, then said, "Laurie I'd like to tell you what happened. Three young women, all about your age were sold into slavery last night. Sold to your boss, and we think they are still on Bela Bela somewhere. That's why you were drugged, so you wouldn't hear what was going on. But your boss's plans had a sudden change, a bit of unseen bad luck and they are at the hospital right now, but not for long.

"Laurie we are going to search the hell out of that yacht today, and if those girls are onboard we will find them, but until then, I need you on that boat to be our eyes and ears. Please listen to what I'm telling you and try to understand. I'm asking you to climb back on Bela Bela for us."

The fork fell from Laurie's hand as she stared at the detective not believing what he just asked of her. "Don't ask me that," she finally managed to say ". . . god you're freaking me out . . . please, please don't ask me to get back on that yacht!"

Chapter 54

"McBain, it's Commander Leboske, you awake son?"

Jimmy brushed some hair off of his face as he sat up on the small sofa in his living room. He glanced at the clock in the kitchen, it was a little after noon. Lester came stumbling out of the bedroom the call waking him from a troubled sleep.

"I'm here, did you find them?"

"We did. The yacht is called Bela Bela and it is in Royal Bay Marina right now."

Jimmy slumped back on the sofa relieved beyond words.

"Great, Commander, what now?" he glanced up at Lester and gave him a thumbs up sign as Lester sat down on the sofa next to him.

"The police have been contacted, a Detective Klein, I believe you remember him."

Jimmy stood up, too anxious to sit, his mind trying to focus on every word Leboske said, "he's a good guy, okay so now what? When do you search the boat?" Jimmy asked.

"Well . . . that's up to the police. They can probably come up with some reason to go through Bela Bela, so right now the Coast Guard is sitting back and letting them handle it."

"Commander, we need to get the girls off that yacht now. They must be so freaked out, can't you just send a bunch of Coast Guard guys and go through that yacht with a fine tooth comb?"

"Listen McBain, it's in the cop's hands and that's the right place to start, at least for now."

"What can I do?"

"Nothing just sit tight. I'll keep you posted."

"That's about the hardest thing you could ask of me right now . . . to sit and do nothing."

"Listen Jimmy, you found the girls, you made this happen and by the end of today I think you will be able to take the three of them out to the finest restaurant in St Thomas, just be patient, alright."

"Alright, but call me if you hear anything."

"Will do," and Leboske hung up.

Jimmy stopped his pacing and smiled at Lester, "let's get going, they found the boat it's at Royal Bay Marina and I'm not going to sit around here doing nothing."

*

As Tigran and Louis climbed out of the cab Detective Klein and his partner were sitting on a small bench ten feet from the beginning of the outer breakwater. Tigran paid the driver then they started walking across the parking area toward the breakwater and his yacht. Tigran and Louis were talking to each other and didn't even notice the detectives until they stood up and started walking next to them.

"Tigran," Detective Klein said and the Russian and Louis both stopped and looked at them, then glanced at each other, their conversation coming to an abrupt end.

"Who are you?" the Russian asked with no fear in his voice.

"Detective Klein and Detective Ochee," he didn't bother to extend his hand.

"What do you want?" Tigran asked.

"Just a few questions."

"I don't have the time," then Tigran started to walk away, followed by Louis.

"Oh I think you will find the time for this."

Tigran stopped, looked back at the two detectives then a slight smile appeared on his face.

"I don't have the time as I already said. I have a departure that I must keep. Sorry. If you have any other questions contact me through my lawyer. I'm sure he can be of help."

Then he turned and started walking away, his back to the cops, Louis again right beside him. He took five steps before Klein caught up with him, grabbed his right shoulder and spun him around, his face inches from the Russians.

"Listen asshole. I've got a swat team en route, with a warrant and we are going to tear your fucking yacht apart, so don't give me shit. You're a fucking drug dealing, perverted, son of a bitch, and today we'll find the girls on your piece of shit boat and when we do your ass is mine."

Tigran rotated his shoulder breaking Klein's grasp on his arm. He swung his arm back away from Klein, took a step away and spit his words out with such venom that Klein was taken back but he didn't show it.

"Arrest me if you want, but get out of my way. I've got lawyers that will eat you up, they will eat your little piss ass police department, and shit you out as garbage. Understand me, so fuck off detective whatever your name is?"

He turned once again and he and Louis headed for Bela Bela.

Klein stood for a moment watching them walk away, glanced at his partner, then reached into his pocket, whipped out his cell phone and called Boschulle's private number.

"Desmond, it's Klein, they are heading back to the yacht. I think they're going to be out of here before you can get that warrant. I'm thinking ten minutes and those engines will be running and in fifteen they'll be casting off the dock lines."

"Stall em," Desmond said not sounding very concerned.

"This guy is no fool."

"I don't know what to tell you. We have to go by the book, its out of my hands Frederick."

"Bullshit, that asshole is going to pull out of here, waving goodbye to us, and before we know it they will be in international waters and those girls are going to be gone."

"We don't even know if they are on board. I can't just rush out there and break the law."

"Desmond, you're a gutless pussy," Klein said then he hung up.

"Wow, what did you just say?" Ochee asked his mouth open as he looked at his partner.

"Fuck him, I've been wanting to tell him that for the last four years."

"Well you picked a hell of a time, now what?"

They both glanced down the breakwater to see Tigran and Louis reach the steps to Bela Bela and climb aboard.

"Call the Coast Guard" Ochee said.

Frederick grinned, shaking his head up and down, "good idea, damn why didn't I think of that?"

He punched Commander Leboske's number which he had programmed into his phone a few days ago, and had a short wait, before a woman with a pleasant voice answered the phone "United States Coast Guard Commander Leboske's office."

"Yes, this is detective Frederick Klein I think the commander will recognize my name. I need to speak to him, it's very urgent."

"One moment sir."

Klein knew there would be hell to pay for calling the Coast Guard and going outside the department but at the moment he didn't give a damn.

Twenty seconds later, "Commander Leboske here detective."

"Commander . . . good morning."

"What can I do for you?"

"A lot and real fast. I can't get a warrant and Bela Bela is about to depart from the marina. I think we have five minutes before she's gone."

"Jesus detective, you can't stop that yacht for probable cause or something?"

"Boschulle doesn't want to, so there's not much I can do. I can't run down the damn dock waving my pistol in the air and demand that they stay in port."

"You think I can? You think I can just stick my nose in a police matter. It's your baby, think of something, damn it."

"Listen Commander, that yacht is departing soon, the engines are running and I can't get my asshole of a boss to do a damn thing.

Call in your people. Do a safety check for god sakes something, just don't let that boat leave the dock."

"Christ almighty, Frederick."

"It's the shits, I know, I should have been able to handle this but I can't and only you can stop that boat now."

"Alright, I'll think of something."

"Commander . . ."

"What!"

"Make it fast."

Chapter 55

It took Jimmy and Lester thirty minutes to drive from Red Hook to Royal Bay Marina. That was a record. Jimmy had driven like a mad man, racing through the narrow mountain roads of St. Thomas, running stop signs and forcing three cars to come to a screeching halt or else there would have been a crash. As they finally pulled into the marina parking lot they could see the upper superstructure of a yacht in the distance, her hull and the breakwater itself hidden behind the large row of shrubs that lined the parking area.

"I hope that's her," Lester said.

"So do I."

Jimmy pulled into the nearest parking spot, a ten minute loading zone, turned the engine off, and slammed the emergency brake on. He had his door opened before the car had come to a complete stop.

Lester jumped out and they both started running. Racing around the last of the shrubs they could finally see the yacht and with a sense of relief that stopped them both in their tracks they could see two Coast Guard boats both with lights flashing tied up to it. On the dock a few people stood around while a woman and a man who was wearing a Captain's uniform sat on the wooden toe railing of the dock in the shade. A young man in a Coast Guard uniform stood in front of the yacht's boarding ladder holding a weapon in his hand.

"Thank God," Jimmy said as he looked at Lester.

"Let's find out what's happening," Lester said and they started walking at a fast pace toward the yacht.

Half way down the dock Jimmy recognized Tigran. The Russian was watching him, and Jimmy had the almost uncontrollable urge to run up and continue beating the hell out of him but he didn't, instead he and Lester walked to the boarding ladder and stopped in front of a young man wearing a Coast Guard uniform.

"There's no one allowed on board, sir," the young man said, his weapon held firmly in front of him.

"What's going on?" Lester asked, trying to keep his excitement under control.

"That I don't know, sir."

Jimmy looked at Tigran and saw Louis standing a few feet away from him. Two other men stood close by and he realized that he had seen one of them before. Briefly, last night when he came out of the darkness with a shotgun pointed at him and the girls. Tigran continued to stare at him, the others standing around looking over the water or glancing nervously around the marina. The Russian mocked Jimmy with his eyes and that little smile of his. Jimmy couldn't stand it and he walked up to him, "I want the girls," he said his face inches away from Tigran's.

"What? . . . Girls. I'm sorry, try the whore house in town, for girls," the Russian replied and Jimmy knew he was enjoying taunting him.

"You asshole," Jimmy said his anger growing, as his self-control faded away.

"Enjoy this, we will be departing soon. That I guarantee."

McBain brought his face even closer to the Russians, his eyes inches from the dark sinister eyes of Tigran.

"No way in hell. We know all about Cantelle Bay, Frankie Balero and the girls. You are going down you drug dealing piece of shit."

Tigran smiled even deeper, then puffed out a short laugh that pushed Jimmy over the edge. Jimmy grabbed the Russian's shirt and without even thinking closed his right hand into a fist.

"Jimmy," Lester yelled out, as he had been watching the two of them.

Jimmy pushed Tigran away from him then turned and walked back to stand next to Lester.

"That asshole," Jimmy said before he heard, "McBain, Lester," from above them.

They looked up and saw Commander Leboske standing on the upper deck, "come on up," Leboske shouted, then he looked at the guard standing at the boarding ladder.

"Let those two on board."

"Yes sir," he replied, as he stood aside making room for Jimmy and Lester to walk past him.

Lester and Jimmy climbed aboard, stood on the back deck for a few moments before Commander Leboske came walking through the open sliding door that lead into the interior of the yacht.

Behind Leboske they caught a brief glimpse of two uniformed Coast Guard men walking down the steps that led from the pilothouse and then they disappeared down the hallway.

"Follow me," Leboske said and they walked into the main salon.

Jimmy looked around and he couldn't believe how rich everything looked.

"Sit down," Leboske said as he waved his left hand at the sofa, then he sat down on a small chair across from them.

"I've got five men going through this yacht, we've been here for fifteen minutes and we haven't found a thing."

"What?" Jimmy exclaimed.

"Nothing Jimmy, not one sign of the girls."

"They have to be here."

"Why?" Leboske asked.

"Because. This is the yacht that was anchored last night at Cantelle Bay. We watched them take the girls out in a dinghy, they have to be here."

"Just because you think they have to be here doesn't make much difference if we can't find them. They could have dropped them off somewhere last night before they came in."

"Can't you get more men to search," Lester asked.

"Why, how many do I need to go through this yacht? We start at the front and work our way to the stern, if they are onboard you'd think we'd find them, wouldn't you?"

"Commander," Lester said, "can you get some dogs, there could be a lot of hiding places on a yacht this size."

"Well, Lester, I thought about that. I'd have to fly them in from Puerto Rico and right now I'd have a hard time justifying that."

"This man is a known drug dealer. There could be enough drugs on board to make it justifiable," Jimmy said hopefully.

"Maybe. But suppose there isn't. This guy is no dummy. I doubt he would come into U.S waters to kidnap three women and have drugs onboard," Leboske replied.

"Maybe he would," Jimmy said hoping against hope.

"Listen, guys like this don't run drugs on their private yachts, way to risky. They have freighters, or planes, or small boats for that," the commander said, his voice soft, almost sad.

"How long can you keep him here?" Lester asked and Jimmy was shocked at the question.

"You might let him go Commander?"

"Listen McBain, I'm not done searching this boat. We can keep it going for hours. I'm calling it a safety check. Believe it or not we found that this guy's flares have expired. So that gives us more reason to search this boat, but I can't keep him here forever."

"How long sir?" Jimmy asked.

"I don't know it's a little after one now," he said looking at his watch, "I guess a few more hours at least."

"Only a few hours," Jimmy couldn't believe it as he felt the girls once again slipping through his hands.

"If the girls are here we'll find them. If they're not then this yacht will have had one of the most extensive safety checks I've ever been involved in. That's about it."

"Can we help search?" Lester asked as he looked around, feeling Jimmy's hopelessness.

"Sorry," Leboske replied as he stood up, "but I'm going to have to ask you two to get off the boat now."

Chapter 56

Jimmy and Lester sat on the small bench at the head of the breakwater. They'd been sitting there for over two hours, watching Bela Bela and any sign that the girls had been found.

"Suppose they did transfer them last night before they arrived," Jimmy asked Lester thinking about Leboske's earlier comment.

"It's a possibility, but let's think it through. They didn't expect us last night. I doubt they were planning on leaving Three Cove Island until this morning and I doubt they were going to head to St. Thomas. No. I think we wrecked their plans and they needed medical attention bad enough that they had to come here. I just can't understand how they could hide the girls so good."

"It's a big boat."

"Yeah I know."

A car suddenly pulled up a few parking stalls away from the walkway to the breakwater and Detective Klein stepped out. He had a surprised look on his face when he glanced up from locking the door and saw Lester and Jimmy.

"Just who I wanted to see," he said as he walked up to them and sat down on another bench across from them.

"Where are things at?" he asked as he looked down the breakwater to Bela Bela.

"Not sure. We talked to Commander Leboske a couple of hours ago. He was just starting to search the boat."

"That's not good."

"I know," Jimmy said, looking at Klein, "you'd think they'd have found them by now."

"If they are on board," Lester interjected, thinking that maybe they had overlooked something very important.

"Well I've got bad news, once the Coast Guard started searching Bela Bela, Boschulle cancelled the warrant."

"Why?" Jimmy asked.

"Because he doesn't want to get his hands dirty, the asshole. He told me to let the Coasties do it and if they couldn't find anything then neither could his people."

"Shit," Lester said realizing more and more that this search could prove futile and Bela Bela would sail away and there was nothing they could do to stop her.

"Where's Detective Ochee?" Jimmy asked.

"He's working on something back at the station. If anything comes up he'll call me."

An unwelcome silence settled upon them, each lost in their fearful thoughts, each struggling with what to do next. Jimmy was stunned thinking that Bela Bela was soon going to be allowed to depart and there wasn't anything he could do about it. His mind started running away as he sat there staring down the breakwater studying the yacht. What could he do if they didn't find the girls? He didn't give a shit about the law any more, he didn't worry about somebody's rights, he was way past worrying about right or wrong. There was only one thing that mattered right now, and that was Bela Bela could not sail away. If she departed and the girls were on board they would be lost forever. Yet how could he stop her? If the Coast Guard couldn't find the girls then there was no legal reason to keep the yacht from departing. Nothing that Leboske could do could keep her from casting off her dock lines and heading out. Panic started to race through him as he sat there, knowing that there had to be something. He had a thought just for a fleeting moment before he discarded it about walking up to Tigran and slamming his right hand into his throat, which would kill him on the spot. At least the boat wouldn't go anywhere, but he would, probably to prison for a long time and that wouldn't help the girls.

"See the lady sitting down next to the Captain?" Detective Klein said breaking the silence and bringing Jimmy back to the moment.

"Yeah," Jimmy and Lester replied at the same time.

"I had a long talk with her this morning. Her name is Laurie. I told her what's going on."

"What'd she say?" Lester asked.

"She was leaving the boat, had her bags packed when we talked. She had had enough of Bela Bela."

"Well she's there now so what does that mean?" Jimmy asked bringing his gaze from the crowd around the yacht back to Klein.

"Well what that means is we have somebody on board who we can trust. I have no idea what we do with that but I just wanted you to know she's on our side."

"What about the Captain?" Lester asked not taking his eyes away from the group of people down the dock.

"I don't know, I didn't talk to him. But Laurie told me she thought that they drugged both of them last night."

"Drugged them?" Jimmy asked.

"Right, which makes sense if they were transferring the girls onboard and they don't want any crew to know what's happening," the detective said.

"So we don't know if the Captain is aware of what's going on or not," Lester said, trying to find anything or anyone that he could possibly use.

"It's unknown. Although Ochee did some checking on him this morning and he seems good. Been a Captain on yachts down here for the last eight years, never had any trouble. He's only worked for the Russian for two years. So I'd guess he's not involved."

"I hate guessing," Lester said looking at Klein.

"Me too but it's all we got."

*

It was after four when Commander Leboske walked up the breakwater and sat down next to Jimmy and Lester, Detective Klein had left a half hour earlier. The two Coast Guard boats were pulling away from the dock and Tigran and company were now back on board Bela Bela. The look on Leboske's face told Jimmy and Lester everything they needed to know and feared about the outcome of the search.

"Sorry, guys, but they are not on board."

"Oh God," Lester moaned and Jimmy slumped back on the bench feeling defeated and beaten down so low that he didn't know what to think.

"I know they are on board," Jimmy finally said a minute later.

"We can't find them," Leboske replied feeling as bad as Lester and Jimmy.

"So now what Commander?" Lester asked "does Bela Bela just sail away into the sunset?"

"Basically yes, although not as quickly as she would like. We found a violation that needs to be fixed before she can depart. It seems there's a lot of oil under her port engine, it's in the bilge and that has to be properly taken care of."

"What does properly taken care of mean?" Lester asked.

"Well, probably they would just pump it overboard once they were at sea and nobody would be able to do a thing. But I wrote it up so it has to be removed before they can depart, and only a licensed and bonded hazardous removal company can legally do it."

"You're kidding, just to remove some oil from a bilge," Jimmy asked dumfounded.

"It can buy us some time," Lester said softly, then continued, "if we can think of what to do with it."

Leboske ignored Lester's remark, "the law's written for supertankers and freighters. One of those baby's could dump thousands of gallons of contaminated bilge water into the ocean. So . . . I took a few liberties and wrote them up but I don't think that will keep them here for long."

"Why not?" Lester asked.

"Because Tigran was already on the phone with a company in St. Thomas that does that kind of work and I think he'll throw enough money at them that they will stop whatever they are doing and get their asses out here as soon as possible."

"How many companies in St Thomas are licensed to do the removal," Lester asked his mind running fast.

"Two on St. Thomas, why?"

"The longer we can stall, and keep that boat from leaving the better our chances are of doing something," Lester replied.

"Something, like what? I already told you the girls are not on that yacht," Leboske said, somewhat irritated that they refused to accept the outcome of his search.

"I don't know, I just don't want that yacht to sail away," Lester said but his thoughts were already racing in another direction.

"Okay. So what do we do?" the Commander asked, knowing that Lester was working on something.

"Can you contact the two company's? Ask them to stall as long as possible. Maybe they could wait until tomorrow to do the job?"

Leboske thought for a minute, "I can't. It's not something I can do legally and I've stretched this investigation as far as I dare, but call Detective Klein he might be able to convince them to take their time."

Jimmy was about to say that was a good idea when he suddenly saw the captain climb off Bela Bela and start walking up the dock carrying a small daypack. Leboske and Lester followed Jimmy's gaze down the breakwater.

"I wonder what's up?" Lester said, not looking at Jimmy or Leboske.

"We'll it looks like we will soon find out," Leboske replied, as the captain continued walking toward them. When the captain reached them he stopped, dropped his bag and sat down on the bench next to Jimmy and Lester. He exhaled a deep breath, ran his fingers through his hair then looked at the three men sitting around him, "that asshole," he said then for some reason looked right at Lester, "that asshole told me he was going to take the yacht back to Antigua and for me to get a hotel and fly back tomorrow. What a bunch of shit."

"Why would he do that?" Lester asked looking at him but he had a feeling he already knew.

"Hell if I know, because he's an asshole," the pissed off captain said.

"What about Laurie?" Jimmy asked.

"They need her. She's the cook for god sakes, those helpless bastards couldn't make a peanut butter and jelly sandwich if they had to."

Jimmy looked at Lester, and somehow they both suddenly understood, the girls were on board, the captain was not part of the plan, and they had to do something fast.

Chapter 57

"Just try to stall them, that's all I ask. I just need a few hours," Jimmy said holding the phone in one hand his other waving in the air as he tried to explain to Detective Klein why he needed him to call the hazardous materials company.

"Listen, McBain, there's not much more we can do here. The Coasties are gone, the yacht is clean and as soon as some oil gets pumped from her bilge Bela Bela's going to be gone, that's about it."

"Just call them. There are only two companies in St. Thomas that can do that kind of work. You can find out which one Tigran hired and just ask them to take their time, tell them its important police business, hell, I don't know. I just need a few hours."

Jimmy could hear the exasperation in Klein's voice, "alright I'll call them."

"Thanks," Jimmy closed the cell phone and looked at Lester, Leboske was already gone.

"I've got to stop by a friends dive shop, let's go," Jimmy said.

As they walked to the car Lester asked him, "what are you thinking?"

"That we can't let Bela Bela leave the dock."

"Well we know that, so how can we stop her?"

"We can't."

"Am I missing something here?" Lester said as he closed the car door behind him and Jimmy pulled out of the parking space.

"Lester my brain is going a thousand miles an hour, and it's mostly all blanks. I don't know how to stop that yacht but I do know that if it does leave I'm going to be onboard."

"How are you going to do that?"

"I have a plan."

"I bet you do."

*

Tigran paced inside the pilothouse. He was impatient, he needed to get out of St Thomas and he had to get to the girls immediately. They'd been out hours longer than he had anticipated and he feared that permanent brain damage could have occurred, maybe they were already dead. He had never kept anybody unconscious for so long. But he couldn't do a thing while Bela Bela was still tied up on the breakwater. Not with the people coming aboard to remove the oil. No. He couldn't do a damn thing, not yet. Once they departed St. Thomas and if the girls were alright he would move them to the large forward master stateroom and lock the hallway door that led to them. He'd probably post Vonderick at the door to make damn sure that Laurie never got close, but if she did, and she found out they were on board well . . . she just might have an accident, like falling overboard, things like that happen aboard yachts he knew.

It was now five-thirty, the last time he had called United Alliance they told him that a pump out boat with a thousand gallon capacity holding tank would be leaving Crown Marina by five and it was a short two miles to Royal Bay Marina. It easily should have arrived by now, and somewhere in the back of his mind he feared that games were being played. He'd wait another fifteen minutes, that's all then he'd leave . . . to hell with them.

*

Blue Water Divers was only three miles from Royal Bay Marina and Jimmy had already called his buddy and told him that he was coming and what he needed. Hopefully, Jimmy thought, they had everything in the warehouse. Jimmy drove his car into the parking area and hit the brakes hard causing gravel, dirt and dust to fly. He jumped out of the car followed by Lester and they rushed inside the dive shop.

"Nobody's here," Lester said looking around.

"Yeah, they had to leave. I told them I'd lock up when I left."

"They must be good friends."

Jimmy looked at Lester as he headed through swinging doors that led into the back warehouse away from the retail store.

"They're good people we've been friends for a while. Lester, wait here for me, I'm going too fast to talk and I know what I need, just wait, alright," then the swinging door closed shut and Jimmy disappeared.

Lester sat down and looked around the shop, grabbed a magazine but he didn't read it, he just held it in his hand wondering what the hell Jimmy was thinking. A minute later Jimmy came out carrying a small surfboard and he had a wet suit over his shoulder. He put the board on the floor, threw the suit on top of it then turned and walked back through the door. Lester could hear him rummaging around, and a minute later the door opened again and Jimmy was dragging a huge coil of black rope. The coils were so long that as he walked out of the front door of the dive shop large loops of rope were still piled on the floor inside the store.

"Let's go, Lester," Jimmy said.

Lester jumped up, grabbed the dragging coils and keeping the door opened with his other hand, helped Jimmy get the rest of the rope outside before he followed Jimmy out into the parking lot.

"I want to stretch this rope out," Jimmy said as he dropped the coil of rope and knelt down digging through it until he found one of the ends. Then he stood up and walked to the last car that was parked in the lot.

"Start unfolding it Lester, I need it to run free," Jimmy said as he tied the end he had just found to the cars bumper. He stepped back and tied a small loop about ten inches long in the rope then another about two feet away. Lester dragged the huge coil of rope, paying it out as he went until he reached the end of the parking lot and he still had a huge amount left.

"What do you want me to do now?"

Jimmy turned, stopped tying a loop and said, "wrap the rope

around the tree then start dragging it back toward me. We need it completely stretched out."

"How long is this thing?"

"I'm not sure, but it's at least a couple hundred feet. I told him I needed the longest black line he had."

"Why black?"

"Lester I don't have time, just unfold the rope, please."

"Right, sorry."

The rope was so long that it reached back across the parking lot to the car that Jimmy had used to tie off the fixed end of the rope and Lester pulled the remaining rope through the first loop and then continued unwinding coil after coil trying to untangle the mess as he went. By the time he reached the end he was just a few feet short of the tree that he had taken the first wrap around. The rope was almost four times as long as the parking area. Jimmy was still tying loops as fast as he could, concentrating, making each knot the correct one.

"Want me to tie some loops Jimmy?"

"Yeah Lester, use a double bend, the loops can't come loose with that knot."

"Alright," even Lester knew a double bend knot.

Twenty minutes later the entire length of rope had loops every two feet.

"Lester, you load the rope in the car. I'll run back and lock up," Jimmy said as he headed toward the front door of the dive shop.

The rope was incredibly heavy and Lester guessed there was at least four hundred feet of it as he crammed the rope in the backseat. By the time he was finished Jimmy had locked the dive shop, and was carrying the surfboard, which Lester realized must be a boogie board because it was only about four feet long and the wet suit with him. He ran over to the car and threw them in the back seat.

"Get in Lester," Jimmy said as he raced for the driver's door and Lester climbed in feeling completely clueless at the moment.

Jimmy opened the driver's door, hopped in, started the car and spraying gravel headed out of the parking lot.

"What are you thinking, Jimmy?" Lester said once they hit the main road.

Jimmy looked over at Lester and shook his head slightly, "if I told you, you wouldn't believe it. We're almost there, just hang on, Lester."

It was dark when they pulled into Royal Bay Marina. Jimmy pulled behind Tickles Bar and the grocery store, and drove down to the end of the parking area near the fuel docks. He pulled into the last parking space nearest the water and turned the car off. Dock lights glared casting distant shadows, and they couldn't see Bela Bela from where they parked because the fuel dock and marina office blocked the view.

Once the engine was off and the car parked Jimmy turned and looked at Lester.

"Lester, here's my plan and I need your help. I'm putting this wetsuit on, then I'm going to tie one end of this rope to the leash holder on the boogie board. After that I'm going to swim through the marina with you feeding me the line as I go. Once I get near Bela Bela I'm somehow going to tie the other end of this pile of rope to her stern."

"Christ, Jimmy, you're going to be towed behind that thing. It'll pull you so fast you wont be able to even hang on."

"That's the reason for the loops. I can pull myself up the rope with them."

"Jimmy that boat will be going twenty miles an hour a couple of minutes after it leaves the marina, nobody could pull themselves through the water at that speed."

Jimmy looked over at Lester and said softly, "Lester, I'll pull myself aboard . . . or I'll drown," then he stepped out of the car and started hauling out the coils of rope.

Chapter 58

Jimmy tucked his hair under the wet suit hood then pulled it tight over his head and smoothed out the bottom of it on his neck. He stretched to his left, rotating his hips and pushed his arms high over his shoulders trying to get the wet suit to fit right.

Lester hadn't said a word since Jimmy had stripped down to his shorts and started putting the suit on. This plan was crazy Lester knew but unfortunately he didn't have a better one, and so he didn't try to talk Jimmy out of it. Once the suit was snug and as comfortable as it was going to be Jimmy reached down grabbed the boogie board and a hand full of rope and walked to the edge of the fuel dock. He sat down on the rough concrete, the water three feet below him then he turned and looked at Lester.

"Feed me the rope once I start swimming. Try to keep it from tangling up."

"Jimmy . . . be careful," Lester said suddenly knowing that this could possibly be the last time he ever saw his friend.

"Lester, I'm going to get the girls. That's all there is to it," then he turned and lowered himself into the water. Lester walked to the edge and grabbed a handful of rope and threw a pile of it on top the boogie board. Jimmy started swimming away, pushing the board in front of him as Lester fed the long black rope into the water. Jimmy disappeared into the darkness before he reached the first row of boats tied up on the closest finger pier. Lester kept feeding rope until the end of it fell from his hand with a splash. The black rope disappeared and he felt a sudden surge of fear as he lost the last of his connection with Jimmy. God help you, Lester thought, standing there looking into the darkness.

Pushing the boogie board in front of him Jimmy reached the second dock which was completely full of boats. He continued kicking with his feet being careful trying not to make a sound as he pushed the board alongside a large sailboat. The lights were on inside and he could hear people laughing, and music playing. There was complete darkness on the water except for the few places where the dock lights shined a low glow. He kept himself in the shadows and started swimming toward the next dock. Royal Bay Marina had five docks each able to berth thirty boats, fifteen on each side, plus the outside breakwater. As he kicked his way toward Bela Bela the rope started getting tangled around his feet, making it almost impossible to swim. He tried a scissor kick but it didn't help, finally he stopped kicking and floated for a minute before he reached out and grabbed a loop of rope in his right hand. Holding the line as far away from himself as he could, he started once again toward the yacht.

Once past the fourth dock he turned to his left and started swimming toward the deep end of the breakwater. He could see Bela Bela now, lights casting strange shadows about the yacht. Reaching the last dock he swam alongside a large, dark powerboat and stopped. He hid in the darkness, treading water softly with his hands as he looked at the Bela Bela seventy feet in front of him tied to the inside of the breakwater. The water between him and Tigran's yacht was pure darkness.

Still treading water he started pulling the rope to him, trying to find the end. The more he pulled the more rope started to bunch around him and soon huge limp coils floated around his chest some sinking down toward his feet and he knew that in this darkness if he ever got tangled up it would be impossible to free himself. Finally he found the loose end. Holding the free end in his left hand he swam around a concrete piling pushing the boogie board ahead of him and then tied a fast knot securing the board to the piling. Then still holding the free end he kicked off and started toward Bela Bela, the black line snaking behind him through the dark water. He swam until he reached the yacht then swam down her long side until he was at the stern. Once there he treaded water, his head under the wide wooden stern platform that extended three feet out from the end of Bela Bela and ran the width of her hull. There was less than a foot of space for him to breathe and his head banged into the wood as he looked around trying to find something to tie the rope to. He couldn't see a thing in the darkness and the saltwater kept splashing in his eyes, burning them, and making it difficult to even keep them open. He ran his hands along the stern where the boarding platform was bolted to the hull. He couldn't find a thing to tie the rope to. Suddenly a deep rumble echoed through the water scaring the hell out of him and in the next second a surge of water exploded out of the starboard exhaust vent. Then another rumble and the port engine started shooting a stream of steam and exhaust water out of the port engine thru hull. The stream was only a foot from his head. Exhaust fumes hung under the transom and started to choke him. Bela Bela was leaving and he had to find a way to tie this rope off now. He looked down and saw the two large three bladed propellers with their tips about three feet underneath him. If they engaged the engines right now he'd be sucked under and chopped like he was going through a vegamatic. Frantically he took a breath, and swam under water trying to feel anything to tie the rope to. He came up gasping for air, choking on fumes, the rope still in his hand and suddenly he heard a voice on Bela Bela. The man was talking in a strange language, Russian he guessed, and he was walking to the stern of the boat. Jimmy froze, exhaust fumes suffocating him as the footsteps grew closer. Jimmy reached up and grabbed the slot between the teak boards that made up the stern platform and stopped kicking. The footsteps were right over him and he suddenly saw to his right one of the huge fenders that protected the hull being pulled out of the water. He heard the man say something, then the fender was dropped on the deck and the footsteps started walking away.

Jimmy looked around. He had to tie this line off now, he had to leave, those props were going to start spinning and he couldn't be here when they did.

He released his grasp of the teak boarding platform, reached out to the end and ran the rope through the second to the last gap between the boards. He pulled the loop through then ran the rope back underwater and tied the loops together with a bowline knot. The instant the knot was tied he pushed himself away from the stern of Bela Bela and started swimming away from her with all of his strength, heading for the dock and the boogie board. He could hear voices now on Bela Bela and suddenly he felt the deep vibrations of propellers slowly spinning underwater. He glanced back over his shoulder as Bela Bela started pulling away from the dock. He swam as fast as he could, every second counting, he had to untie the boogie board before the rope was stretched tight. If he didn't something would break, either the rope or the boarding platform would rip apart but he knew before that happened Bela Bela's stern would swing wide when the rope was pulled tight and whoever was at the helm would instantly know something was wrong.

Jimmy reached the boogie board and started untying his knot as fast as he could. The black line was whipping through the water behind him. His fingers felt frozen, unable to accomplish the simple task of untying a knot. He fumbled with the knot and finally he managed to pull it loose. Seconds later the boogie board flew around the concrete piling slamming into his rib cage and he barely had time to grab it before he was being pulled through the darkness. Kicking as hard as he could he stretched himself and grabbed the board with his right hand. Slowly he pulled himself up until he was laying on the board. He tried to balance himself, knowing that if he put his weight too far forward the nose of the board would dip into the water and he would flip over. His feet trailed behind him bouncing over the water as Bela Bela reached the end of the breakwater and he could feel her surge faster as whoever was driving increased the throttle. Jimmy was hanging on for his life, terrified that the front of his board would hit a wave, flip over and throw him off. As the lights of Royal Bay Marina started to dim in the distance Jimmy look a quick look behind him and he was scared to death.

Chapter 59

By the time Bela Bela left Royal Bay Marina Vonderick had already moved the anchor chain and opened the small hatch that led to the starboard anchor locker. One small light cast shadows in the room as he looked at the girls who were unconscious, each of them looking like pale angels. He hoped they were alright. He brought his ear down to each of them listening to their breathing and he felt the pulse of one of the blondes. It was steady, slow but steady.

Reaching behind him to his right he opened a small drawer, only three inches deep, eight inches wide that came out of the side of the hull and lifted the top up until the long arm of the hinge locked in place. He pulled out a small vial only an inch high then stuck a hypodermic needle into it and drew out the amount Tigran had told him to use. He jabbed the needle into one of the blonde's forearm veins, injected her then stuck the needle back into the vial and pulled out another dose. He gave all three of the girls the same amount before he closed the lid of the drawer after replacing the syringe and then stood there looking at them. In a few minutes hopefully they would start to stir. In five minutes they would be awake and semi-coherent. In fifteen minutes he would have them in the forward stateroom, locked up good and tight, he hoped.

*

The boogie board bounced like a rodeo bull and Jimmy knew it was only going to get worse the faster Bela Bela went. His hands kept slipping as waves poured over him, the water tugging at his body trying to tear him off the board. He had to arch his back up just to keep his head out of the waves and be able to breathe. They hadn't even reached the first buoy at Shipwreck Rocks yet and once past that reef it was open ocean, and the waves would be a lot bigger. The yacht would very soon start going faster and he could hardly hang on now.

Jimmy pulled himself higher on the board, feeling the front of it start to dip, only to find the first loop was further away than he had planned. Damn, he thought. He was afraid to reach for it but he knew he had no choice. Keeping his body arched trying to keep the weight behind him he slowly reached out, stretched his right arm as far as possible and finally he was able to grab the first loop. He ran his hand inside then rotated his wrist locking the loop around him. Laying there on the boogie board, water flying all around him he knew it was time to jump off this board and start pulling himself toward Bela Bela if he could.

The waves were now getting bigger and further apart, there started to become small valleys between the surging troughs where the board would surf down the front of the wave taking the strain off of the line and his arm. He waited until a large wave rolled over him and the board started to surf then he lunged to his right kicking the board away with his left foot. Instantly the water pressure grabbed at him, trying to pull his arm from his body as the next wave rolled over his head. He pulled with everything he had, every ounce of his strength. The water flew in his face, a rooster tail shooting over his head as he was pulled through the waves. He could no longer use the board to arch his back and he couldn't raise his head high enough to get a breath. Fighting with everything he had he reached for the second loop and managed to grab it, then the third. Still he couldn't get his head high enough to get out of the water and take a breath. His lungs were exploding, and soon he knew his body would force him to breathe regardless, and if he had any water in his face he would drown.

In a last frantic effort he brought his legs up tight against his chest then felt with his toes until he found the first loop and he kicked his right foot into it and then stretched his leg out. Suddenly his face came out of the water and he took a long precious breath. He rolled on his back his weight on his foot, his face finally clear of the rushing water. Clinging there in the darkness he had a sudden uncomfortable feeling about sharks. It was as if Bela Bela was trolling and he was the bait, and he couldn't get Tommy's screams from his mind. Forcing those thoughts away he reached out and grabbed another loop then kicking his foot free he pulled himself further up the rope. Every time he did this he panicked as he tried to lock his right foot back into a loop. Wave after wave rolled over him as he slowly, painfully pulled himself until he reached the boarding platform on Bela Bela's stern. Releasing the last loop he grabbed the teak board with his right hand then reached out and grabbed it with his left and with a desperate kick he pulled himself aboard.

*

Laurie was in the galley making a quick meal of pasta and frozen chicken. She hadn't seen Tigran or the two crewmen since they pulled out of the marina but Louis had been pestering her ever since they left. The yacht wasn't even out of the marina and already he had started demanding dinner. What an asshole, she thought.

Right now he lay on the sofa in the main salon with the music blasting, his right arm in a cast that ran up to his shoulder. He kept smiling at her whenever their eyes met, a smile that really freaked her out. She hated him, she realized, he was worse than Tigran. The Russian scared her, there was something very sinister about him but somehow in some strange way she could sense a predictability about him, that the Russian operated on reason, even though it must be warped as hell, but Louis was just a spoiled rotten prissy asshole, flaunting himself at her like he turned her on or something. She felt like slugging him every time he looked at her.

She dumped the pasta in the boiling water, set the timer on the stove and leaned back against the counter. She had ten minutes before the pasta was ready and she was going to stay in the galley. It was the only place she even remotely felt safe.

Standing there wondering what the hell she had gotten herself into she started thinking about her conversation with the cop in the restaurant. White slavery... god she didn't think that happened. Yet as she thought about the last twenty four hours, she knew something was going on. She definitely had been drugged by Tigran, she had no doubt about that anymore. Waking up in St. Thomas, when last night they anchored at some little island miles away, how the hell did that happen without her knowing it? Then there was the Coast Guard, searching Bela Bela for hours, what was that about? The Captain being kicked off the boat and flying back to Antigua, that really scared her. There was no way she would even be onboard right now if she knew the Captain wasn't going to be here. There definitely was something really strange going on and she was scared to death.

Her palms started to sweat as she realized how dangerous her situation was. If Tigran was capable of doing what the detective told her, then he would have no problem hurting her, or even killing her, and somehow she just knew that was true. Suppose she stumbled on the girls, then what? Tigran would not leave any witnesses, she knew. As the pasta boiled away she knew once back in Antigua it was goodbye Bela Bela. That is if she made it that far.

Chapter 60

When dinner was ready she walked to the bottom of the stairs that led to the pilothouse and called to Tigran, "dinner, would you like it in the pilothouse or down here?"

"I'll be right down, just let me get the auto-pilot going," he said sticking his head around the corner.

Laurie figured wherever Tigran was eating the rest of the crew would eat as well. She set four placemats on the table each with a rubbery back so things wouldn't slide off in the boat's rough motion. Louis just smirked at her the whole time. She brought out four plates, set them on the mats, grabbed a bottle of red wine and put it in the wine holder in the center of the table. She heard footsteps behind her as both of the crew came from the forward area of the boat. They both gave her a little smirk as they sat down around the table and Louis finally pulled himself off of the sofa and sat down as well. Tigran came down a minute later from the pilothouse, pulled out a chair and sat.

"Won't you join us?" he asked Laurie.

"Oh, thanks anyway" she said hoping he would leave her alone, "I have a lot of clean up to do and I've already eaten."

She turned away before he could insist and hurried back to the galley. She started cleaning taking her time, there was no hurry, there was no place else she could go. Trapped in her little cubicle she started thinking about how crazy she was to be here. She never should have listened to that detective in St. Thomas. What could he do on this yacht as it sailed through the Caribbean night, if things turned to shit anyway she thought? How was she supposed to keep an eye out for three girls who according to the Coast Guard were not even on board, and what if she found them? Then what? She was stupid to be here, she knew it, she should have just kept going, told the detective to shove it, and right now she could be in some nice hotel laying by the pool with a pina colada in her hand. Now because of that cop she was still on Bela Bela with four creepy guys and not even the captain was onboard to help her out if she needed him. Damn, she sure screwed up she thought.

Dinner was finished before she had the galley cleaned. Everybody got up without saying a word to her, leaving the table a mess and disappeared. Even Louis was gone which was a blessing. She figured he had gone forward with the crew members. Tigran was probably back up in the pilothouse. Just as long as everybody left her alone she didn't care where they all went.

Her back was to the sliding glass door as she gathered plates and silverware. Just as she turned behind her to grab the last of the mats she saw the door slide open. She almost screamed and the plates started to slide from her hand but she caught them moments before they shattered on the table. Standing there was a man in his underwear, dripping wet, with a strange smile on his face holding his right index finger up to his lips. Laurie remembered seeing him earlier this afternoon talking to the Coast Guard. He reached behind him and gently slid the glass door closed.

"Laurie," Jimmy whispered as he moved from the sliding door to where she stood. He glanced down at his feet and saw he was leaving puddles behind him.

"Laurie don't freak out. Remember me, from this afternoon?"

She just stood there with her mouth open, her mind racing wondering if this night would ever end, and what the hell she should do.

"Listen, Laurie, I'm here to rescue the girls, I know they're here. I'll get you off too. I need a place to hide right now, help me please."

Laurie absentmindedly shook her head as if this was just a dream and she would snap out of it. Jimmy stood there dripping water knowing that in two seconds he was going to find a place to hide with or without her help.

"Follow me," she whispered as she turned and headed for her galley.

Jimmy silently walked behind her then stopped once inside the small galley. She put her arm full of dishes down in the stainless sink then turned and looked at him.

"Laurie, you need to wipe the water up from the floor."

"Right," she replied looking at the salon and seeing a trail of wet leading to the galley.

"Hide in here," she said as she opened a small door under the sink. Jimmy took one look and almost told her to forget it but instead he crouched down into the little space so he was somewhat hidden, except the door wouldn't close because his right knee was in the way leaving a three inch gap. It was the best he could do. Laurie grabbed a towel and disappeared from Jimmy's view. She came back a minute later and threw the wet towel in the sink.

Jimmy opened the door enough and he twisted his body so he could look up at her.

"Where do you think the girls are?"

"I don't have a clue . . . God. I don't know what you're going to do."

"I'm going to find the girls and get them off of this boat I think you should come with us."

"How?"

"There's a powerboat on the aft deck next to the jet ski's. We can all escape in it."

Laurie thought it through for a minute then knelt down and looked Jimmy in the eye.

"How can you get the boat in the water? Bela Bela would have to stop before you could use the hydraulic arm to lower it down."

Jimmy had been wondering the same thing. There was no way to put the speedboat in the water with Bela Bela doing twenty knots.

"I have a plan," he lied.

"Good . . . you'd better. They'll kill you if they find you aboard."

"Yeah, so I'll be careful. Where's Tigran?"

"He's up in the pilothouse."

"Where's the crew?"

"I think they're all forward."

"Alright."

"Now what?"

"I'm working on it."

"Well you can't stay here, that's for sure. Maybe I'll just pretend I never saw you, how's that?"

"Whatever," Jimmy said as he climbed out of his hiding place and looked around.

"Listen, Laurie, if things get out of control just hide in here," he pointed to the space he just climbed out of.

"This is insane," she said in a whisper.

Chapter 61

Jimmy put his ear to the closed door that led to the forward stateroom trying to hear above the noise of the engines and the slapping of the waves on the hull. He couldn't hear a thing. There was no way he could open the door without knowing what was behind it. Suppose the crew were all there, waiting, then what? Carefully he walked back to the galley and found Laurie leaning against the small counter, her face ashen, and he knew this was all too much for her to handle. Which made it that much harder for him because he needed her now.

"Laurie, I need you to open the hallway door."

"What?" she whispered snapping back from her deep thoughts.

"You need to open the door for me."

"No way, I'm not involved in any of this James Bond shit!"

"Listen I can't do it without your help. Make up some excuse, bring them some cookies. I just need to know what is on the other side of that door."

"Oh God, you could get me killed."

"Laurie, listen, three women that I love are going to disappear forever if I don't get them off of this boat right now. Do you understand me? They might as well be dead because the life that they will have to live won't be worth living if I don't rescue them. I need you, Laurie. Just tell me what is on the other side of the damn door."

"Shit," she whispered then grabbed a platter from an overhead cupboard, poured some cookies in it from a plastic bag and started for the door. She knocked once, then hearing nothing she opened the door just enough to stick her head around it and peek down an empty hallway. There was one closed door on her right and another on her left and each led to private cabins, Louis's was on the left. Fifteen feet in front of her was another closed door that led to the owner's master stateroom. Carefully she knocked on the door to her right. She waited a second then knocked again. She opened the door slightly, looked inside then closed the door behind her, nobody was in there.

She took three steps to her left and knocked on Louis's door. She heard movement then the door opened and Louis stood there. He was naked and when he saw her a big grin grew on his face.

Laurie forced herself to act nonchalant.

"My, what a treat," he whispered as he glanced at the tray of cookies then brought his eyes back to Laurie, "a little midnight snack," he said then blew her a kiss.

Laurie smiled, her mind racing not knowing how to play this, his body growing hard before her.

"Thought you might like a little something Louis, it seems I owe you a favor or two, don't you think?" she said softly almost gagging on the words trying to think if there was any way out of this mess that she just created.

"Oh my, darling, why don't you come here," he reached his hand out as he smiled at her.

"Well," she hesitated playing him along, "I have to get back to the galley. I left the stove on."

He reached out grabbed her and pulled her to him, forcing his lips on hers. There was nothing Laurie could do but return the kiss.

"Louis please, I'll be back in a minute."

"Laurie, I want you, you can see that."

She smiled as she looked at him, forcing herself to go through the motions while her mind screamed at her to turn and run.

"One minute, I have to turn the gas off," she whispered then stepped back away from the door and partially closed it, before she turned and hurried back to the galley.

"Louis is waiting for me in his cabin, the door on the left."

"Waiting for you?" Jimmy asked.

"Listen. He was standing there naked and I didn't know what to say . . . so he thinks I'm coming back and he thinks I'm all hot for him."

Jimmy smiled, "listen, I'll be right behind you. The moment he opens his door I'll take him out."

"I don't think I can go back in there, this is just too much."

"What else can you do? You know he's going to come looking for you if you don't show up."

"God how do I get into these things?"

Jimmy grabbed a heavy cast iron frying pan out of its holder then spun Laurie around so she was facing out of the galley.

"Let's go," he whispered pushing her in front of him.

Louis's door was open a few inches when Laurie reached it. She pushed it open a bit more then stuck her head inside. Louis was laying naked on the bed. He was too far away for Jimmy to do anything. She had to get him to the door, but how?

"Come here, Laurie, I've been wanting you for a long time."

"Louis, I think you need to come here."

"Why is that my love?" he said as he stood up.

Laurie smiled, trying to keep herself in the game, knowing that if he got suspicious both her and Jimmy would die tonight.

She leaned against the door jam and slowing started unbuttoning her blouse. Then she ran her hands down over her hips before she brought her hands up and held them out to Louis.

"Because I like it standing."

With two steps Louis was at the door, his arms reaching out to her as she took a step backward and he followed her out past the door. Jimmy swung the frying pan with all of his strength and smashed it into Louis's face. He never even saw it coming, he never uttered a word as the heavy skillet smashed him backward into his room, shattering his skull and he was dead before he hit the floor.

"Oh god," she uttered as she looked at him, blood pouring from his face, his nose pushed flat against his left cheek, a bloody froth oozing out from his lips, his head twisted back at an ungodly angle.

"Alright, now we find the crew. There's only two of them. Right?" Jimmy asked her but she didn't respond, she just stood shell shocked looking at Louis who stared at her with open eyes and a destroyed face.

Jimmy grabbed her shoulders and shook her, snapping Laurie back.

"Where are the crew?"

Laurie just pointed to the large wooden door in front of them.

"Alright, grab the cookies let's go," he whispered as he grabbed her by the shoulder, spun her around and pointed her to the master stateroom.

"I can't do this," she whispered, tears rolling down her face, she was close to hysterics, her breathing coming in great gasping gulps.

"Laurie, it's the crew then I stop this yacht and we are out of here."

Forcefully he pushed her forward, jarring her mind from its frozen state, and she took one hesitant step, glanced at Jimmy then turned and walked to the door. Jimmy reached down and flipped the lock button on the inside of Louis's door then closed it behind him. He followed her until they were at the master suite door.

Jimmy reached down and tried to turn the handle. It was locked.

He stepped to the left of the door and leaned against the wooden bulkhead. The door swung into the stateroom and he would have about one second to do this right or else.

"I can't," she whispered her blouse still undone.

"Listen Laurie we die or we live in the next two minutes. Button your blouse," then he reached over and knocked on the door. Jimmy could hear voices through the wall and suddenly the door opened. Laurie was suddenly all smiles as she held out the plate of cookies. He watched her expression as it turned to one of concern then fear, then panic, and suddenly an arm reached out from the open door and grabbed her wrist.

"Don't hurt her," Jimmy heard from inside and he knew it was Megan.

The arm started to pull Laurie into the room as Jimmy leaped from behind the bulkhead wall and pushed Laurie out of the way and slammed the frying pan under the chin of the unsuspecting crewman. His feet flew off the carpet and he didn't uttered a sound as he flew backward and crumpled into a heap on the floor. But in the next instant Vonderick was up off the bed charging Jimmy.

Jimmy spun inside the door but the frying pan was too heavy for him to swing back before the crewman was upon him. Vonderick slammed his right fist into Jimmy's stomach, then let his left fist fly catching Jimmy on the chin, but it did little to slow Jimmy down. Jimmy twisted to his left as his fist crashed into the Russian's kidney, dropping him to his knees. Jimmy's fist flew again, this time connecting under Vonderick's chin snapping his head back forcing his body up and away from Jimmy. Then with his left hand Jimmy grabbed the back of the Russian's head and jerked it down as he brought his knee up exploding Vonderick's face, sending him crashing back into the bed. The Russian gave a slight moan but didn't move. Jimmy charged, grabbed his shirt and pulled him off the bed, then slammed another right into his stomach before letting him drop to the floor like dead weight.

Vonderick landed with a thud crashing on his back. Jimmy waited, sensing that the fight was over, and he never should have done that, he should have finished it right then. The Russian rolled on his side, lay still for just a second then surprising everybody he jumped to his feet with a knife in his right hand. Jimmy couldn't believe how fast it all happened, the blade almost screaming as its sharpness cut the air in front of him. Jimmy moved but not fast enough and the blade caught his naked chest slicing a thin ribbon of blood open against his tan skin. Just as Vonderick tried to bring the blade back again Jimmy grabbed his knife hand and, holding tight with both hands, he kicked the Russian's feet out from underneath him, which sent him crashing to the floor. The moment Vonderick hit the cabin floor Jimmy used the leverage that he had from being on his feet to twist the blade around and push it through Vonderick's heart. The man gasped, tried to move but then his eyes rolled to the back of his head and he just lay there, blood pouring from the wound. Jimmy jumped to his feet, pushed Vonderick's body away and rushed to the girls.

One of the twins, he couldn't tell which at the moment, started to say something but he cupped his hand over her mouth then looked at all of them.

"Not a word. We're not out of here yet."

Chapter 62

With Jimmy leading the way holding the bloody knife that he pulled from Vonderick they reached the outside sliding glass door. Jimmy turned and looked at the four women whose lives depended on what he did in the next few minutes. He wanted so much to stop and hug them, to tell them it was going to be alright but he couldn't, not yet. They weren't off of Bela Bela and Tigran was one adversary that he would just as soon not tangle with. Just get off the boat kept echoing through his mind.

He slid the door opened and motioned for the girls to follow him outside, then he closed the door behind him.

"This way," he whispered as he headed for the speed boat.

"Jimmy," Megan whispered as she threw her arms around him.

He pushed her away, scaring her, "not until we are off this yacht," he whispered, his voice cold, unemotional.

"Listen we have to do this right. I can't get the speed boat into the water until Bela Bela is stopped."

"How are you going to stop this boat Jimmy?" one of the twins asked in a whisper.

He ignored her as he reached down and with Vonderick's knife cut the two wide strips of webbing that attached the speed boat to the deck.

"Once this yacht stops all you do is push this button," he said to Megan as he pointed to an inch wide red button on a small electric box mounted on the wall next to the hydraulic arm, "push the top one, it should raise this arm up," he said as he reached out and grabbed the arm that held the cables that were attached to the dinghy floor.

"Alright," Megan whispered.

"Raise the dingy high enough to clear the rail then push it overboard and hit the bottom button which will lower the boat until it hits the water. Once the boat is floating it will take the pressure off of these two hooks," he pointed to the two stainless steel hooks attached to the cable coming from the dinghy's floorboard.

"Unhook them but make sure the boat is tied off to Bela Bela, you can't start floating away yet. Not until we are all on board."

"Jimmy," Megan whispered, "please . . . be careful."

He ignored her.

"Just get the boat in the water, climb in, lower the engine and be ready."

"Alright," Megan whispered.

Jimmy's mind was racing, getting the powerboat in the water was only the first part of a plan that had to work flawlessly or else they could all end up dead tonight.

Even in the dim light Megan saw the fear and doubt on Jimmy's face as he stood there. She reached out put her arms around him and pulled him to her. In the next instant the twins and Laurie reached out and hugged Jimmy, the girls wrapping their arms around him, holding him tight, each one knowing he was their salvation. Jimmy was the Cavalry and nobody was going to get them off this damn yacht but him.

*

Tigran stood in the pilothouse looking at the radar screen feeling tired. The last twenty four hours had taken their toll. The auto pilot was on course and he had the GPS waypoints all pushed in. It was about time for one of the crew to take the helm. All they would have to do was watch and make sure no boats got in their way. He walked over to the captain's chair and sat down, putting his feet up on the instrument console. He made sure his foot didn't hit any switches then he glanced over and looked at the engine monitor screen which flashed pictures from four different cameras in the engine room. All looked good. He stretched out and closed his eyes, just for a second, he never dreamt he would fall asleep.

*

Slipping back inside Jimmy slid the glass door closed even though his first thought was to keep it open in case he needed to make a fast getaway. But he had to leave the boat exactly as he found it. Still holding Vonderick's knife, which he knew would do nothing against bullets, he walked to the main salon and stopped. The engine room had to be below deck. Turning to his right behind a large glass cubicle full of fishing reels and spear guns he saw a small stairway that led below. He walked over to it, stopped at the top and listened, then slowly he started down the stairs. After eight steps he landed on a small carpet and a hallway that led to a large watertight door.

Jimmy walked to the door and looked in through the small window. It was the generator room and on the right was a small workbench with lots of tools hanging above it and he saw another door leading out of the room and he figured that had to be the entrance to the engine room. He opened the door and walked into the generator room then closed the door behind him. The noise assaulted him, and as he opened the engine room door the noise was almost unbearable. The room was well lit and he thought that was strange but he put the thought out of his mind. The engine room was meticulously clean except for some oil underneath the port engine. Jimmy turned to his left and walked to a huge electric panel then looked at the ceiling and that was when he noticed the video camera high on the wall.

"Shit," he said under his breath and he knew he didn't have a second to spare.

Turning around looking at the engine nearest him he suddenly had a thought and he raced over to it and looked at the large external fuel filter mounted on the side of the engine. The glass dome was full of fuel with a little water separator on the bottom. Holding Vonderick's knife he twisted his wrist and slammed the back of the knife handle into the glass. It didn't break.

"Damn," he whispered as he turned and raced into the generator room and grabbed a large crescent wrench off the wall. He ran back inside the engine room and swung the wrench at the glass fuel filter and it shattered in a thousand pieces. He raced to the other engine smashing the glass filter on it then charged out the door. As he climbed up the stairs to the main salon he knew that there should be enough fuel in the engines to run for a few minutes before they would run out of fuel. He wondered if Tigran had seen him on the camera monitor but he didn't hear him and he wasn't going to wait around. He threw the sliding door open and raced out to where the girls stood. He reached up and hit the red button on the electric switch and the hydraulic arm started to rise. It seemed incredibly slow and just as the arm pulled the boat high enough to clear the rail he felt the first hesitation as one of the engines started to run out of fuel. Jimmy swung the boat out over the water then looked at the girls.

"The moment it hits the water I want you four in the boat hugging the floor."

Bela Bela's diesel engines coughed again, then in a matter of seconds both motors stopped running and suddenly Bela Bela was gliding through the darkness in an eerie silence.

Chapter 63

As the port engine gave its first cough Tigran woke with a start. His feet slipped off the instrument console and he fell off the chair and landed hard on the floor. Instantly he was up looking at the instruments his mind not really focusing on what was around him, but he saw that the port engine tachometer was zero. His legs felt like rubber as he stood there trying to figure out what was going on. Then the starboard engine faltered and stopped. He looked at the camera monitor for the engine room and at first everything looked normal, then suddenly he saw the shattered glass from the starboard fuel filter spread out over the floor and he knew somebody had sabotaged his yacht. He raced to the chart table, wrenched it open, and pulled out a 9 millimeter Uzi machine pistol. He grabbed a second clip, jammed it in his pants pocket then charged down the pilothouse stairs.

*

Jimmy knew he couldn't wait for Bela Bela to come to a complete stop. There simply wasn't enough time. Reaching down he grabbed the thick rope that was connected to the front of the speed boat with a stainless steel carbineer clip and tied the free end off on the rail. The yacht was still moving at least ten knots when he pushed it out over the water, jumped in and cut the thick webbing strap that held the boat to the hydraulic arm. Instantly the speed boat plunged into the waves slamming hard and throwing Jimmy off his feet. He jumped back up and pulled on the dinghy rope until he was back to the rail.

"Jump," he hollered at the girls and they all leaped over the side of the boat and landed with a crash. Jimmy was reaching up starting to cut the rope holding the speedboat to Bela Bela when suddenly he saw Tigran come racing through the open sliding glass door with a weapon in his hand. Jimmy sliced through the rope and the speedboat instantly started drifting behind Bela Bela. The Russian stopped and stood on the aft deck looking into the darkness, searching, trying to see, and Jimmy was praying that Tigran wouldn't notice them as they continued to drift farther away from the yacht, but he was wrong. A moment later the Russian noticed the speedboat was gone, the hydraulic arm leaning overboard, telling him all he needed to know about where his enemies would be found. He raced to the edge grabbing the webbing to support himself and fired a burst from the machine pistol. The speedboat was fifty feet behind Bela Bela and she was lost in the darkness, but Bela Bela was slowing down and she would come to a stop at any moment.

Jimmy didn't know what to do. The girls were huddled down in the bottom of the boat and he stood with his right hand holding the rail of the boat steadying himself as he watched Tigran hesitate. Then the Russian turned and raced back inside. The moment he was out of sight Jimmy reached back and gave the engine a pull. The large outboard roared to life and Jimmy threw the shift lever forward and they started racing away into the darkness. A minute later Bela Bela seemed to explode with light and Jimmy was almost blinded. Suddenly the lights from the yacht lit up the night sky and them as well. Jimmy pushed the throttle all the way forward and the bow of the boat raised as the motor pushed harder. Suddenly a spray of little eruptions exploded around them and the sound of machine gun fire echoed through the night. Fiberglass blew into pieces as the bow of the boat was riddled with bullets. Jimmy turned the boat hard to his left as the explosions suddenly stopped. He looked behind him and all he could see was the blazing lights of a motionless Bela Bela. He kept the throttle going full speed thinking that maybe they just might make it, although somewhere in the back of his mind he knew the Russian wasn't going to give up this easy, not that bastard.

Turning his attention forward Jimmy thought he could see in the distance the flashing light for Shipwreck Reef, but it was hard to tell because the background lights of St. Thomas hovered on the horizon. He spun the boat toward the flashing buoy then looked behind him at Bela Bela, and what he saw put the fear of god in him. He couldn't believe it as he watched Tigran slide one of the jet skis overboard off the stern then pull it along side Bela Bela. In the next instant Tigran jumped on and was racing after them. Jimmy had no idea how fast a jet ski could go but he knew it was a hell of a lot faster than a small speed boat with five people in it.

Tigran fired a wild burst from the machine gun, the bullets never getting close to Jimmy and the girls but the sound of the shots exploding through the night air scared them all. Jimmy had the speedboat at full power, the lights of Shipwreck Reef still far away. There wasn't enough time to do anything. Another burst shattered the night, this time a round hitting the transom sending more fiberglass flying. Jimmy weaved the speedboat to his left then his right but that was only making him go slower. If he kept a straight course he was too good of a target but if he weaved the boat it would slow him down too much. God, he realized, they were all as good as dead and he knew it.

Glancing up at the lights of Shipwreck Reef he suddenly realized that something was wrong. The glare of St. Thomas had fooled him, he wasn't seeing the buoy light of Shipwreck Reef, no, he was looking at the stern light of a large barge which was being towed on a half mile cable by a huge tug boat. He knew the tug would be slowing down as she neared St. Thomas and he knew that soon they would start reeling in the barge.

Another burst from the machine gun shattered the night sky. One of the girls screamed filling everyone with terror, but that scream filled Jimmy with a new resolve. He hadn't come this far to lose again.

The outline of the tug was now barely visible in the darkness and

Jimmy knew he was only minutes from it. He looked behind him and he could see the jet ski's silhouette reflected against the blazing lights of Bela Bela. Tigran was maybe a hundred yards behind him, if not closer and coming fast. Jimmy knew he had only minutes left to live. The tug was still doing a good five knots as Jimmy reached it, then turned the speedboat to starboard and raced for the front of the barge. Reaching the front a few moments later he could see the thick steel cable leading off of a three way bridle that hung from the top of the barge out over the water. The inch steel cable was attached to the bridle that slowly arched downward before it hit the water and disappeared about thirty feet from the front of the barge. Jimmy knew he had one chance. He looked behind him again and Tigran was rapidly closing the distance between them. When he turned back forward he couldn't see the cable. It was lost in the darkness and at that moment a blast from the machine pistol forced Jimmy to act. Guessing where the cable must be entering the water and knowing that its weight would pull it low below his propellers he swung the speedboat directly in front of the barge. The rail dug deep as the boat suddenly changed her course and raced right in front and on a collision course with one hundred and fifty tons of floating steel. Jimmy was guessing now, and suddenly he saw the cable fifteen feet to his left and the speedboat flew past it then he turned again to his left trying to put the barge between him and Tigran. If he planned it right the Russian might be able to see the dim outline of the fleeing speedboat and not notice the steel cable that was all he had, his last hope. Jimmy knew it was all coming down in the next few seconds. He watched as the Russian came flying around the front of the barge and he was now only sixty feet behind them. Jimmy could see Tigran's right hand up holding the machine gun, a blast of light then bullets shattering fiberglass on the stern of the speed boat. The shooting suddenly stopped when Tigran saw the cable directly in front of him. The crazy Russian frantically swerved away from the barge. The steel cable was pulled so tight by its heavy load that it didn't budge when it slammed into the Russian. Tigran was flung off the back of the jet ski. Jimmy could only imagine his fear as in the next second the huge barge slammed right over him and then over the floating jet ski smashing it underwater and breaking it into a hundred pieces. Jimmy backed off the speedboat throttle and stopped. The girls slowly climbed off the floor and they just stared as the barge slowly continued by. It seemed like it took hours for it to pass, but it was only a few minutes as they floated in stunned silence. Finally Jimmy engaged the motor and slowly the speedboat started back to the destroyed jet ski which was nothing more than a few plastic pieces floating in the wake of the barge. Tigran was nowhere to be seen.

"Are we safe?" Amy asked, clutching Jimmy's arm as she looked at the destroyed jet ski.

Chapter 64

Bela Bela looked like an eerie ghost town as she floated upon the dark ocean with all of her lights shining. Jimmy drove the speedboat up to the stern then tied it off on a cleat. He pulled the boat close, then had the girls climb on board. Laurie was the last to leave the speedboat. She stopped when she reached Jimmy and looked at him, "It feels really wrong to climb back on board," she whispered so the other girls could not hear her.

"Well, it probably does but it's safe. I guarantee that."

She smiled at him, touched his shoulder and said, "you'd make a great captain. I'd sail with you anywhere."

Jimmy laughed, "just get on board, Laurie."

It took Jimmy twenty minutes of searching through the engine room before he found one replacement bowl for the fuel filter. It only took five minutes to install it on the starboard engine. It took another ten minutes before he figured out how to bleed the air from the engine. All the time the girls just sat in the main saloon, drinking tea that Laurie had made and not saying much.

Jimmy walked back upstairs and saw the girls and smiled, "Ladies, what a lovely crew I have." he said.

"Jimmy, you couldn't handle us," Megan said with a sexy look on her face that almost melted him right there to the floor.

"That's for sure but I think I could do a damn fine job with one of you," he smiled again as he winked at Megan, who turned a slight shade of red.

"But for now I'm going upstairs to get this boat rolling. Once it starts, I'll call the Coast Guard and let them know we are all safe and we don't need any assistance."

"Jimmy, you're our hero," Sarah said and the girls all laughed and made swooning sounds as he disappeared up the stairs to the pilothouse.

It took some cranking before the starboard engine sputtered once, twice then finally roared to life. Jimmy engaged the throttle and slowly Bela Bela started moving. He spun her around and started on a heading that would take them back to Royal Bay Marina. Only then did he feel some of the fear, the tensions that he had held so close for such a long time start to leave him, and suddenly tears rolled down his cheeks and he couldn't stop them.

Soon Bela Bela was making about eight knots on one motor but that was fast enough. Jimmy slumped back in the pilot chair and took a deep breath. He couldn't believe that it was over. He started to reach for the radio to call the coast guard when suddenly from down below a chorus of screams erupted all at once.

Jimmy threw himself from the chair dropping the radio microphone and raced to the steps that led down to the main salon. The girls were still screaming as he charged down the steps three at a time. The girls were now clambering over the back of the sofa trying to hide pointing past the galley toward the front of the boat and in that instant Jimmy remembered the one crewman that was still alive.

Jimmy dove as he hit the bottom step landing hard on the floor then spun to his right and jumped to his feet. A shot exploded in the room but Jimmy was moving too fast to even think. He slammed his right elbow into the glass case that held the fishing poles and spear guns, hoping it would break, but it didn't. He looked past the galley and saw the last crewman, supporting himself against the wall pointing a pistol at him. The glass in the case hadn't shattered, but it felt like his elbow did, then in the next instant the pistol fired another round and the glass exploded as a bullet meant for Jimmy missed him by an inch. Glass flew across the room as Jimmy dove, grabbed a spear gun, hit the floor and spun toward the galley. The crewman was leaning against the wall trying to support his broken body. He tried to line Jimmy up with the pistol barrel but Jimmy fired first. The three foot spear, pushed by its CO_2 cartridge, flew across the room and slammed into the crewman's chest who gave a scream then started to fall but he didn't because the spear went through him, part way through the wall into the galley and he hung there like a macabre three dimensional piece of art, the pistol lying at his feet.

Jimmy sat stunned, then tried to get up but his right arm gave out from underneath him and he fell back landing with a crash on the floor. Megan was the first to reach him. She threw herself down at his side and brought her hands to his head. None of the girls knew if Jimmy had been shot or not, everything had happened so fast. Tears streamed down her face, "Jimmy, are you alright?"

He slowly opened his eyes, wincing at the pain, then a smile grew until he laughed, "an angel, right before my eyes, my god . . . I know I can't be dead, I'm too horny."

Megan burst into laughter, and the rest of the girls hovered over her and Jimmy, and soon everybody was laughing in hysterics. Megan brought her lips to his and gave him a deep passionate kiss. When she pulled away from him she knew without a doubt she would love this man for the rest of her life.

Then she gently pushed his head over and stood up, "horny . . . my you are going to have to go to confession . . . you naughty boy."

The girls started laughing again and all Jimmy could do was lay on the carpet laughing with them even though every time he did his entire body hurt like hell.

*

It took almost an hour before Bela Bela reached the breakwater at Royal Bay Marina. Jimmy had called the Coast Guard and asked them to notify Commander Leboske, and have him contact Lester.

As Bela Bela pulled up to the dock Jimmy could see Lester, Flip, and both the detectives, plus a score of flashing police and ambulance lights and enough people standing around to fill Bela Bela to capacity. The moment the dock lines were secured and the boarding ladder locked in place the twins rushed off Bela Bela into their father's waiting arms. Tears flowed from everybody on the dock. Laurie climbed off and for some strange reason walked up to Detective Klein and gave him a big hug. Jimmy stood on the fly bridge looking down at everybody below him. His body was a wreck, his elbow probably broken, his shoulder ached, his gut felt like it had been ripped open by all the fear and emotions that he had faced the last few days. Trying to stand there watching the joyful reunion below him he suddenly wondered where Megan was. Then somehow he knew and he turned and there she was standing three feet in front of him.

"Come here," he whispered and she flew into his arms, smothering his lips with hers. Jimmy pulled her tight, tears streaming down his face as he felt a rush of emotions that overwhelmed him. Gently after that first kiss he softly pushed her away and looked into her deep beautiful brown eyes. A slight grin appeared on his face as he ever so slowly pulled her face back to his.

"Want to go sailing?" he whispered in her ear.

"Sailing hell, Jimmy McBain, I want you!"

THE END

WILLIAM F. CARLI and his wife share their time between a small island in the Pacific Northwest and an even smaller island in the Caribbean.

Other novels by W.F. Carli are *Sunset Run* and *Stone Totem*.

To contact the author or to purchase books please email him at wfcarli@gmail.com.

CPSIA information can be obtained
at www.ICGtesting.com
Printed in the USA
FFOW03n0945190814
6937FF